HELL HATH NO VENGEANCE

LOUISA LO

TIN CAN
PRESS

Cover Design: Jacqueline Sweet

Cover Photo: Sara Eirew

Content Edit: Joshua Essoe

Beta, Copy/Line Edit: Help Me Edit

Proofread: Help Me Edit

Hell Hath No Vengeance/Louisa Lo—1st edition

ISBN: 978-0-9952302-8-6

To hubby,

For always believing in me.

ACKNOWLEDGMENT

To Joshua,
For pushing me to reach for that next level.

❧ I ❧
THE KIDNAPPING

WHEN A LOVED ONE WENT MISSING, some people raged in helplessness, while others retreated into themselves. I was fortunate enough to have a third option.

Keeping myself busy by kicking some vengeance butt.

"You know, what he's doing is just a step up from stealing candies from a baby." I wrinkled my nose, staying in the shade with Gregory as we watched our target cross the intersection and head toward our hiding spot. The shade also served as relief from a blistering sun. It was unusually hot for what is supposed to be the beginning of summer on the human plane. A good thing, too. Most people had the good sense to stay indoors, leaving the area surrounding the side entrance of a grocery store relatively deserted.

Gregory, clad in his trademark dark jeans and black sweatshirt despite the heat, shrugged. His sensuous lips parted in amusement. "Megan, is there ever a more ethical way to steal?"

I rolled my eyes. "I guess not."

Today marked the three-month anniversary of my career as a mercenary and my partnership with Gregory. The mercenary life turned out to be a lot like my old life at the co-op program of the University of Demonic Studies. Granted, there were less textbooks and bigger paychecks, but I had to work just as hard to keep up.

The Prince of Darkness could be one demanding customer.

Our latest target was Boyce Armstrong, a mean-looking dwarf-giant thug who adapted a human-sounding last name for his official records.

And what a record. The guy had the rap sheet the length of a person's arms, including grand theft auto, B&E, and to crown it off, the murder of four people. To keep up with the stereotype, the guy looked like he was straight from the villain catalogue of Central Casting. He was all biker jeans, tattooed arms, enormous build, and facial scars. According to the photo attached to our work order, there was one particular scar that went from his forehead to his cheek, missing his left eye by a narrow margin.

I liked it when they made the verification process so easy, helping me get to the capturing part all that faster.

Mr. Armstrong was supposed to be serving time in Hell, but he made an escape two weeks ago during a massive prison break. And now here he was, resorting to stealing from little old human ladies right off the street of downtown Toronto. It was as wrong as it was sad.

We watched as Boyce smiled at an elderly woman carrying five bags of groceries, and offered to hold her stuff for her so she could concentrate on using her walker to cross the street. I barely resisted tapping my foot on the ground, as I hated witnessing anyone in the process of being charmed and conned, knowing in most cases the likes of me weren't there to prevent the fallout.

We waited until Boyce got onto our side of the road with his would-be victim. Then I grabbed the front of his shirt, pulled him into the small alleyway I was hiding in, and banged him against the wall before the old lady could let out a scream—and before the grocery bags could hit the ground. As dwarf-giants were tough SOBs, I relied on the element of surprise to quickly plant a temporary weakening spell on him.

"Get off me!" Boyce spat when I flipped his body so that his back was facing me, and restrained him using a pair of Unbreakable Cuffs.

With well-oiled coordination that we'd perfected in the past few months, the moment I engaged our target Gregory started calming down our innocent human bystander. With a light touch on her shoulder, he made the last few minutes of her memory blurry. Then he gathered the grocery bags, tied them onto her walker, and sent her on her merry way; he even threw in a boost of energy for her to enjoy for the next two hours. The old lady complied, moving away with a spring in her step.

Gregory turned his attention back to Boyce just when the latter tried to pull himself free of the Unbreakable Cuffs. It was all to no avail. I purchased the goblin-made cuffs with my first paycheck. They were expensive but impossible to break once they were on, making my job safer as a result.

"What the hell do you want?" Boyce yelled.

"Hell is the right word here," Gregory said dryly.

Comprehension dawned on Boyce's face as he took in Gregory's vengeance wings, fully extended as mine were during a confrontation, from his vantage point. Our target growled.

"Boyce Armstrong, we're sending you back to Hell," I informed him, using the dispassionate voice I learned from school. "You have the right to remain silent. Anything you say or do may offend the assigned vengeance demon and lead to a more severe punishment—"

Gregory coughed discreetly.

My cheeks heated. Damn, I did it again, giving the guy his Belinda, the vengeance demon version of the Miranda rights. Mercenaries didn't do that, as we weren't exactly legal ourselves under the existing vengeance laws. Old habits died hard.

Luckily, our target didn't seem to care about my present embarrassment whatsoever.

"I can't go back there," Boyce howled. "I didn't do those things they say I did. I mean, I did all the small-time stuff when I was younger, but I'd turned my life around since then. I didn't kill those four people."

"Yeah, and I guess taking that old lady's groceries is really making you believable here." I snorted.

"I was *helping* her," Boyce insisted.

"Yeah, right." I waved off his words and nodded at Gregory, indicating that I was ready to teleport whenever he was. He looked around to check for any other human witnesses, found none, and started opening a portal to Hell.

During those few seconds, Boyce went deadly quiet. That should've triggered some alarm in me. But I was confident with the Unbreakable Cuffs and my own weakening spell. Probably a little *too* confident.

Anyway, one moment he was calm and docile, the next he turned around and blasted me with an ice energy that knocked me right off my feet. Then he started running away.

Lying sideway on the hard concrete of the alleyway, I directed every magic I had at the retreating back of my target. With the weird angle and the growing distance, I wasn't sure how good my aim would be, but a girl's gotta try, right?

I didn't have a chance to check if I hit him, because a bone-numbing cold started settling into my limbs. It was a strange sensation, to have my skin sweating from the surrounding heat and my insides getting frostbite. Who would've thought a dwarf-giant, from a species known for their brunt force, would know such strong, sneaky magic?

"Megan!" Gregory's voice sounded like it was from under water. I didn't have the energy to answer him.

Gregory kept calling my name. One more urgent than the other. Oh, come on, couldn't he chill? I sure was. All I wanted was to drift to sleep...

Someone was slapping my cold cheeks with scorching hands that came straight out of the oven, hot and relentless. It threatened to tear off the top layer of my skin with the friction. I opened my eyes.

And realized I didn't remember closing them. That should have scared me, but all I felt was numbness.

Gregory was holding me in his strong arms, his warmth surrounding me. His hair had grown since we started our partnership, and as he leaned down to look at me, strands of brown hair kept falling over his eyes and chiseled cheekbones, giving me the urge to smooth them back with my fingers. With the weakening of my body bringing down my mental resistance, I greedily took in two large breaths of his body scent, which reminded me of clean citrus soap, before I was able to stop myself.

I needed to get a grip. He practically ran away after our first and only kiss. I'd always known that I fell short on the vengeance demon beauty standard—with my wild mud-colored hair, olive complexion, and child-bearing hips, I wasn't classically lithe and graceful. I didn't think Gregory would've cared, but something turned him off and I had no idea what. My physical attributes were as good a possibility as any.

"Megan, you alright?" His voice tight, Gregory propped me in a more upright position and offered me his hand. "Here, take some of my energy."

Figuring this wasn't a time for pride, I clasped his hand

and drew his power into me. Gregory didn't just have the blood of one of the oldest vengeance families flowing in his veins—he was also a powerful vengeance demon in his own right. His power, a rich and potent Earl Grey tea, filled my senses.

Immediately a picture of me being wrapped in a blanket and sitting in front of a crackling fireplace came to mind, making me feel safe and content. It was the perfect imagery to chase away the cold that had sank deep into the core of me.

As rejuvenating as the act of energy-taking with Gregory was, though, it wasn't as intimate as it was with Esme, my half-sister. With Esme, it was "no holds barred" when it came to her emotions. With Gregory, there was a boundary there neither of us was willing to cross.

I took just enough energy and stopped, before I became too overwhelmed by his essence and got right into wishful-thinking mode. He wasn't interested in me, and that was that. He'd been a valuable business partner, and I just had to learn to be content with that.

Even if it killed me.

"Thank you," I said to Gregory rather formally, with no small measure of awkwardness. I got up quickly, desperate for some distance. "Whatever happened to our target?"

Gregory pointed at a space some twenty feet away, and I looked toward that direction. There was Boyce, trapped in a prison made of flaming rods, which nicely cancelled out his ice energy. The garbage cans next to the prison were melted, their contents fused with their grey plastic exterior like gooey ice cream sandwiches under a hot sun.

"Your magic hit the garbage cans," Gregory said dryly, "and enough energy bounced back onto Boyce to delay his escape so I could imprison him.

So my less-than-perfect aim did manage to find purchase, kind of. Oh, well, as long as the job got done.

Boyce kept trying to touch the bars and kept bouncing back, his hands singeing. He didn't look very happy about it, as he demonstrated with his endless stream of curse words.

"Go ahead." I gave him a smug smile. "Make all the noise you want. This whole alleyway is sound and sight proofed from mortals. They see nothing. They hear nothing."

That was the advantage of choosing the place of confrontation—Gregory and I had set up all the precautions beforehand.

I knew I should rejoice over not losing Boyce, but something was bothering me.

So let me get the sequence of events straight. After I was struck and Boyce was down, Gregory figured out the appropriate spell to offset our target's ice energy and promptly trapped him with it, *then* he came to my aid.

All of which was understandable, as the profit and reputation of our business came before the well-being of any individual partner. Totally reasonable.

Then why was it a tiny, illogical part of me wished that his priorities had been slightly reversed? That maybe he would be so focused on my state of being that all else was forgotten, including the escape of our target, once I had fallen?

Because that would've been the expected behavior of a *solus iungere*, a vengeance soul mate. Total devotion and putting that person above all else.

During our one-and-only kiss, I was so sure that Gregory was my true mate. Except he wasn't. He made that clear when he pulled away as if my skin burned him.

Anyway, I really couldn't dwell on that. I straightened and briskly walked to one side of Boyce's prison, and Gregory got to the other side after transforming the garbage cans back to their original state. He waved an enchantment that would allow us to touch the prison bars without harm. Then he opened up a now-familiar cross-dimensional portal. Straight to Hell.

Knowing what was coming, Boyce paled. "No, no, no. Listen, you really don't want to do this."

"Don't want to do what, return you to Hell and collect our bounty?" I pulled back my upper lip. "You know how many all-nighters we've pulled in the last few months taking your kind back? I would gladly get this assignment done and over with."

"And how's serving Hell working out for ya?" He grit his teeth.

"We don't *serve* Hell." My nostrils flared. "We *do business* with Hell."

"Yeah, keep telling yourself that." Boyce sneered.

I had to admit, Boyce's comment struck a nerve. Granted, a big part of the reason I wanted to become a mercenary was to build up contacts in the fight against the Greys, aka the Council. There was no contact as big as the Lord of Hell himself. But in the past months it was increasingly looking like he was the *only* client we had time to satisfy, given the sheer frequency of the prison breaks that were fast becoming the norm. Nobody knew why Lucifer was having a hard time keeping his prisoners in check, but Gregory and I had handled at least two dozen cases, and we weren't the only mercenaries Hell had contracted.

I was a big believer in not keeping all my eggs in one basket, but it was hard to say no to these assignments—and not only because they were extremely lucrative. It was more like riding on the back of a potentially ill-tempered beast, and it was a lot easier getting on than getting off. Not that our interaction with Hell had ever been anything but professional and civilized, but the devil's reputation spoke for itself. If the just and mighty Council hadn't turned out to be such bull, I would never imagine making such uneasy allies.

Not wanting Boyce to sow any more seeds of doubts into my head, I pursed my lips and grabbed hold of a pair of prison bars. Gregory did the same on his side, and together we dragged Boyce through the cross-dimensional portal, prison and all.

We arrived at Hell through one of its service entrances, being the freelance service providers that we were. This reception desk of the Underworld looked like one from a library for rare books, all tall, oversized, and polished dark mahogany wood.

Boyce rattled his prison bars, desperation seeping into his voice now. "Let me out of here!"

We ignored him, and he cursed wildly in an unfamiliar language. It had to be cursing, from its rough sounds and the universally rude hand gestures that came with it.

A small man with a frog's head and an elf's body, undoubt-edly perched on a high chair, sat behind the desk. He had thick-rimmed glasses and a beer belly, and was bending over a large, thick volume with a fountain pen, making small notes here and there. Even with the ruckus Boyce was making, the man at the desk seemed to have difficulties tearing his eyes from the text to pay us any attention. There was a disturbingly obsessed look on his face as his head remained bowed. A tall, stick of a man stood behind him, holding onto an ink pen and parchment.

"Hey, Leonard," Gregory greeted the man reading the text, forcing him to look up at him. There was a power in saying someone's name and I was glad to see Leonard responding to it.

Leonard was the bookkeeper of the Book of Life and Death, which recorded the activities of all souls in existence, physically live or dead, supernatural or otherwise. The Book kept track of the estimated arrival dates of sinners in Hell, the expected duration of their torment, and where they were headed after the punishment was through—the cleansing fire of reincarnation for mortals, or a possible return to their old lives for the supernaturals.

The data in the Book were ever-shifting as every choice a living person makes took them closer down one path or another. Everything from the decision to cheat in an exam, to pocketing a tiny screw from the hardware store instead of coughing out the required twenty cents, set the stage for the next round of choices and the round after that, which eventually determined a person's eligibility for Heaven or Hell. Leonard's job was to keep track of Hell's occupancy status based on all these variables.

A monumental task for such an unassuming slip of a man. His legions of assistants, like Tatus, the tall man behind him, were only ever trusted with manual tasks such as filing and miscellaneous note taking.

"Megan. Gregory." Leonard's eyes were clear once he looked up from the Book. He glanced at Boyce. "This is faster than I expected."

"Thank you." I beamed at the compliment. As concerned as I was about the jobs from Hell taking up too high a percentage of our total business activities, I was nevertheless pleased that Leonard was impressed with our work. For one, he was our way in to meet the ever-elusive Lucifer. Secondly, what vengeance demon, mercenary or otherwise, didn't like to be told that they'd done an efficient job?

Leonard glanced at Tatus, and the latter rang a small silver bell. A pair of guards materialized. They were both muscular and nearly naked, with a piece of cloth over their loins, which made them look like a cross between a stripper and a romance novel cover model. I heard that the higher rank you got, the more clothes you'd be allowed on the job. I wonder what the guards looked like at the grand entrance of Hell, which was rumored to be a place of super glam.

"Guards, can you take our prisoner back to his punishment? He has"—Leonard wetted his thumb with his tongue and flipped through the pages of the Book—"two years, five months, eleven days, and fifteen hours to go on Level One. After that he will be eligible for early parole."

Looking at Leonard causally reading someone's fate off the Book of Life and Death had always given me the creeps. To know that there was a database out there keeping track of all the good and bad things people did in their lifetime, which in turn determine the amount of time they might stay in Hell, was unsettling to say the least. I dreaded what the Book might say about me, and about my family and friends, especially since a lot of us were against the Absolute Good. If the Book followed the same "naughty or nice" standard as the Council, then we were so screwed. Just because Hell used me as a hired gun didn't mean it wasn't my eventual destination. Maybe it even made it more likely.

One of the guards waved his hand, removing the fire prison while the other took out a piece of yarn and wrapped it loosely around Boyce's wrists. I'd learned over the past months not to underestimate the fragile looking thread. It was more powerful than ten Unbreakable Cuffs.

Speaking of Unbreakable Cuffs, it was time to remove mine. I reached toward Boyce, knowing that I—the rightful owner of the cuffs—could release the locking mechanism with my touch. But the guard on the left beat me to it. And by that I meant he waved his hands over the cuffs, and the darn thing just fell off Boyce's wrists and into the guard's open palm. Then the guard handed it back to me.

My jaw sagged. I looked at Gregory and he shrugged. How the guards could pull that off, I would never know, but it must be an inborn talent for the servants of Hell or something. I couldn't help but wonder what other things we might get blindsided by if our friends here ever turned on us.

Boyce hadn't even left the room when Leonard's gaze started drifting back to the Book of Life and Death like a moth to the flame, his mouth gaped as he lost himself in it again.

Tatus gave a discreet coughed, and Leonard looked up again, seeming almost surprised by the continued presence of Gregory and me. He blinked rapidly a few times. "Oh, right. Well, thank you for your help. The fee will be transferred to your account within the next twelve hours."

Having prompt payments from Hell was never the issue. It was what other hidden costs this working relationship might carry that kept me up at night.

2

COMPLICATED

GREGORY and I teleported to the front of the duplex I shared with Rosemary, my human roommate, on the west end of Toronto. Whenever we returned from Hell, we always traveled to the same destination first even if we were to split afterward.

I would love to say that was done because Gregory was a romantic and wanted to escort me to a safe place before taking his leave, but the truth was he did it for business reasons—some spirits were known to be able to hitch a ride back from Hell, but their ability to do so decreased drastically if the traveler wasn't alone. Something about multiple people being able to ensure that all the blind spots were covered during teleportation.

The last thing we wanted after returning a fugitive to the Underworld was to provide passage out of there for another one. Leonard, ever the accountant, would probably consider it a wash and refuse to pay us for our work.

I cleared my throat after my feet landed on the front steps of the duplex. "So, er, that went pretty well."

"Yes, it did," Gregory agreed.

Awkward silence, in which we shifted our gaze everywhere except each other's eyes.

"I'm sure Leonard will call us when he's got something else," I said finally.

"He will."

Silence again.

Now that the responsibility of delivering the target was over, my mind veered to how Gregory held me in his arms earlier, something he hadn't done since that night three months ago. We'd been careful about avoiding physical contact with each other ever since then.

Under the waning sun, the sharp angles of Gregory's cheekbones made the contours of his face even more defined. His long-limbed body, usually relaxed with confidence, hunched with hesitation. His midnight-blue wings were only half-extended, as if they, too, weren't sure what the next move was.

If I didn't know better, I would say he was as confused and conflicted as I was. But Gregory wasn't exactly the contemplative and tormented type. I must be reading what I want from the situation.

Steeling myself to keep things light, I swallowed and said brightly, "Alright then, I'll keep Marv with me for tonight and let you know if anything comes up."

My comment had the desired effect. Gregory grimaced. "I wish you wouldn't call the Phone by that ridiculous name."

Marv, aka the Phone, was for the 24/7 vengeance hotline we set up for the business. We usually took turns holding onto that little communication device through the night. A few weeks ago I decided to rechristened it to Marv, which stood for Mercenary Assistive Response for the Vengeful. It was way cooler than its old name.

"You should be glad I'm not calling it Vermin." I smirked.

"Vermin?" he raised his eyebrow.

"You know, Vengeance Emergency Response Management Initiative, with the 'n' from the word 'initiative' forming the last letter of the acronym."

"Marv it is," Gregory said quickly, probably hoping to discourage me from coming up with more names for the little gadget. "Anyway, I reprogrammed it so it doesn't make that chirping ringtone if you don't answer it within a minute. Your roommate won't be disturbed again."

"Thank you." I dropped my cocky act and said gratefully. Always the optimist, Rosemary really thought that those abandoned eggs up in the nest under her bedroom window were still capable of hatching, though we were well past spring. I didn't need her getting excited by mistaking the chirping for the sound of baby birds only to be bitterly disappointed.

Gregory looked like he was going to say something else, then stopped himself. Without a further word, he took Marv out of his pant pocket and handed it to me. The little device, which fit right into the palm of my hand was warm to the touch, and I tried not to think about Gregory's body heat that was just right next to it.

I ducked under the porch as Gregory teleported away, and opened the front door to the divine smell of pot roast and grilled vegetables. My stomach rumbled in anticipation. At least no matter how my day went, I could always count on a hearty meal at the end of it.

"I'm at the back. Come on out, Megan!" The distant voice of Rosemary, my roommate slash chef extraordinaire, called.

I walked through the living room and kitchen and stepped out onto the deck. A setting for two was laid on top of a yellow tablecloth, with a small vase of fresh cut daisies on the side. Rosemary was in the middle of pouring homemade lemonade into two glasses. In the center of the table were two large covered pots.

"Just in time for dinner." Rosemary smiled, uncovered the pots, and started spooning vegetables and pot roast slices onto the plates. A petite blond with a round face, my room-mate was a culinary student who could bake like a team of angels and cooked like a temptress from Hell. I was so, so lucky to have found her. "I made chocolate molten lava cake for dessert."

And I officially didn't deserve her.

I just had to be glad that I had the metabolism of a super-natural, or I wouldn't have been able to fit through the front door, let alone catch any fugitives, with the way Rosemary had been feeding me. She called it experimentation, I called it Heaven.

Unfortunately, Rosemary also had a nosy side. "Hey, was that Gregory I saw walking you home?"

Living with me meant that Rosemary was bound to witness something supernatural at one point or another, be it catching me in the act of casting a spell, or seeing me talking to Sassy, my feline shade. Rather than dealing with these inci-dents on a case-by-case basis, I'd placed a perception filter on her to help her mind ignore things that it couldn't under-stand. That meant that she didn't actually see Gregory and I teleport onto the property, or him teleport away. All she saw as she peeked out of the window was him walking me home, then leaving.

"Yeah, that was him," I replied.

"Gregory, your *business partner*?"

"Yep." I told her Gregory and I had started an event plan-ning business together. It explained all the weird hours I kept, and it was true in a way—we planned events in which people got sent back to Hell.

"Uh-huh." Rosemary studied my face like I was an expensive restaurant dish she was trying to reverse-engineer.

"So how's the canning going?" I asked quickly. "Are you onto the grape jelly now? When is the peach batch ready?"

"The peach will be ready in another week. I'm already halfway through the grape jelly and started on the raspberry jam."

"That's a lot of new stuff to sell." Rosemary ran a side-business of jams, organic fragrance, and soap products, not to mention really awesome dog biscuits.

"I'm only keeping half. We're running a bake sale at the shelter next week. Why not tempt them with some jam when people are going to be buying breads and buns?" Rosemary got herself an extra portion of pot roast and offered me the same. I obliged. "Looks like I'm going to have tons of left-overs tonight. You should have asked your *business partner* to stay for dinner. I told you before that he's welcome to, remember?"

I should've known that Rosemary wouldn't be so easily deterred. Someone who created baklava from scratch by methodically building one sheet of phyllo over another twenty times over, without them drying out or sticking together, wouldn't have given up so easily.

Though my roommate had met Gregory briefly several times, I'd always managed to get her away from him before she could extend any dinner invitations. It would be just like her to grill him over a delicious meal about the state of things between Gregory and I, and that would've just killed me with embarrassment.

"Er, he's busy," I lied.

"That's what you said the last three times. You didn't ask him, did you?" She narrowed her eyes at me.

"It's...complicated," I admitted. What an understatement.

"What's so complicated? He's single. You're single." Rose-mary stopped the forkful of meat that was halfway to her mouth. "Wait, he's single, right?"

I nodded. "As far as I know." Whatever the reason that made Gregory step away, at least I knew it wasn't because he had a girlfriend back home waiting for him—the essence of cheating had a distinctive flavor to it, and as a vengeance demon, I would've been able to detect it, and I didn't, either during or after the kiss.

"Then what's the problem?" she persisted.

"As I said, it's complicated." I envied the human in front of me. She could choose whomever she wanted as a mate. There was no weird vengeance chemistry, or the misread of such vengeance chemistry, for her.

"Just drop it, okay?" I begged Rosemary.

My roommate must've heard the weariness in my voice. She chewed on her lips. "Sorry. I just keep seeing how your eyes light up every time you mention him and I thought... never mind. Here, these came in for you today."

Rosemary hurried into the kitchen, picked up a stack of letters from the counter, and handed them to me.

"One from U of T, one from Election Canada, and one from Ontario Health." She commented, "I betcha that last one is a health card renewal notice. I just got mine done last year. The lineup wasn't too bad, but the picture was horrendous."

With her perception filter, Rosemary only saw what she was meant to see as a human being. The three letters were actually from the University of Demonic Studies, Election Vengeance, and the Department of Vengeance Health, respectively.

The fact that they got the letters delivered here, my address on the human plane, rather than to my parents' house, was in itself a bad sign.

I was glad I was a super-fast eater and had already polished off the main course, or I would've surely lost all appetite.

The letter from the University of Demonic Studies confirmed my withdrawal from the Faculty of Arts and Vengeance, and that for the time I'd spent there, with three completed school semesters, two tuition hikes, and an GPA of 3.7, they were granting me the transferrable course credits of...zero. It would be like I'd never attended a day there.

I clutched the paper so hard my fist was shaking. Rosemary shot me a worried look.

I tried not to let it get it me, to tell myself that this was such a small matter in the grand scheme of things. But dammit, I earned those credits fair and square. I'd slaved over the school works, pulled all-nighters for the midterms, and almost gotten killed over my first co-op assignment.

I didn't deserve to be treated as if I was expelled. I walked away voluntarily, and they were pretending that I left in disgrace.

The letter from Election Vengeance informed me that since I wasn't living, going to school, nor engaging in eligible employment on the vengeance plane, I wasn't qualified to vote in the upcoming mayoral election.

Eligible was the operative word here when it came to the employment status. I worked plenty, just not in a legitimate, Council-approved sense.

Not that I cared about the mayoral election—all the candidates had pretty much the same platform—but it would be nice to be able to *not* exercise my right to vote.

The letter from the Department of Vengeance Health was not about the renewal of my health card at all, but the cancellation of it altogether. They cited the same reasons as Election Vengeance. Then, to put a cherry on the top, attached to the letter was a bill for the annual checkup I did two weeks ago.

A bill. They'd sent me a freaking bill. Nobody said anything about refunding my tuition, but they took the time to create an invoice for my annual Flap test—like a human Pap test but for my back where my wings were stored.

Three letters. Three fallouts from the fight against the Council, aka the Greys.

What do you expect, Megan? You denied their chance to annihilate most of the population in existence.

True enough.

"Are you alright?" Rosemary's words pulled me out of my reverie. If my frowning roommate could sense supernatural powers, she would've been able to feel the sudden energy spike in the air resulting from my anger and ran the other way. I forced myself to take a few deep, calming breaths.

"Yeah, I'm okay," I reassured her. "How about that dessert?"

Sometimes the only thing a girl can do was dig into her chocolate molten lava cake, then move onward.

I was helping Rosemary put away the dishes when the doorbell rang.

"I wonder who that is?" Rosemary frowned as she wiped her hands on the dishcloth and hurried out to the front door.

"Could it be Jordon?" I asked. Rosemary's boyfriend was a regular fixture here—whenever he wasn't working two jobs on top of volunteering at the local animal shelter.

"No, he's working tonight."

I stayed put and wiped down the kitchen counter. I suppose I could use magic to do it, but I found the manual labor calming.

Not to mention, I was a bit stingy on magic use, especially with the three letters reminding me how unpredictable life could be. Better save up some power like humans would with blue chip stocks.

Rosemary came back with a vase of flowers. Not a huge one, but a tasteful tabletop botanical creation, with bright yellow carnations, purple Matsumoto asters, and pink Asiatic lilies. A single blood-red rose stood proud in the middle of the cheery beauty, adding a sense of mystic to the floral offering. I so happened to like carnations and lilies quite a bit. Was it just a coincidence?

"It's for you," Rosemary proclaimed.

My heart rate sped up. For me? My first thought was wondering if it could be from Gregory. He didn't seem like the flower gifting kind, but I couldn't think of anyone else who would be sending me something like this. Unless it was from my trickster brothers, and the flowers were time-released stink bombs.

"Oh, look here, there's a card." My roommate pointed at the small envelope tucked behind the rose. She looked at me expectantly.

I suppose that was the part where I fulfilled the social obligation of reading the note out loud so a friend could share in the thrill vicariously. I reached for the envelope and opened it. There was a note and what looked like a movie ticket inside. Handwritten in a calligraphic style that was masculine and fancy at the same time, the note said:

Dear Megan,

Would you consider doing me the honor of joining me for an evening at my casino? If you play your hand right, I might be able to help take all your troubles away. If so, please come to the front of the casino and present the guards with the red armband with the enclosed VIP pass.

Until then,

L. Morningstar

p.s. Wear something nice.

Through the roar in my ear, I asked myself, *L. Morningstar, as in Lucifer Freaking Morningstar?*

My breath caught. What the hell is he doing inviting me to the grand casino of Hell? I mean, I'd been to the Underworld plenty of times in the last three months, but it was always through the no-frill service entrance, never the front door. What was the devil playing at? I was a pay-by-assignment freelancer. A professional. I worked as a team with Gregory. Why had Lucifer approached me individually, flowers and all?

And what the hack did he mean by "I might be able to help take all your troubles away"? Was he talking about my issues with the Council? The timing sure seemed suspicious given the letters I just received.

Or was he talking about helping me find Grandma? If so, the devil sure knew how to tempt me. Wondering how Gran was faring while trapped inside the Internet was what had been keeping me up at night. I had no idea how he would've found out about Gran, but he was the devil, after all.

"So, what did it say?" Rosemary asked impatiently, cranking her neck to look over my shoulder.

"I—it's nothing. Just a client." I stuffed the note back to the envelope along with the all-access pass to Hell. I hate disappointing my roommate, but a message from the Underworld wasn't exactly the stuff the mortal should see.

Rosemary's eyes went saucer-sized. "A client? So not Gregory then?"

Guess that was her first thought as well.

"No, not him." I shook my head.

"What does he want?"

I decided to give her a half-truth. "He wants me to meet him at his place of work."

"For business?"

"I don't know."

"Do you like him?"

"Rosemary!" I gasped, horrified by the idea.

"Hey, you're the one who keeps insisting Gregory is just your business partner. What's the harm in saying yes to this other guy?"

What's the harm in mixing up with the devil? Oh, let's see, how about losing your soul?

Was that it, he was hoping to make a trade for my soul? Maybe as a half-vengeance demon, half-trickster hybrid, my soul was like a collector's item? Or was this something else altogether?

I glanced at the flowers again. The single rose, plus the suggestion to wear something nice, seem to indicate an interest of a more personal nature.

Eww, creepy.

Everyone knew that Lucifer was the ultimate seducer. Question was, was it my heart, soul, or body that he was going after? A light tremor made me shiver to my very core. Whatever it was, I was now officially singled out by the Prince of Darkness himself.

How the Hell was I supposed to respond to it?

✳ 3 ✳

THE WITCHING HOUR

I TOOK THE FLOWERS, the letters from the Council, and Lucifer's envelope to my bedroom. Then I paced around for what felt like an eternity, which was tougher than it sounded given my tendency to be just a teeny little bit messy. My dresser drawers were half open, stuffed with fresh laundry I never bother folding, their corners perfectly positioned for my elbows to bang into. A pair of pants and a bunch of shirts I only wore twice were on the floor. They would eventually get washed when I got sick and tired of tripping over them, or be worn again if I got desperate enough rushing out of the house one of these days.

As I paced, I contemplated Lucifer's offer. To say I wasn't tempted would be a lie. With a simple *yes*, I could get Gran back, or get much further along in my fight against the Council. What was a little heart and soul, when I'd already been threatened with my share of bodily harm in the past year?

But Grandma taught me better than this. No good ever came out of taking the easy route. I would hold on, and I would stay the course.

Even if it killed me.

Besides, I became acquainted with Hell through Gregory, and it just didn't feel right connecting with Lucifer directly and skipping over my own business partner.

Now that my mind was made up, there was just one tiny, teeny problem.

Just how did one say to the devil, *Thanks, but no thanks. Mind if we just keep it professional? Er, no hard feelings, right?*

I eventually decided to scribble on the note:

Thank you for the offer, but I'll see if I can handle it myself first.

There. A "no," without sounding too closed-minded, but not open-minded enough to provide a lot of hope, either. Hopefully that would do the trick. I guess someone far more cultured—or had spent time at law school—could come up with something far more elegant and with double or triple entendre, but that wasn't me and there was nothing I could do about it.

I tear the note apart and watch it burst into flames spontaneously, knowing the message was now sent to Hell.

I would have to tell Gregory about this. But not tonight. I would tell him tomorrow. A tiny, petty part of me was looking forward to seeing if he would be jealous of the devil's gesture, which was exactly why I didn't want to give into that and call him right over tonight. It just seemed a bit too...desperate.

I left the vase of flowers on my dresser. Plants grown in Hell were nearly indestructible. I would have to look into how to dispose of it safely. The very least I could do for now was not leave it in the common area, lest Rosemary cut her finger on a thorn and grew a horn or something.

For some reason, I couldn't bring myself to tear up the

VIP pass, though. So I shrunk it to the size of a microchip with an enchantment and magically attached it to the clasp of my necklace. I couldn't imagine ever using it, but stranger things had happened.

I wish I could at least go and find out exactly what Lucifer was after, but everyone knew better than to accept the Devil's invitation. That would be like Hansel and Gretel accepting the witch's invite to get inside her gingerbread cottage, except much worse because at least their souls were still theirs after the witch killed them.

I took a few deep breaths. Once I was convinced I'd calmed down enough, I made the call I'd been making every night for the last three months. Right around now habits were welcoming, even an unhappy habit.

With the existence of cell phone contact lists, I never used to memorize any numbers. But there was one number I'd been dialing so often that I'd now memorized it without trying.

Esme picked up on the second ring. "Hi, Megan."

"Any news?" I asked her the same question I'd been asking her every night without fail.

"No. I'm sorry." Frustration was clear in Esme's voice. "Mother and I keep getting close, but there's always something blocking us from making direct contact with Gran."

My grandmother used to be a distinguished member of the Council before she was betrayed by her closest friends and allies. Weakened and injured, she escaped into the one place she'd hated the most—the World Wide Web.

Gran's mistrust of the Internet had less to do with a senior's natural fear of technology, and more to do with a general suspicion regarding all things that sprung up and took over the world too quickly. Never trust something that was more than the sum of its parts, she always said, and what was the Internet, beyond programming codes, electricity, and a willingness of people to devote a good portion of their waking hours to it?

And now she was trapped in there. The irony wasn't lost on me.

It was sheer dumb luck that Cynthia, Esme's mother and my grandmother's ex-daughter-in-law, happened to be a pioneer of punishing wrongdoers on the Internet. Besides the classic cheating men, she kept her finger on everything from revenge porn uploaders to cyber bullies. Because of that, she was able to sense Grandma's presence in the web and notify us right away.

Esme, anchored by her mother, had been making regular trips there in search for Grandma. Without a guide of my own in the vast sea of information, I had no choice but to step back and let my half-sister take over the lead.

There was a good reason why I took on all those mercenary assignments. It was either working myself to distraction or staying home and biting my nails off.

"I'm the one who's sorry." I swallowed. "I'm being a pest, and I know it."

"You're worried sick," Esme said gently. "We all are."

Just how long could Gran stay in the land of the substance-less before she could no longer rejoin the physical world? Just where the heck was her body right now anyway? Stashed somewhere in a safe house in the middle of nowhere? What if some wild animal got to it and she came back with a limb missing or something?

"And you're sure she still exists?" I forced myself to ask the very question for which I most dreaded the answer.

"Yes," Esme said firmly. "Mother said she's not truly lost if she's remembered by those she loves."

"Just how does that work?" I asked, wanting so much to believe that.

"You know how the more often a certain keyword is typed

into a search engine, the higher it raises in the ranking? Just like that, the more our grandmother is remembered and thought of by us, the less likely she's to fade away in the land of the Internet."

"Well, I sure as hell refuse to believe that she's gone for good." I blew out a breath. "So she better not fade away."

"I'll keep trying, I promise," Esme vowed.

"I know you will." I hesitated. I was never sure how much concern I could show someone as disciplined as Esme without sounding like I was doubting her ability to be in control of her emotions. Well, screw politeness. "How are you holding up, sis?"

A short pause, then Esme sighed. "It's been a trying few months."

The understatement of the year.

"Thank you for what you're doing. I mean it. I don't know what I would do without you. And please convey my thanks to Cynthia." My dad's ex might not have been the warmest person I'd known, but I had to admit she had been very gracious in helping us in this matter.

"I will. Good night, Megan." Esme hung up.

I forced back the tears that always threatened to spill out of my eyes during this part of the evening, when I found out, yet again, that there was no update regarding Grandma.

One thing was clear in my mind—I had to remember and honor my grandmother by keeping myself together.

I had to focus on the important stuff, and choose my battles wisely. That meant getting the minor things out of the way and not get so hung up on them as to be used as leverage by anyone, may it be Lucifer or the Council.

I reached over for the invoice from the Department of Vengeance Health, which I'd placed on the top of my dresser with the rest of the letters. Refusing payment was futile—as they had ways to take the funds right out of my bank account

—and would only give the Council an excuse to throw more roadblocks my way.

I quickly paid the invoice through electronic transfer. I had more than enough money to cover it, thanks to the payment from Hell that had already arrived in my account. It was just money. Taking care of the bill—and letting go of the bitterness associated with it—helped me concentrate on the end game, which was to fight against the Council.

Even if it meant working as a mercenary, and doing some fancy footwork with Lucifer.

———

I had just come out of the en suite bathroom and was about to slip into bed when I noticed a slight movement under the lump that was my unmade blankets and sheets.

The motion was almost too minuscule to detect, and there was no energy disturbance to indicate the presence of any supernaturals. Not to mention, my magical safeguard for the house was supposed to be top-notch.

But then the best ones were those who could bypass everything, weren't they?

Bit by bit, I expanded my wings. Usually, I pulled them out fast in case of emergency, but doing it excruciatingly slow meant whoever hiding under my bed couldn't detect the gathering of my power. Or so I hoped.

I quieted my mind and held back my power like a floodgate to a dam, in perfect control like Grandma had taught me, but ready to let go at a moment's notice. Then I carefully grabbed a corner of my blanket and yanked, prepared to blast my intruder with everything I had.

It was a good thing I gave my eyes a split second to suss out my enemy before I attacked.

A pair of large green eyes blinked at me, from the face of a young girl no older than seven. Blonde curls danced around her forehead and shoulders, disturbed by my displacement of the blanket.

"Candy!" I exclaimed, hastily pulled back my power, and folded my wings inward. "I almost killed you. What are you doing here?" In the last few months, I'd gotten to know the little rascal more, and hiding her energy signature and breaking through the duplex's safeguard like a pro were just some of her many skills. That girl was going to be a spectacular witch one of these days. Heck, she was already one in many ways.

"Hey, Megan." Candy, in her pink jammies, sat up on the bed. She was holding some kind of zombie-looking plastic doll, with dark circles under the eyes and scars all over the face and arms.

I was momentarily distracted. "What is that, a voodoo doll? Whatever happened to *My Little Pony*?"

The little witch whom Gregory regarded as a baby sister rolled her eyes. "Oh, *please*, it's Monster High."

She looked at me as if expecting me to know what she was talking about. I had no idea. Technically being a supernatural meant we were all monsters in one form or another. To use the words "Monster High" would be like saying something obvious like "edible food" or "wearable shoes."

"You're elementary school age," I reminded her. "High school is a bit far away."

"It's not like I'll be going to either, so what's the difference?" she said defiantly.

That was, sadly, the truth. Until Candy grew up enough to defend herself, her incredibly potent yet raw talent would attract very bad attention from the wrong people. There were vampiric supernaturals out there who would want nothing more than to make a meal of her and her magic. Enrolling in school run by the four major witches' unions didn't protect her. Monsters still came to her home. That was why she was on the run with her mom and younger brother. Mel took them in and gave them shelter, and Candy's mom became his jack-of-all-trade assistant.

I sometimes found Candy sounding a few years older than her age, if not in the choice of words then in the emotions behind them. But that was because she'd been through a lot. I also know that behind Candy's bravo hid a longing for a normal life she would never have. So I repeated my question from earlier, but gentler this time, "What are you doing here?"

Candy grinned. "I came to help you."

"Help me with what?" I frowned. I wasn't exactly in the mood for tea with dolls just about now, of the zombie variety or otherwise.

"Finding your gran. In the Internet," she said smugly.

That stopped me short.

"Who told you I want to do that?" It was supposed to be hush-hush. First Lucifer implying that he knew, now Candy *saying* so. Did the whole Cosmic Balance know about Grandma's whereabouts or something?

"I heard the grown-ups talking about it. You forgot I'm there." Candy added, "And I can help you."

"No way." I mean, how could she? Esme's mother had been searching for months, and Cynthia was one of the pioneers of online vengeance, starting from the early days of dial-up modem and sites such as Hot or Not. If she couldn't do it thus far, how could Candy?

"Yes, I can."

"How?"

"The Witching Hour." She grinned.

"That's the time when witches are supposed to be at their most powerful, right? I thought it's all a myth."

"No, it isn't." Candy shifted her body to sit on the edge of the bed, kicking her feet from front to back. "Witches *are* more powerful during that time, and so are ghosts."

"Ghosts?"

"Your gran got no body, right? So she's a ghost."

"I don't know what happened to her body, but she's no ghost. She's *not* dead yet." When I realized I was practically baring my teeth at the kid for vocalizing what I'd been fearing the most, I softened my voice, "She's not."

But Candy's words had gotten me thinking. Grandma was currently substance-less. So she was, in a way, no different than a ghost. What if, as another supernatural whose power was also enhanced during the witching hour, Candy could indeed reach out to Gran? What if she could truly pull off what Cynthia couldn't?

"So, you're going to let me help?" Candy asked.

There was something in her voice that was just a touch too eager. "Er, does your mom know you're here?"

Due to Candy's witch nature, her mom was never too straight about bedtime. And she'd done a sleepover with me once before when her younger brother got sick and required her mom's full attention. But still, if the little girl hadn't lured me with all that talk of help, I would've asked if she got her mama's permission to be here right away.

She pouted. "What does it matter?"

Uh-oh. "You sneaked out, didn't you? Candy, what were you *thinking*?"

Due to the potential danger of her being feasted on, Candy's mom and Mel generally guarded over her quite zeal-ously. And then there was Gregory, the self-designated big brother, who was even more protective than them.

Candy bit her lips and cast her eyes downward.

I sat down on the edge of the bed next to Candy, and in a softer voice, asked, "What happened, kiddo?"

Candy's fingers pulled at the purple and black hair of her

zombie doll. "Tonight Mel was going to show me how to astral."

"That's awesome!" I whistled. It must be a big step for Mel to be teaching her astral projection, an act that could potentially put her energy signature on the map, so to speak, if they weren't careful, "Wait, did you say 'was going to'?"

Her fingers fisted around the polyester hair, Candy sniffled. "Gregory wouldn't let him. He was being a jerk."

So Mel thought Candy was ready, but Gregory didn't. Since Mel wasn't the reckless type, I would have to assume that Gregory was being overly cautious. Or not. We were living in a dangerous world. I shuddered as I remembered the succubus queens that, up to a few months ago, I never even knew existed.

"I'm sure he'll turn around." I tried to sound neutral. The business of guarding Candy was a tough call—held too tight, and it would undermine the young witch's confidence, not to mention hurt her feelings; held not tight enough, and she became an energy snack bar.

"I told him I'd be careful," Candy said. "He wouldn't listen."

"You being here won't exactly convince him," I pointed out.

"I hate you." Candy glared at me, finding a new target for her frustration.

"No, you don't." I shook my head and ruffled her hair. "Come on, let me call Gregory and he'll come take you home."

"No, not until I get you into the Internet." Candy's little shoulders were set.

"Why is it so important?" I asked suspiciously.

"Because it'll prove to them I can handle it."

"But what if you can't?" The last thing I wanted to do was

put her in danger. Mel would kill me, and Candy's mom, too. Not to mention Gregory. And most likely not in that order.

"Yes, I can. And I won't go into the net myself. *You* will. Let me show you," she coerced. "Come on, you want to find your gran, right?"

Damn. That little kid tempted me even more so than Lucifer. With Lucifer I had no idea what he could offer, let alone what he wanted in return, but Candy's offer was specific, and her intention sincere if a bit pride-motivated.

I glanced at the clock. The witching hour was between midnight and 2 a.m. It was now just half an hour before it started.

Without waiting for my answer—or confident in my inability to turn down her offer—Candy took out a small laptop with a bright green exterior and colorful, large keys. It almost looked like one of those Leap Frog learning toys for young children, but I wasn't fooled—that little machine had speed and memory that was essentially espionage-grade, and it was operated by the world's youngest and cutest witch-slash-hacker.

Candy's fingers flew over the keyboard in a blur, then she turned the machine over and showed me the screen. I didn't even bother to hide my eagerness as I leaned forward.

There was a picture of Grandma in a grey designer suit, standing with her arms crossed, in what looked like a profile in an official-looking website. Then I read what the domain name was.

"Wait, there's an official site for the Aequitas family?" My jaw sagged.

"Yes. Encrypted for supernaturals only," Candy confirmed.

Well, they sure didn't tell me about it. I guess the hybrid-mercenary black sheep of the family wouldn't be featured on such a site.

I clicked around and did a cursory scan of Grandma's

profile. There was no mention of her being missing, just a contact email address that obviously got directed to the main server. Who knew if anyone really checked that? Maybe not for months.

"Okay, now what?" I asked. I didn't see anything that would help me get into the Internet. There was a veil separating the living and the virtual world, making me only able to surf the net, not enter it. And no, breaking the screen wouldn't help, either. Believe me, I tried that in the early days of Grandma's disappearance.

"Now we wait until midnight, then we write her an email."

"An email?" I echoed incredulously. How would that accomplish anything?

"You can even do the typing," Candy offered. "See, I'm not putting myself in danger."

"What danger?" I rose my eyebrow. "It's just an email."

"No, it's more. It's a way into the net," Candy corrected. "I already put my witch power into the laptop. It's all set to go. When you press 'send,' you'll piggyback ride on the email. Straight into the web."

"That's it? That's the way in?" It sounded too easy. If so, why would Esme and her mom spend months searching? As a matter of fact, it looked like even Mel could've help me out a long time ago. Granted, none of them had the witching-hour angle, but still.

Candy bit her lips. "I think so."

The slight hesitation in her voice gave me pause. "Whatever happened to your confidence earlier?"

"I've never done it before, so I'm not a hundred percent sure. But I'm pretty sure."

"Okay, let's say I really could get in, and by some miracle find Grandma, how do we even get back home?"

Candy's face brightened. "That's easy. The email will be your anchor. When you're ready to come back, just think the word 'reply.' It'll generate another email that will take you back here."

"So let me get this straight." I put up a hand. "You're more sure about getting me out than getting me in?"

"Yes," Candy admitted. "So the risk is low, right?"

She had a point. The worst thing that could happen was me failing to get in at all. Or at least so I hoped. For all I knew, I could end up stuck in some in-between places and be lost forever. And there was the fact that I had no idea what to do to actually search for Grandma once I got there.

"Let me talk to my sister, if you don't want me to ask Mel," I told Candy.

"You can't," she stated.

"Look, I understand how you feel when it comes to Mel, but Esme is okay—"

"—no, you really *can't,*" Candy emphasized. "My witch power is only strong enough to break the veil once every month, and tonight is the night."

The clock showed it was now only a few minutes away from midnight. I glared at Candy. "How convenient. And you're only telling me this now *why?*"

She wouldn't look me in the eye.

"You're hoping that I won't want to wait another month just to get the other people involved, do you?"

And she would be right. Another month of waiting help-lessly for Gran would be torture.

"No Mel. No Rullies." Candy set her lips into a stubborn line.

Rullies was a mercenary term for professionally licensed vengeance demons, mocking them being sticklers for rules. If Candy was telling the truth about only being powerful enough tonight, then there really wasn't enough time to call Esme here, explain everything, and get her support for this crazy plan. My meticulous half-sister always made sure all the *i*'s were dotted and the *t*'s were crossed. By the time she deemed the venture worthy, the window of opportunity would be over.

Misgivings warred with the irrepressible ray of hope that was blossoming in my heart.

Just a peek. I'll just get there and come right back. You know, like a recon mission. Afterward, I'll find a way to duplicate what Candy did with Esme.

Maybe it was the relative attractiveness of Candy's offer compared to Lucifer's. Maybe I just got sick and tired of sitting back and letting others handle the matter, but at the stroke of midnight I found my index finger on the touch pad of the laptop, pressing down on an arrow on the screen that would send a simple email titled "Hi." Just as Candy had claimed, she'd already put her witch power into the laptop, which carried the signature of scented bubblegum and orange-flavored popsicles.

Instantly I felt my spirit drawing toward the screen, leaving my body behind. I was weightless, and time ceased to exist. I could "see" the email racing toward the Internet in slow motion, and I hopped on it as if it was a magic carpet and I was Aladdin.

Yet I was going forward, but not at the same time. Something was stopping me from fully leaving my corporeal body behind. It was like there was a barrier of Jello between me and my designation. Everything turned sluggish, and the sound was muted.

Then my spirit slammed right back into my body, hard, and a blast of energy from the direction of the screen sent me flying in the air and I hit the wall behind me three feet above the ground. I slid down onto the floor unceremoniously.

A sly voice spoke, its coldness slithering on the surface of my skin, "Where is shhhhhe?"

Misty fingers filled my bedroom, sending its temperature

plunging. My heart rate, instead of speeding up in the face of this invisible threat, slowed down while my muscles relaxed, my power being drained out of me and poured into the unnatural mist.

I tried to pick myself up off the floor, but I couldn't get my body to move more than a few inches, and that was with crawling. I glanced around frantically for Candy, afraid that she was the one the voice was seeking. It would fit with the energy-sucking nature of the misty fingers.

My fear was confirmed when I looked up and saw her being held up by the waist in midair, imprisoned by the misty fingers which grew and merged into a thick vertical tree trunk. She screamed, her short chubby legs kicked out in futility. Streams of energy were being pulled out of her and into the mist. The menacing entity must've prevented sounds to escape from this room, or else Rosemary would have come running by now. I was grateful not to have my very human roommate dragged into this.

The little girl's earlier words rang in my ears. *I already put my witch power into the laptop. It's all set to go.*

Oh hell, was that how the unknown nemesis tracked her here? Was the online access like a back door of sorts, over-riding the safeguard placed around my house? Could it be that not only was I unable to get into the net, I'd drawn a monster out of it? What the hell had I done?

Monsters had come for Candy, and it was all my fault. How was I going to fix this? And fix it I would have to. Not only because Gregory would have my head, but because I would never forgive myself if something happened to the little girl.

I inched toward the laptop. If only I could get a hold of it and smash it, maybe it would send the misty fingers back where they came from?

Candy continued to scream, but in a much weaker voice

now that made it more of a whimper. I wasn't doing so swell myself, my limbs felt like lead and my eyelids kept threatening to close on me. My bedroom continued to fog up, most likely a sign of increased power of our unseen enemy as Candy was being fed on.

The cold voice crackled in delight.

The door of my bedroom blasted open, and a familiar silhouette filled the doorway.

Gregory. With his wings fully extended.

I wanted to yell, or gesture, or do something that would alert him to target the laptop. But I needn't try. He made a beeline there and sent the machine crashing onto the floor, breaking the screen right off. And no, it wasn't the type that the screen could naturally come off. Then he wrapped the two parts in a spell that reduced the laptop to its microchip components.

The mist started to fade, and I felt better almost immediately. With a renewed burst of energy, I scrambled to get up. As Gregory casted some sort of spell to dispense the remaining mist, Candy no longer had anything holding her up and dropped to the floor. I rolled to her side and checked her over. The little girl looked shaken, but there was no physical damage from the fall. Thank Hades for the carpet.

After assuring myself that she was okay, I turned my attention back to Gregory.

The last of the mist regrouped and wrapped itself around Gregory's waist, racing over and over his middle like an ever-tightening snake coil. Then it poured itself into his belt buckle. Upon the entry, Gregory doubled over as if someone had punched him.

Then it was his turn to drop to the floor.

❧ 4 ❧

GUILT AND DREAMS

SADLY, I had a pretty good idea of what had just happened here.

Gregory's belt buckle wasn't just your run-of-the-mill fashion statement—it held a secret compartment that imprisoned a pair of succubus queens. Unlike their more common counterpart, who thrived on sexual energy, the queens prayed on pain and misery. Last time we encountered them, I was able to put them in a post-food coma of sorts when their bid to feed on my friend and I backfired. Gregory then miniaturized the cocoons they hibernated into and had been carrying them around his belt ever since.

It was a bit weird, having him basically having two women right around his middle at all times, but it couldn't be helped. Despite discreetly consulting as many experts in the matter as we would dare to do so, we'd yet to figure out how to deal with the queens without unleashing them right back into the world. By keeping the queens close, we could ensure that they were still where we wanted them to be.

The kind of monsters that would suck on Candy's energy would be related to the succubus queens in one form or another, and it was conceivable that once Gregory broke the web access to which they came from, the mist would be naturally drawn to its nearest brethren.

The question was, would they awaken the queens? If so, then we were talking about three enemies instead of one.

I rushed to Gregory. His limbs were flailing, and his skin took on a shade of greyish purple. I had no idea what to do for him.

"Let me," Candy said. With the resilience of young children, she had made it to Gregory's side and was now nudging me out of the way and had her hand hovering above Gregory's belt buckle. Streams of energies, like the ones taken out of her earlier, were now returning to her. Once that process was finished, a single, tiny wisp of black smoke—must be all that was left of Candy's attacker now that her power was taken away from it—snaked out of the compartment, then faded into nothing with an almost inaudible scream.

Nothing else came out of the belt buckle. Guess the queens must be still sleeping.

Gregory blinked his eyes and sat up, his gaze focused on Candy and checking every inch of her over. "Are you hurt?" he croaked.

Candy shook her head. Then Gregory was on his feet, glaring down at the two of us. We probably looked a little worse for wear, with sweat coating our foreheads and our bodies weak from the recent involuntary energy donation. And he wasn't much better, thanks to us.

Well, thanks to *me*.

I blurted out the first thing that came into my mind. "How did you know to come here?"

Gregory bit out, "Mel. He foresaw the whole thing—just barely—and told me to come and destroy the laptop."

"Oh." I didn't know what else to say. A lecture seemed to be coming, and I was never that good at listening to one of those. On the other hand, what happened was indeed my bad. I shouldn't have listened to Candy. I didn't intend to put her in danger, but I did.

Gregory's voice was unexpectedly gentle when he gestured us to sit down on my own bed. Given the circumstances I could hardly protest.

"There's something Mel and I hadn't told you." Gregory looked at both Candy and I. "Precisely because we were afraid you'd try to find a way around it. But given what happened, you might as well know."

"What are you talking about?" I asked.

"Mel has always been an observer of the happenings on the Internet, as he is with the Cosmic Balance. There's a reason why he only ever does the reading and monitoring. In order to access the Internet, and I mean physically enter and exit that realm, you need to master its two major components."

"Two?" Candy echoed.

Gregory nodded. "One is Hardware and Facts, which allow someone to *interpret* information. The other is Lies and Illusions, which allow someone to *create* information. That's why your action tonight failed—Candy has ever only learned how to do the first part from Mel because that's all he could do. Not to mention, the percentage, intensity, and consequences of each component are different for every entry, and require precise calculations for safe passage."

That explained a few things, like why Mel had never offered to help me locate Grandma. It wasn't through a lack of willingness. It also made me realize, for the first time, how complicated a task Esme and her mother were doing. Nothing like a little appreciation that truly humbled a person.

Gregory brought himself to Candy's eye level. "Enough excitement for a night, kid. Time to go home."

Candy's head lowered. "Sorry for all the trouble." Then, just as quick, she lifted it. "But that just shows you we should be honest with each other. And you should trust me more."

Gregory sighed. "Let's talk about this tomorrow, all right? Mel and your ma are waiting and probably worried sick. Off you go."

"What about you?" Candy asked.

"I'll be by shortly, but I have to speak to Megan first."

Uh-oh.

With a pout, Candy allowed Gregory to help her teleport home. My safeguard had by now tagged Candy as friend rather than foe, and the teleportation was allowed.

So there was Gregory and I, standing in the middle of my bedroom for the first time. And it wasn't like how I'd imagined it in the far and rare occasions when I caught myself fantasizing before quickly shutting it down. At least the current messiness of the room wasn't my doing, so I was spared the embarrassment on that front.

"Megan, I don't have to tell you what almost happened tonight. And I know firsthand how persuasive Candy can be. But please, I must ask you not to involve and endanger her from now on."

Everything he said was logical, and the tone he used was more flat than condescending, so why did I feel my ire rising?

Because he'd lied to me about the true nature of the Internet. He had hid the truth from me, and a *solus iungere* wasn't supposed to be able to do that to his true mate. Never mind that I wasn't his true mate. Maybe. Probably not.

"Well, I wouldn't have endangered her if I had all the facts," I retorted back, the shame of what almost happened was making me a little defensive. "We're business partners. I thought that meant something. And my grandma is freaking missing. So pardon me if I'd grabbed Candy's offer like a lifeline without thinking it through."

"Megan"—Gregory closed his eyes briefly, as if struggling to come up with something to say—"I—"

"Ju—just go." I wanted to say that I was shaking with anger. But after that little flare of temper, all I felt was an utter sense of fatigue. I was weary to the bone of getting nowhere with finding Grandma. I was sick and tired of going around in circles when it came to convincing my heart and instincts that there was nothing between Gregory and I. I was so done for the night. Yes, a part of me recognized that Gregory had good reasons for being mad at me, and in fact I'd probably be even more outraged if I was in his shoes, but I was too tired to care. "We'll talk tomorrow, okay? And I'll let you know if I get any calls from Marv."

Gregory bit back whatever the hack he was going to say and teleported away.

I pushed back the pang of longing I always had now whenever he left and got ready for bed. Again.

I did a reversion spell to turn the bedroom back to its pre-attack state. Screw doing it manually, right now I wasn't in the mood to save a few magical credits.

I hopped into the second shower of the evening and let the hot water ease some of my guilt, anger, and frustration. Then I used a bit more magic to zap dry my hair and got into bed.

It might as well be that I'd chosen to take Marv that night, because sleep didn't come easily for me. I was so wired up that, despite the fatigue, I wasn't able to simply shut off my mind.

Truth be told, it was hard to fall asleep most nights these days, but I generally used a spell that was equivalent to a human sleeping pill. Tonight, even that had failed me.

Scene after scene of what I'd been through in the past few months played through my mind as I stared at the ceiling, waiting for sleep to come.

...my friends and family fell around me one by one, cursed by the Council to experience a thousand kinds of pain. The helplessness that overwhelmed me as I watched them suffer...

...the moment when I realized that Grandma was in trouble. The sense of utter shock I felt because she had always seemed so indomitable to me...

...the deal I had had to make with the Council to get my friends out of the vengeance headquarters alive. My fear that it would all come back and bite me in the butt...

Then came that kiss with Gregory.

I shouldn't even be thinking about that in the face of all the other much more serious stuff, but half asleep, my defenses were down.

We were in front of the hospice where I just handed over my active co-op case to a school official, effectively putting an end to my time at Demon U. Gregory had agreed to take me on as his mercenary partner. I was wondering if I should suggest that we go grab some shawarmas when he wrapped his arms around me, his lips closing in on mine, the distance a mere half an inch away and getting less by the millisecond...

I was abruptly pulled out of that memory and submerged in another one. This one from my early childhood.

I was nine, and Mom found me crying under the desk in my bedroom. She was a gorgeous woman at any age, with flawless, glowing olive skin, and long, black hair swaying to her curvy hips.

"What's wrong, sweetie?" My trickster mother quickly put down the box of animate-on-demand plastic spiders she had taken up from the basement. For the sake of my dad, the arch vengeance demon, she no longer got involved in any major-league trickery since her marriage to him, but she always made sure to update her inventory to prepare for any small gigs that might come her way.

"Everyone hates me, why?" my younger self pouted, tears

streaked down my cheek. I was wearing my elementary school uniform, so I was at a stage in life where I was old enough to have gotten my share of cold shoulders, but not old enough to understand that things weren't going to get any better with time. Not with the vengeance lot. My heart ached for the day in the not so distance future in my younger self's timeline when she found that out the hard way.

Mom grimaced. "I'm so sorry, hon. They're like this because your daddy married me."

"And that's a bad thing?" The younger me frowned in confusion.

"Because I'm not a vengeance demon. You see, everyone believes that vengeance demons should marry each other."

"Why?" my younger self persisted.

Mom shrugged. "Because they think only vengeance demons could be *solus iungere* to each other."

My younger self frowned. "What's that?"

"A soul mate. When a vengeance demon meets his or hers and they kiss, they just know."

"How?"

"They just *do*."

"But you're not a vengeance demon." My younger self was chewing on her lower lip, clearly upset. "Does that mean you and daddy are not supposed to be together?"

Mom laughed, her voice as clear as silver bells. "Hon, believe me, your daddy and I definitely belong together. You'll feel it in your heart when it happens. Sometimes, just the scent of a true mate is enough to let you know."

"Does that mean Cold Cynthie wasn't Dad's soul mate?" My younger self seemed relieved by the idea. It was under-standable. Who would welcome the thought that their birth parents belong to other people?

Mom grasped. "That's not a very nice name to call Esme's mom."

"But she *is* cold," my younger self insisted.

"Doesn't matter. Listen, your daddy met Cynthia when he was very young and it's easy to mistake other stuff as love. This kind of mismatch happens more often than you think. It's not like there's a test they could run to make sure all the engaged couples are true *solus iungere* to each other. Most people realize their mistake too late and just live with it. Your daddy's divorce from Cynthia was quite the scandal back then. Well, until he topped it off by marrying *me*."

Mom's mischievous wink dissolved, and I was suddenly back to the memory of Gregory's lips pressing down on mine. First there was still a little bit of heated air between us, then our lips touched.

Then I felt it, and I knew.

There was the lust that I'd experienced to a degree before when kissing other boys in the past. But what was new was this undertone of delicious slow-burning fire, like hot apple cider on a cold winter night. It felt solid and grounded.

Ever and always. True and never extinguished.

Gregory deepened the kiss, tenderly stroking the small of my back. I sighed.

The sweet sensation made me want to shout my joy to the world and twirl in dresses in the full spectrum of the rainbow, which might explain the vengeance demon's out-of-character fashion choices during the time of courtship.

This, what I experienced right there, was why I'd had the urge to act like a lovesick teenager ever since that kiss happened. By all right I should be allowed to, even the strict vengeance society norms allowed that. I'd found my soul mate and it was a jubilant time.

Except Gregory disagreed.

Out of the blue, he pulled away without warning. No, *jumped away* was the more appropriate description. He acted like I was a hot potato and he'd forgotten to put on his oven mitts before touching me. Or like I was a toxic spill and he was afraid of getting chemical splatter on himself.

I was left with my jaw open, staring, which was as inelegant as it sounded. I shivered, and it wasn't just because Gregory's warm hands were no longer on me.

I closed my mouth, then opened it again, but words failed me. What could I possibly say?

Err, did you hate kissing me that much? Was my half-trickster saliva giving you an allergic reaction or something?

Or worse—*Hey, did you feel what I just felt? You want to meet my dad for our traditional Sunday night dinner? How's six o'clock sound?*

For a long moment we just stared at each other while our breathing returned to normal.

Then he cleared his throat and took out a black cell phone I'd never seen before. He kept his eyes on it and started talking, not looking at me. "I, er, took the liberty of setting up a 24/7 vengeance hotline for our business. The ads are not running until tomorrow afternoon, so I don't expect there will be any calls before then. Still, I'll keep the phone on me for now. That'll give you some uninterrupted rest to get ready for our engagement with Hell tomorrow morning. I'll pick you up at your place at eight thirty. It's better if we travel there together because..."

He went on and on about the details of our very first assignment together, talking very fast and very long, which was not like him at all. The Gregory I knew was measured when it came to his movement and speech, the deliberate slowness a mark of his self-assurance and confidence. This guy in front of me was babbling, and I wasn't paying attention to a word he said. Was this guy for real? After what we'd just shared, he recoiled and then started *talking shop*?

I wanted to kick him.

Back on my bed, the present-day me kicked off the sheet.

I'd been reliving that sense of utter bewilderment for months now. It was something that I'd puzzled over and over during my quiet moments. And I was no closer to an answer as I was right after it happened.

I sighed into my pillow. I just had to resign to the fact that I'd mistaken physical attraction for something far deeper, and Gregory obviously didn't feel the same way. Even if he did, what was to become of a union between a full-blooded vengeance demon and a hybrid? Like, get half a soul mate out of each other? Soul Mate Lite? Maybe what my parents had was nothing but a fluke, and there was nobody out there for me.

Or I was fated to go crazy one day and have six babies fathered by six different guys. You never knew. Ugh.

Eventually exhaustion won, and deep, dreamless sleep claimed me.

In the early morning hours I fell into another dream. It felt like a memory, but if so, it wasn't one that was familiar. It felt foreign, the force behind it cold and unnatural.

I was in a park, having a picnic with Jordon, my boyfriend. He handed me a portrait to look over. It was a pencil sketch depicting me in an apron at the kitchen of the animal shelter, having just taken out a tray of freshly-baked dog biscuits from the oven.

"I drew this for you long before we started going out." Jordon grinned.

I traced my finger over the tiny pencil strokes that formed the smile on my face in the portrait. "Is that how you see me?"

"Yes," Jordon murmured. "You're always beautiful to me."

There were two problems with this memory. One: I couldn't bake to save my life. Two: Jordon was Rosemary's boyfriend, not mine. The portrait he drew was of my roommate, not me.

How the hack did I end up experiencing Rosemary's dream?

And by all accounts, this looked like what ought to be a happy memory. I mean, the food from the picnic was delicious-looking, and Jordon was being super sweet and professing his love and everything. Then why was a sense of foreboding and queasiness coming over me as if a pet had just died? Or the half-eaten egg salad sandwich on the picnic cloth was off or something?

I saw the memory to its conclusion, where Jordon and Rosemary kissed, chased each other around the tree in laughter, and packed up before heading off to a local farmer's market. There was absolutely nothing there to indicate food poisoning or death of any kind, but the negative vibe persisted like a low hum that just wouldn't go away, coloring the happy times with imposed darkness.

Then the hum grew louder, higher pitched, until it became the speaking voice of a female. Cold, sly, and full of rage.

I could turn good dreams into bad dreams, and bad dreams into nightmares. Release my Boyce, mercenary, or your roommate will never wake up again.

5

KIDNAPPING OF THE MINDS

I HAD TO WAKE UP. Now.

I would've had a much harder time swimming back to wakefulness, had I not been helped by the sharp pain from a pair of claws digging into my side. I recognized the claws as belonging to Sassy, my feline shade, as she had a habit of kneading me when we cuddled in bed. I bitched about it, but she did it anyway. The difference this time around was the urgency and bluntness of the clawing, as if she, too, knew something was terribly wrong.

"Ouch!" I jumped out of bed, dislodging the cat from my side. I rubbed the scratches that Sassy gifted me with during her departure. My pajama top was torn and slightly blood-stained. Luckily as a supernatural I did heal fast. But still. "That hurts! And I actually mean it this time."

Sassy just hissed and started running toward the bedroom door. To put it correctly, she ran *through* it, being the shade that she was. Looked like my cat wanted me to follow her, and given the contents of my nightmare, I had a very good idea where she was headed. Ever since I moved in with Rosemary, Sassy had been looking out for my roommate, considered the human hers to protect.

Rosemary's bedroom was across from mine. Unlike the pigsty that was my sleeping area, she organized hers like she did with her kitchen—clean, neat, and not a dirty undergarment in sight.

My roommate was lying perfectly still on her bed, her eyes open but unseeing. There was a glassiness in them, as if she was gazing into infinity. I dropped onto the bed, set her upright on it, and gave her a little shake. "Rose," I used the nickname she insisted I use but never did. "Can you hear me?"

No answer.

Sassy jumped onto Rosemary's bed, sniffed at her toes, and meowed. The sound was pure rage. Something had gotten to her human, and the feline knew it. She was probably pretty pissed that whatever it was had gotten past her. She was a shade and it was supposed to be impossible to elude her.

I shook Rosemary again and she remained unresponsive, which was not entirely surprising. Whatever it was that could get past Sassy and invade my supernatural mind in the sanctuary of my own dreams had to be very powerful indeed. And that scared me more than the vacant look in my roommate's eyes.

I raced back to my room, picked up my cell, and pressed the speed dial of Gregory's number. I told myself that he was the first person I thought of because I'd just spoken to him, despite the fact that my own arch vengeance demon daddy would be more than qualified to deal with the situation at hand. If I wasn't so freaked out, I'd be horrified at how I'd come to lean on Gregory in such a short time, even right after we had a nasty fight.

"Gregory," I said as soon as the phone was picked up.

"What's wrong?" Not, *What have we got?* Which was what he usually said when we got a call in the middle of the night. My tight voice must've alerted him to the fact that this had nothing to do with new businesses generated from Marv.

"Come to my place. Now." I barely managed not to scream into the mouthpiece.

No sooner did I hastily change into something that was *not* ripped and bloodstained than there was a banging on my door.

I ran downstairs, yanked open the front door, and there was Gregory. He had on a wrinkled shirt and simple blue jeans that he must've thrown on before rushing here. His hair was disheveled, his face unshaved.

"What happened?" he asked urgently, his eyes raking up and down my body as if checking for injuries.

"It's Rosemary." I let him in, lowering the safeguard for the house. Following his example, I got right to it without discussing our previous disagreement. "She's gone. I mean, physically she's still here, but her spirit has either left or got locked inside her. Her eyes got all glassy, and I can't wake her up. And there was a ransom note of sorts. She's been—"

"Kidnapped," a man interrupted, having teleported directly into my living room, taking advantage of my temporary lax in security while inviting Gregory in. "Miss Aequitas, we meet again."

I inhaled sharply. A man with salt and pepper hair and nearly the same facial bone structure as Gregory stood in my living room as if he owned it. He could be anything from middle aged to elderly—with supernaturals it was often hard to tell after a certain point. It was summer, but the man was dressed in a three-piece black suit. I wondered if he had embedded a cooling spell tailored right into the clothes itself.

He was Macallister Sebastian Sumpsi, aka Minister of the Vengeance Ethics Commission. As if being a Council member wasn't bad enough, he was also the biological father who made a bastard out of Gregory. The gall of the man to just waltz in here at this ungodly hour.

"What are you doing here?" Gregory bit out, clearly sharing my sentiment.

Minister Sumpsi focused on me, refusing to spare his own flesh and blood even the briefest of glance. "I'm addressing Miss Aequitas."

"Okay, what the hell are you doing here?" I snapped. I didn't have time for this. "You know about Rosemary. Did you have something to do with the kidnapping?"

"Of course not." Minister Sumpsi looked offended. "The matters of insignificant mortals are beneath me."

"What have you done?" Gregory's words came out as a low growl. His vengeance wings were at full attention, his stance low and ready for a fight.

"I didn't *do* anything. I was visiting your mother—" Minister Sumpsi began.

"By visiting you mean you were hitting her up for a booty call in the middle of the night." A muscle jumped on Gregory's face. I promised myself I would drag the story out of him one of these days.

But not today.

"Such crass language." Minister Sumpsi *tsked.* "Anyway, I was visiting your mother and found her in the same state as how Miss Aequitas had described her roommate here."

"What? Mom is in trouble?" Gregory yelled. With a quick wave of his hand, he opened a cross-dimensional portal and looked ready to dive in headfirst. But he aborted at the last minute, letting the portal fade away as he grabbed my shoulders instead. "Megan, tell me exactly what state your roommate is in. I need to know what I'll be walking into."

"As...as I said, she's unconscious." I swallowed. Boy, Gregory's face was a picture of thunderclouds. Even though I knew his anger wasn't directed at me, being in such close proximity to it, I still shivered. Out of all the times I'd faced sticky situations with him in business, I'd never seen him like this. Professionally annoyed and outraged, yes, but not this deep-in-the-gut anger. This was personal. "Her mind is hijacked, with good memories being turned into bad ones. There was a voice there, telling me I have to give Boyce Armstrong in exchange for Rosemary."

"Boyce Armstrong, our target." Gregory's jaw formed a grim line.

"Yep." And there it was, the consequence of working with Lucifer. If I didn't have doubts about the arrangement before, I sure did now. The generous pay dirt we took home held hidden risks far beyond a simple, cut-and-dry client/free-lancer relationship.

Gregory forced a calming breath into his lungs, then he waved his hand and got ready to teleport again.

"Don't bother going to her," Minister Sumpsi spoke at the last minute. "I've brought her here."

The asshole sure knew how to hold back information.

Minister Sumpsi took a green bubble the size of a marble out of his suit pocket and threw it toward my living room sofa. Despite the momentum, the bubble moved away from his hand slowly, enlarging exponentially until, by the time it reached the sofa, it was as big as the furniture itself. Being blown up to this size, I could see that the bubble's thick texture and relative lack of transparency was similar to the type of air pockets that humans like to produce when they chewed bubble gum.

Then the bubble burst, revealing a woman. She dropped onto the sofa none too gently, her neck bent in an awkward way that would most likely give her the crick of a lifetime. She appeared to be in deep sleep, her body limp and relaxed.

"Mom!" Gregory ran to the woman and tenderly rolled

her head into a more comfortable position. The look he gave his father promised retribution and pain. "How dare you transport her like a piece of cargo!"

Minister Sumpsi shrugged. "She isn't hurt by it whatsoever."

Yeah, but that wasn't how one should treat even someone they'd called just for booty call, let alone the mother of their child. Bastard. Minister of Vengeance Ethics, my butt.

I narrowed my eyes and crossed my arms, looking at the old man. He had come here, to my own home, to see *me*. I bet he didn't even know Gregory was going to be here. "So let me guess. You found your would-be lover of the night unconscious upon your arrival. You went into her mind, found the message left there, and figured this is related to your son's mercenary business. Instead of solving it yourself or having the guts to go to Gregory, you came to my doorstep to dump this onto me so *I'll* go tell him."

"I'm here to show you the consequences of your new life, you insolent child!" Minister Sumpsi huffed. "You keep working with the mercenaries, and you're bound to drag those you love into your mess. I'm trying to make you take responsibility for the path you've chosen."

"To what end, so that I'll realize what a better alternative it is to help the Council destroy the world? After what you've done to my grandmother? Seriously?" I snorted.

Minister Sumpsi's usually civilized face twisted into a sneer. "You can delude yourself into thinking that you're free of us, young lady, but you're a vengeance demon, and you are ours. You better hope you never get injured from your *new job*. I'll make sure that every hospital triage desk from this plane and beyond knows to treat you last."

With that parting shot, he teleported away.

I raised the safeguard while Gregory continued stroking his mother's hair. In the faint early morning rays I could tell that she was a woman in her forties, clad in a nightdress and a white bathrobe. I was glad of the presence of the bathrobe, because from the hot-red lace trim peeking out of it and the generous showing of legs, I got a feeling the nightdress would match the "booty call" nature of the foiled visit a little too well. Not exactly the kind of things I wanted to see from the parent of my maybe soul mate.

I could see the resemblance between mother and child. Her curly chestnut hair was the same shade as Gregory's, and they shared the same chiseled cheekbones. Despite the lines on her face that betrayed a not-so-kind life, she was still an attractive woman. Her vengeance power, however, was nowhere near her son's, let alone Minister Sumpsi's. Her signature was weak and all over the place, though I had no idea if that was due to the kidnapping of her mind, since I'd never met her at her normal state to establish a baseline. Her open, unfocused eyes were so like Rosemary's that I wanted to rush upstairs to check on my roommate right this moment.

"Give me every detail on what happened with Rosemary," Gregory said softly, his eyes not leaving his mother's face.

I told him.

"So this lover of Boyce Armstrong's took someone from each of our lives as hostages in exchange for him." Gregory's eyes glinted like dark chips of ice on a cold January highway.

I shivered. Gregory's mother was a supernatural and it didn't stop whatever it was enthralling her from taking hold. What chance did Rosemary have to get out of this?

As if sensing my train of thoughts, Gregory said softly, "My mother is weaker than most supernaturals. Her entrapment doesn't mean your roommate is without hope."

He didn't elaborate, so I concentrated on the matter at hand. The associates of hardened criminals were usually also, well, hardened criminals. Add that with a little bit of crazy, obsessive love, and it was a recipe for disaster. Judging from the almost simultaneous attacks on Rosemary and Gregory's mother, this one seemed to have the ability to be in two places at the same time.

"What do we do?" I asked, squeezing my hands together until they hurt. "You heard the minister. I doubt taking them to the hospital would be the best choice right now, even if Rosemary was a supernatural."

"I agree." Gregory nodded. "We have to see if we can free them ourselves. Your roommate and my mother are either ejected from their minds or being trapped inside them. Either way, the answer could be in there as well."

I had to admit, this "kidnapping" actually had a twisted kind of brilliance, as the women's bodies were still right here with us. If our loved ones were physically missing, there were locator spells we could employ to find them. The working of the mind, on the contrary, was still very much a mystery, even for supernaturals.

Sassy hopped downstairs and stared at Gregory. He leaned down and let her sniff his fingers. She must've decided that he was all right, because she wound around his legs, then turned to me and meowed, tilting her head toward the stairs as if urging me to get back to Rosemary.

"My shade is attached to Rosemary," I explained to Gregory as I started following Sassy toward the stairs.

Gregory stayed rooted, frowning at Sassy with the most peculiar expression. "The invader was able to launch an assault on your roommate, in your house, while your shade was here?"

"Looks like it." I shrugged.

"But you know what that means, don't you?" He blew out a breath heavily. "It means that the invader herself must also be a shade. It takes a familiar to get past a creature that's born into the shadow."

He closed his eyes and ran his palm over his forehead, his eyebrows creased deeply.

I stopped in my tracks, icy fingers caressing my stomach. Even in the worst of work situations—and there had been a hairy moment or two—Gregory had never seemed upset or overwhelmed by the tasks ahead. Yet here he was, coming as close to being unnerved as I'd seen him.

I decided the best way to address it was to treat it like any other case. So I used my most business-like tone and said briskly, "I assume that would make our job a little bit harder."

Gregory picked up his mother to follow me, so I started moving again. It was probably a good idea to have his mom and Rosemary close to each other for whatever it was we were supposed to do to help them anyway. "That's an under-statement. How much do you know about shades in general?" he asked.

"No more than what common sense dictates. They say shades make the most loyal pets if you get them real young. They choose you, you don't choose them. Once they imprint on you, it's for life, and they'll look out for you always."

"But you see, not all shades would choose the role of loyal pets and de-facto bodyguards." Gregory shook his head as he gingerly walked up the stairs while making sure his mother's dangling feet weren't hitting anything. "There is a darker type that could take on corporeal form if they wish, that likes to hide inside the minds of others like a parasite, a menacing presence in the backdrop of memories. They feed on guilt and pain."

"Is that why that voice spoke to me through Rosemary's memory?" I gestured Gregory to my bedroom, and he placed his mom on my mattress. There wasn't any space to put his mom in Rosemary's room, unless you counted a couple of folding chairs.

Boy, was I glad I splurged a bit and did that magical quick

clean on my room. On the other hand, my reversion spell was only able to turn my bedroom back to the way it was before the first attack—yes, I was rapidly exceeding the attack quota de jour—and the original state of my room wasn't exactly tidy to begin with. Maybe it would've been better if I never cleaned up the room. Then my own mess would've been totally hidden by the bigger mess.

"That memory of Rosemary's—was it a happy one?" Gregory asked as he made minor adjustments to make his mother's position more comfortable.

"It was supposed to be, until it turned all dark and gloomy for no apparent reason."

"That would be the shade's doing." Gregory appeared thoughtful. "She was converting a happy memory into a horrible one that needed to be repressed."

"How does it work?" I asked, intrigued despite the current situation.

"A real repressed memory, created from a traumatic event, hides in the shadow of the mind and festers like an untreated wound. A fake one mimics that, making the conscious mind shy away from dealing with it because it feels painful and filled with shame. When I said this type of shade feed on guilt and pain, I mean they often cultivated the emotions themselves by artificially nurturing the environment necessary for it."

"That's why she said 'I could turn good dreams into bad dreams, and bad dreams into nightmares.'" I muttered.

"Exactly. We have to get my mom and Rosemary out before the shade starts corrupting every happy memory they ever had. Permanently."

"So where do we begin?" I asked. We never discussed giving into the kidnapper's demand and actually getting Boyce for the proposed exchange. It wasn't happening and the reason was simple—going up against Lucifer would be suicidal. And then we die, go to Hell, and get slaughtered all over again. The big circle of death. No thank you.

"We have to enter the infected memories and decontaminate them one by one. Only then can we eject the shade once and for all. But Megan—" He swallowed. Talk about guilt—there was a load of it that was evident on Gregory's face right now, and it instantly put me on guard. "Do you mind if we work on Rosemary first?"

"Why?" I stared at him, and he looked away for a second before facing me again. He straightened his spine.

"I could lie and say that it's because your roommate is human, and therefore more vulnerable to the shade's attack and has less time before it's too late. But the truth is, my mother is the more vulnerable one. The kind of extraction we're talking about is tricky, and I dare not risk her until I know what we're dealing with. For all we know, entering and exiting a damaged memory in itself could destroy it, or even hurt the very spirit of the person altogether."

"But it's okay to use Rosemary as a guinea pig?" I asked angrily. Growing up bullied and stigmatized, I didn't have friends by the bucket. Rosemary might not be blood, and I could never be fully honest with the mortal, but she still means a lot to me. How dare Gregory place her at risk over his mother when my human roommate was so obviously the more exposed of the two?

Was everything I came to believe Gregory to be nothing but a lie? Was my initial assessment of him as a scumbag right, after all? Was he *that* willing to throw what was mine under the bus when his was threatened? Was this retaliation for what almost happened to Candy under my watch?

Might as well that nothing came out of that kiss, then.

Bad enough that thanks to my need to defeat the Council, I got into the mercenary line of work, became involved in Lucifer's business, and brought fear and devastation to Rosemary's doorstep, damn if I was going to put her last because I was too busy playing maybe-soul-mate with Gregory.

"Trust me, your roommate is far stronger than my mother," Gregory countered.

"Bullshit," I bit out, "your mother is a freakin' supernatural. Rosemary is only human."

"Believe me, your roommate is the tougher one," Gregory said.

"Why?"

He locked his jaws mulishly.

"Oh, come *on*, don't go silent on me now." He was asking me to trust him. A lot. He better have a darn good explanation.

"Because even though I'd never get to know your roommate well, I heard enough about her through you to get a good idea of who she is. She's mentally strong," he ground out.

"How did you come to that particular conclusion?" I crossed my arms.

"You told me the story about that abandoned nest of eggs under her window and how she believes they would still hatch. She's positive enough to never give up hope on those long-calcified eggs, and she allows herself to be happy again even after she suffers a disappointment. She's tough." The corners of Gregory's mouth turned down, as if he would rather eat nails than to say his next words. "Unlike my mother."

"Because she's weak enough to take a booty call from the man who walked out on her and her child?" As soon as the words left my mouth, I regretted it—or at the very least, I regretted using the word *booty*. Gregory had never talked about his mother other than in a superficial way since I'd known him, and me being insensitive about it when he started doing so wasn't how I'd imagined it.

"Okay, that was out of line," I said. "I shouldn't have—"

Gregory held up a hand, "No, despite the crude way you put it, you were right. My mother never stopped mooning over my biological father. Never allowed herself to love someone else. Never mind that he'd never paid her a single dime of child support. Never mind that he'd moved on and married someone else, she has no pride and no dignity where he's concerned. There's a reason why the shade targeted whom she targeted—she took the people she considered to be the weakest links in our lives. Your roommate is human, and by the natural design of her race she's weaker, while my mother had allowed an unworthy man to ruin her life. An emotional vulnerability, especially a willful one, is always more severe than a physical shortcoming."

Oh crap, it did sound like Gregory's mother was the one who was more at risk once he put it that way.

In a way, it would've been easier if Gregory had lied about why we should try to help Rosemary first. Instead, his honesty was forcing me to be an active participant in the decision to choose the safety of his mother over my roommate. With him being upfront about everything, I couldn't even claim the bliss of ignorance.

Damn him.

✿ 6 ✿

GREGORY and I each stood on one side of Rosemary, holding her hands.

"The actual viewing of memory is no different than the regular procedure," Gregory explained. "But rather than experiencing the recollection after it is downloaded and reformatted onto a flash drive, we'll be seeing it at its source. Since you're already familiar with the infected memory, I'll rely on you to lead the way."

Lead the way. Right. As if a single wrong move wouldn't have a negative impact on Rosemary's psyche, maybe even her life. I didn't want the responsibility. But I couldn't back down, either.

Then something occurred to me.

"Wait, if we're both going in, who's going to be our anchor?" I asked. Even for regular memory viewing, there was always someone doing the anchoring, staying behind in the physical world to make sure that the viewer didn't get lost in the memories. I would assume that would be even more important, given what was awaiting us inside Rosemary's mind.

Stuck forever wandering in my roommate's corrupted memories sounded like a punishment worse than death.

Sassy settled herself right at the foot of the bed and meowed. "Meeee yyyelp!"

I could've sworn it sounded like: "Me help!"

Gregory reached over and scratched Sassy at the back of her ear, "I figured you would want to help, feline warrior."

I rolled my eyes. Leave it to my cat to be chummy with Gregory when I was still trying to figure it all out with him. Our fight earlier might've been put on the back burner for now, but it remained unresolved. It was surprising to see him drawing back his hand with all five fingers intact. Sassy usually wasn't into being patted. I guess that little feline warrior compliment went a long way. I sighed and closed my eyes, willing myself to visualize the memory where the shade had given me the warning.

A park full of trees. A picnic. A pencil sketch.

Once I was certain I got as many details of the scene right, I pushed this "contraband" memory toward Rosemary's mind. The real memory of that event, being attracted to its fake counterpart, surfaced and became front and center in her consciousness.

Willing myself to become as light as smoke, I grabbed onto the thread of the real memory and dove into Rosemary's mind. Gregory, in a similar new form, followed me while keeping a connection open with Sassy. The feline would use her meows to guide us back if we needed to pull out.

Then we were in, and we watched as Rosemary and Jordon laughed and chased each other around the tree. Rosemary shrieked when Jordon caught her in his arms and leaned in for a kiss, the picnic and the drawing lay forgotten at their feet.

The couple appeared very happy, but there was a gloom-and-doom narrative droning in the background, in the same female voice that had spoken to me earlier, "This joyful moment is not going to last. Nothing ever does. Look at his handsome face. Do you think someone like that would stay with you? He's probably figuring out a way to gently get rid of you as we speak. You're going to look back at this memory as a moment of shame, when you were dumb enough to let down your guard and be so blinded by so-called love..."

"Cheerful." Gregory shook his head.

The narrative was all a lie, of course. This memory would be around a year old, and the couple was still together in the present time. As far as I knew Jordon had never been unfaithful. The way the shade colored everything, though, every one of his gestures was suspect, every loving word from him was a falsehood.

I was reminded of what the leading man from that human movie *Casablanca* said, "We'll always have Paris." The actual details of what happened in Paris never changed, but the interpretation of what they meant did. And it changed everything.

What was once sweet between Rosemary and Jordon was now stained with doubt and shame.

Changed memories led to changed mood, which in the long-term led to a whole altered outlook in life.

"I need to find the root of that negative voice," I said. When I viewed memories from USBs, I could just click back to an earlier timeline like I would with any video clips. But how do I do that here when I was experiencing the memory directly?

I visualized the lips of Rosemary and Jordon parting from each other, then had the couple running backward around the tree. It worked! I continued to "rewind" the memory, until we stood before Rosemary and Jordon as he handed her the portrait.

"I drew this for you long before we started going out." Jordon grinned.

Rosemary traced her finger over the pencil strokes. "Is that how you see me?"

"Yes," Jordon murmured. "You're always beautiful to me."

There it was. When he said that, there was the faintest of a snicker in the background, blended in with the rustling of leaves, mocking Jordon's sincere words.

"I think this is where it begins," Gregory said.

"I agree." Then I frowned. "The question is how do we neutralize the negative vibe?"

Gregory pursed his lips. "From what I understand, everyone's brain works differently. You know her better than I. What do you think are her best strengths to fight this?"

Well, there was Rosemary's sass for life and her generous spirit. She could brighten up a room with a smile and whip up a cheesecake from scratch in less time than it would take someone to drive out to the store and buy one. And she would share it with anybody who wanted a piece. That was just how she was.

That stupid shade messed with the wrong girl. The core of Rosemary was filled with positivity. All I had to do was find a way to draw out her real voice and amplify it with my supernatural strength.

There was an old trickster belief that if you were inside someone's head, and you touched the visual representation of that person in their memory, you could hear the thoughts they had during the experience. I tried doing it to Fir once when I was little and ended up with a migraine for my trouble because his thoughts blew by me too fast. My half-brother's brain raced at a thousand miles a second, countless trickery plots twirling in his head. But even if I'd chosen a quieter brain, the end result would've been the same—people naturally talked to themselves without filter, pleasantries, or the need to explain things because they were their own audience.

But with Rosemary being in a state of mental paralysis, her thoughts might just move slow enough for me to follow.

I walked closer to Memory Rosemary and placed my hand on hers as I'd done with her physical body back in her room. Immediately, her true thoughts and feelings from that moment in time rushed toward me like a freight train. Definitely not as fast and confusing as Fir's had been, but still pretty intense.

What I found there was a great sense of awe and wonder. *I can't believe he'd draw that for me. It's very nice. I didn't even know he had feelings for me back then. All that time we'd worked in the shelter together, liking each other and never thought the other would return the feelings. How silly is that?*

I honed in on Rosemary's inherent optimism. She wasn't dwelling on lost times, but rather, looking forward to the future. I poured my strength behind that sunny personality, enhancing it. I felt Gregory doing the same beside me.

Come out, Rose. I called to her spirit. *All this doom and gloom is not who you are. Come out and show them.*

I kept calling her, and soon our surrounding became more colorful. There was a sweet, light breeze in the air. The vibrantly green grass blades swayed. The trees burst to life with white and yellow flowers, bees buzzing by collecting its nectar. All over the park, the natural energy of my roommate was seeping into the very soil, drenching every pore with positive outlook and hope.

A second Rosemary appeared. This one was semi-transparent. Her eyes widened when she saw me, and she mouthed my name. She must be my roommate's spirit.

But before she could fully solidify and take control of her own memory, the happy feeling around us got rapidly sucked away like water going into a sinkhole.

The shade was fighting back.

The tree leaves became dry before our very eyes, dropping onto the ground like it was suddenly autumn. The sky darkened with storm clouds. A howling gust blew across the park, lifting up the dead leaves and twirling them around like they were trapped in a wind tunnel. The park-goers screamed, covering their faces from the razor-sharp edges of the leaves. Jordon put Memory Rosemary behind him, shielding her from the worst of the assault.

Cold and despair once again dominated the landscape, the very anti-thesis of what my roommate was, and no doubt grinded at her spirit like sandpaper. With a silent scream, Spirit Rosemary fell to her knees.

As the sly laughter of the shade rang, and Spirit Rosemary started to fade, retreating from this memory, I grabbed her memory counterpart once more, searching for any authentic, positive thought that was still there. While I was doing that, Gregory kneeled in front of Spirit Rosemary, whispering words of assurance to her, encouraging her to stay just a little longer.

There! I found one of her last remaining positive thoughts from this experience, and I held onto it with everything I had.

That was a really good lunch. I think I'm going to ask Jordon to come with me to the farmer's market before they close. I want to try that new lamb curry dish I found online. I'll see if he's interested in being my guinea pig. Megan already texted me and said she'll be working the night shift again...

Hope. Love. Plus a tiny little hint of naughtiness. Perfect.

I threw everything I got behind those positive thoughts. Sassy anchoring us from the physical world or not, there was no way the shade would release us from this memory if Rosemary's spirit retreated. I wasn't going to get stuck here, and that was that.

Gregory looked at me and nodded, seemingly reading my mind. He put his arms around Spirit Rosemary and muttered under his breath, building up a shield of sorts to block the worst of the wintry assault from her, his will indomitable in refusing to let her slip away.

Another strong gust of wind blew across the park, this one different from the others because it was directed toward Gregory and I, while before none of the things from this world of memory could really touch us. The wind wrapped us in a mini tornado of twigs, leaves, and even contents from a nearby garbage can. I would have time to feel disgusted if I wasn't so busy trying to hunker down.

Soft drink from half-finished cans soaked through my shirt, while saliva-glazed food from Styrofoam containers hit me right on the forehead. The twigs made gashes on my hands and cheeks, the pain worse than a thousand paper cuts. I bit my lips to prevent myself from screaming against the onslaught. The physical pain nearly broke my connection with Memory Rosemary's positive thoughts.

"Megan!" I could barely hear Gregory through the hurricane-force wind, though he must be still only a few feet away.

"I'm here!" I pushed aside all the physical discomfort and concentrated on the faint thread that still linked me to Memory Rosemary. It was weak, so very weak. I supplied it with the essence of my roommate from my own memory of her—all the good times we'd had trying out her latest experimentation, all the things I'd learned about animals by working in the shelter with her.

As the connection built, I crawled my way toward the sound of Gregory's voice. When I reached him, he pulled me close so we were both wrapping our arms around Spirit Rosemary. Just like me, Gregory was looking a little worse for wear, with various nicks and bruises all over his body. Even knowing that they would be gone once we return to the physical world, I still grimaced.

Spirit Rosemary stared at me and swallowed, "Megan, is it really you?"

"Yeah." I cleared my throat.

"I want to go. This is not me. None of this is me." She looked at the devastation around us with tears in her voice.

"I know. But you can't go. There's nowhere safe to hide. You have to fight this," I told her.

"Fight what? Why is there so much darkness here? Are you even real?" It must be hard for the very core of my roommate to understand any of this, when she didn't have any knowledge about supernaturals to know what was really going on.

"Think of it this way"—I struggled to put it in terms that she would understand—"I'm trying to make soup, and I put in too much salt. What do I do?"

"You dilute it." Spirit Rosemary said without thinking. I used that example because it actually happened in our house once. She was making vegetable soup and I wanted to help. I thought the use of measuring spoons was over-rated and... well, let's just say I put in just a little more than the daily recommended amount. Anyway, my roommate switched the whole thing into a larger pot and started adding in extra onions, carrots, celery, potato and such, and the soup was saved.

"Right. That's exactly what you need to do here." I squeezed her shoulder. "Think happy thoughts. Tell me about the farmer's market and dinner after this."

She proceeded to tell me how she and Jordon were able to get fresh lamb shoulders from the butcher, and organic ground turmeric from a spice vendor. Then Jordon surprised her with a bouquet of wild flowers, which she placed on the patio table when the lamb curry was served that night under the stars.

And that was the night Jordon stayed over for the first time.

As Spirit Rosemary talked, more and more positive energies were drawn to this memory, and I stored them up like humans with blue-chip stocks. When I was confident I got enough, I pushed it outward in one fell swoop, reclaiming the memory and ejecting the shade from it.

The wind calmed, the dead leaves and the other debris fell harmlessly to the ground, and the sun came back out.

The shade was gone.

"Hey, look!" I pointed at Memory Rosemary and Jordon, who appeared as happy with each other as ever, and not a hair out of place from the wind earlier. Their joy now permeated the memory without the encumbrance of fake doubts and shame.

Spirit Rosemary stared at the couple. "I think my job is done here."

"I think so," I agreed.

"Am I going to remember any of this after I wake up?"

"No," I admitted. "You won't remember this."

And she won't remember what Gregory and I were capable of. She would go on thinking we were mortals, just like her.

Thank Hades for that.

Spirit Rosemary faded away, and Gregory and I walked through the entire memory twice, from beginning to end, just to make sure that the shade was indeed gone.

Yep, there was now nothing there except the happiness of the moment. Not bad for my first cleansing attempt.

We did a quick check of the rest of Rosemary's mind before pulling out. No menacing presence anywhere else, either. Not to say there was no sad moment in Rosemary's mind—nobody went through life without a battle scar or two, and my roommate was no different. But there was no manufactured negativity and that was awesome news.

Satisfied with the result, we left Rosemary's mind. Gregory did a mental "tugging" at his anchoring thread with Sassy, and the shade pulled him back to the physical world along with me.

"Thank you." I leaned down and scratched Sassy under her chin. She meowed and jumped onto Rosemary's bed.

My roommate's eyes were now closed instead of staring. Her breathing was slow and even, suggesting that she was in a slumber, not a trance.

"Well, at least Rosemary is officially shade-free," I told Gregory.

He didn't look as relieved as I'd expected him to. Not that he knew my roommate enough to care deeply for her actual well-being, but it spoke well for Gregory's own mother's chance of recovery, right?

"That's because the shade is all in my mom now." Gregory's face was drawn.

"What?"

"I could feel it," Gregory said in a horrified whisper. "What have I done?"

Damn.

✦ 7 ✦

BONNIE AND CLYDE

IF GREGORY WAS CORRECT—AND I had no doubt that he was —then this was no longer a game of speed, but a game of patience. The shade was already waiting for us inside Gregory's mother's mind, so it was imperative for us not to blindly rush in there. The more calculated and measured our moves were, the more of an upper hand we would gain.

"It's Sophia," Gregory said as we entered my bedroom again.

"What?" I said, puzzled.

"That's my mother's name. It means wisdom in Greek," he said softly. "I guess I'd always hated the name because she doesn't make the best of choices, and that name sounded more like a cruel mockery. She has no pride, no dignity where my biological father is concerned."

"Why are you telling me this now?" I frowned. Don't get me wrong, I wanted to know every sordid detail, but it seemed odd to be bringing up his reluctance about her name when her very life and spirit were threatened.

Gregory sat down on my mattress heavily, running his fingers over his hair. He closed his eyes and took a shaky breath. "Because I want you to know that to my shame, I haven't always been proud of her. I should've looked in on her more often. I don't, not because I got too busy, but because sometimes it's hard to look at her without being angry about the things that she allowed to happen to her, and allowing to happen to her still. And now, *this*. I should've been there for her more. So yeah, I'm telling you because I need you to kick my ass for what I've done, and the terrible son that I've been."

I walked over to where he was sitting. Yes, he needed to get this off his chest if he was to face the shade with his mind focused, but not in the way he thought it would.

"I'm not going to kick you while you're down. But here..." I kicked his shin. "Here's to thinking that I will. Happy?"

His eyes flew open, and he ruefully rubbed the area where my foot had made contact. "Well, as far as kicking was concerned, that did do it nicely."

"You're welcome." I sat down next to him, taking the chance to place my hand over his. He didn't flinch. "Listen, you're ambitious and proactive about improving your life, and it's hard to understand when someone you love is not as strong as you are. But if you're going to place any blame, put it on your asshole of a biological father. I don't know your mom enough to know why she couldn't just let go of him, but you know what they say, the heart wants what the heart wants."

Gregory straightened himself and said formally, "Thank you, Megan."

I let my hand slide off his, missing the contact but glad that he was looking better. His more business-like tone didn't faze me. It just meant he was more like his usual self. Under the circumstances, that was a great thing.

"My pleasure. Now let's get to work." I moved over to the other side of Sophia and took her hand. Gregory mirrored my move. Sassy was already at the ready for the anchoring, though we weren't going in just yet, just a tentative probe to see where things were at.

Gregory and I closed our eyes and took a first glimpse into Sophia's mind.

Oh, crap.

Trying to tap into her mind was like trying to decide on a starting point in a maze that made no sense. While the picnic scene popped out in Rosemary's mind thanks to my prior experience with it, there were multiple corrupted memories in Sophia's head, like a cancer that had spread out of control. Was it just because Sophia had a full dose of the shade while Rosemary only had half, or was it exactly like how Gregory had claimed, that his mother was the weaker one to begin with?

A person's memories were a series of life experiences with different nodes functioning as interconnecting hubs. Each hub contained multiple sub-nodes, which then broke down to individual scenes. Unlike with Rosemary where we dove into the specific memory, we had to take an overview of Sophia's entire mind.

The unaffected memories were represented by lines of neon blue, while the corrupted memories were an angry red. They crossed and tangled with each other and created one big, hot mess. Rosemary's single-scene infection was child's play compared to this.

I was familiar with Rosemary's personality, and that knowledge had aided me in ejecting the shade. But I knew nothing about Sophia, so this was Gregory's turn to pick whichever of her memory threads should we dive into first.

I didn't envy his task.

"Hard to choose, isn't it?" It was the same menacing voice that I'd heard before, except it wasn't coming from inside my own head anymore.

I quickly opened my eyes.

Sitting on top of the tall dresser with her feet dangling was a lithe female figure, which at first glance seemed to be naked. Closer observation showed that she was dressed in a nude bodysuit of the same material that figure skaters used. The girl looked to be in her early twenties, with a pixie build and a doll-like face, reminding me of those chubby clown toys. She was pouting, but on her face it came across as more bratty than dangerous.

Then the girl's features and outfit changed. The nude bodysuit became a black polyester one, her body became elongated, and the breast cup size doubled. Her chin became more sculpted, her face gained a decade of maturity.

She basically went from cute to smoking hot before our very eyes.

Her neck, which wasn't hidden by the bodysuit, was now covered in tattoos of blood-red roses and thorns. Her nails had grown long and become covered in red polish, and a long tail with a pitchfork end snapped playfully at her feet.

Gregory protectively placed himself in front of his unconscious mother, and I joined him. The stance was only for show, of course. The shade had already been to Sophia's mind, done the damage, and left.

My first instinct was to launch an immediate attack against the cursed woman, but Gregory gave me a look that begged me not to. The shade held a lot of cards, and we had to tread carefully if we were to get Sophia's mind back intact.

"Is this more of what you expect from a dangerous entity who's holding your mother's fate in her hands?" The shade teased Gregory. "I personally prefer this biker-chick look. What do you think?"

"You're quite the chameleon, I'll give you that," I snapped. "So what?"

"So I want my boyfriend back." The shade examined her nails casually. "If that's not too much trouble."

Gregory and I looked at each other. Should we pretend to negotiate, or tell her outright how getting Boyce out of Hell would be impossible? Well, not impossible, since Boyce had somehow managed to do just that on his own, but Gregory and I really couldn't afford to piss off Lucifer when we already made so many enemies.

The shade hardened her jaw. "I went into the store for like, five seconds, and you assholes grabbed him and sent him back."

That explained why we'd found our former target being close to a grocery store—he was "helping" his girlfriend with the shopping by robbing little old ladies of their purchases.

"I know what you're both thinking, but you got it all wrong. My Boyce is just a big, old teddy bear with a soft heart. You two jerks ganged up on him and arrested him for something he didn't do," the shade complained.

Right, the dwarf-giant thug with the long rap sheet and facial scars was a big teddy bear who'd done no wrong. And I was the queen of the fairies.

Seeing the disbelief on our faces, the shade hissed. "I'm telling the truth. He's been a good boy ever since he got out of Don after serving time for that last B and E. We started writing each other while he was still in there, and he told me that being with me changed him into a better man."

Urgh. Better man. Yeah, right.

Boyce Armstrong's record came straight from Hell's Book of Life and Death. As certain as the sun would rise from the east on the human plane, the Book had never been wrong for supernaturals. If it said Boyce Armstrong had to do time, then he most certainly had done the crime.

The Don Prison was a supernatural jail on the vengeance plane, mainly for generic petty crimes that the Council deemed too mundane for a customized vengeance job. So the shade was like one of those women who were into dating inmates, and she harbored him after his escape from Hell. Great. She really wasn't helping his case here.

This was a time I wished for direct telepathy between Gregory and me. I needed to talk to him about how to proceed. It was, after all, his mother who was at risk here and he had the most to lose. And things with the lovesick shade could get messy. Fast.

There was a movement out of the corner of my eye. I dared not turned toward it, but I was pretty certain that it was Sassy—I'd known her long enough to identify her even with just my peripheral vision. She was quietly stalking toward our enemy. Good girl. I forced my eyes to fixate on the shade, and proceeded to keep talking.

I had no idea how to beat a shade, so Sassy was our best hope.

"So you're saying that your boyfriend didn't kill all those people. But why take it up with us? We're just freelance contractors. Can't you like, submit an appeal to Hell or something?" I asked.

"I did." The shade banged her fist on the dresser door. "I got stonewalled by Lucifer's damn bureaucrats. And they're all 'we're just following the Book.' Bullshit. You took him to Hell. You get him out of there for me. Or else this one's mother gets it." The shade pointed at Gregory.

She was going to say something else, but then her eyes were caught by the vase of flowers next to her on the dresser.

The plants from Hell.

The shade plucked the single blood-red rose out of the center of the floral creation and sniffed at it. Then she narrowed her eyes at me, "Lucifer is *courting* you?"

"What is she talking about?" Gregory asked me sharply. Was that jealousy, or professional concern on his behalf, that the big bad of Hell had shown some sort of unspecified interest in me? I found myself secretly hoping for a dash of jealousy.

"Er, I was going to tell you, but with everything that was going on tonight..." I trailed off. I expected to see anger and annoyance, but—was that hurt in his eyes, or was it wounded pride?

"You have that kind of pull with Hell." The shade threw the rose on the ground in disgust. "And you wouldn't even look into this matter for me?"

At that moment—to save me from answering the question or to take advantage of the shade's distraction—Sassy jumped seven feet onto the shade's back.

Except she couldn't exactly land on her target. She got to the shade's back all right, but she managed to reach nothing but thin air, which she sailed through. It was as if the shade wasn't actually solid at all—well, a shade wasn't solid to begin with, but I thought when a shade went against a shade, something had to make impact, right?

My poor kitty expected to be jumping onto *something* and ended up hanging off the front of the dresser by her claws.

The shade looked down and sneered at where a dangling Sassy protruded from her stomach. "Little sister. Do you really think it'll be that easy? You've been domesticated for far too long and you've lost your wild side. You can't hurt me."

Sassy gave the shade an extremely dirty look. *Domesticated* was probably the most insulting word one could use to describe an independent soul like Sassy.

The shade turned back to Gregory, her eyes cold. "Fine, if you and your devil's whore won't help me, then go ahead and try to rescue your mother and see if you'll have the same luck as with Rosemary. My name is Vera, and I'm your worst nightmare."

Devil's whore? Whoa, that was a bit harsh. I received the

flowers from the guy and I turned him down. That didn't make me a whore of anything. And even if I had an in with Hell, which I didn't, that still didn't mean I was obligated to help Vera's unreasonable cause.

Vera laughed mirthlessly and faded away. The iciness of her laughter slithered down my spine in continuous waves even after she was gone. And was she really gone, or was she still in this room? Or did she return to Sophia's mind to meet us there?

I glanced at Gregory and his expression was closed. Was he mad that Sassy had escalated the situation with her attack on Vera? Or was he still processing the sight of Lucifer's flowers in my bedroom?

"Sorry about cutting the bargaining process short," I began.

He shrugged. "There's nothing we could have promised her anyway."

"And, er, just in case you're wondering. This is the first time I've ever gotten flowers from Lucifer, and I already turned him down." It was really a personal issue, and it wasn't like I owed Gregory an explanation, but if Vera thought I could've help and didn't, then it became a business matter.

I wasn't going to dwell on the fact that I felt compelled to clarify because I wanted him to know nothing was going on with me and Lucifer. Well, at least not from my end.

Gregory gave me a curt nod, but I noticed his shoulders relax noticeably. "We'll talk more about it. After."

"Okay, let's go then." I settled Sassy back on the bed and leaned toward Sophia, but Gregory was rooted to the ground. "What's the problem?"

His eyes were trained on his unconscious mother, his voice tight. "Megan, can you do me a favor?"

"Sure. What is it?"

"Pick a thread for us to go into. I don't trust myself

enough to do it. In my current state of mind, I'll probably crash land into a memory and destroy it once and for all."

I couldn't help but feel touched that despite everything that still needed to be said between us, he was trusting me in this matter.

I reached over and took Gregory's hand in mine, then I touched Sophia with my other hand. That way I bore the direct responsibility of selecting which thread to go into, and Gregory was simply tagging along. I sure hoped that I would make the right choice. Talk about pressure. This was worse than doing the same thing with Rosemary earlier, given Sophia's relatively weaker state, Vera's open challenge, and the fact that Gregory was counting on me.

I took a deep breath and closed my eyes. Sophia's mind was even more messy and infected than the last time I checked. There were now many more corrupted memories, making the healthy ones nothing but a tiny minority. The ugly red lines of the corrupted memories tangled with each other, with many broken paths that had turned grey. Ironically, in some places certain damaged memories were held together by other damaged ones, sharing characters and settings for similar scenes in the mental equivalent of duct tape.

Looked like Vera had done a heck of a lot more damage out of spite for Sassy's sneak attack.

Should I go for a memory that was the most corrupted, or the least so? More recent, or deeper into the past?

I couldn't afford to become paralyzed with fear. Gregory was already too close to it. I had to make a choice. At this point, any choice was better than inaction.

In the end, I made the call using the very scientific and clinical method of *eeny, meeny, miney, moe*.

❧ 8 ❧

SOUL MATES

WE ARRIVED in a little boy's bedroom, painted in royal blue. There was a night lamp casting a silvery glow over the ceiling, and the walls were covered in stickers brushed with fairy dust, which allowed them to change shape and color on command. The stickers were set to a series of trains, at the moment. The train cars raced around the room producing puffs of steam and making choo-choo sounds.

A fair bit of money had gone into decorating the room. It was there in the night lamp projecting the illusion of dancing fairies chasing each other across the room. It was there in the magically-enhanced wall stickers. It was there in the small bed by the window, which was made of imported dark wood from the Grimmian Forest that was supposed to accelerate early childhood development. It was probably all just a marketing gimmick, but there was no denying the ridiculous price tag.

A boy of about four or five lay on the bed under a blanket that matched the wall's color, an oversize children's book over his chest, with a woman leaning over him from the chair beside the bed.

I recognized the kid as a younger Gregory because he was a miniature version of the man that I'd come to know: the same rich brown hair, the same dark brows, though his cheekbones were rounded by chubbiness typical of children his age. His eyes were unguarded and sparkling with hope, and there were dimples on his cheeks as he beamed at the woman.

That must be his mother, though she was far less recognizable when compared to her modern-day counterpart. It wasn't so much due to her physical appearance, because the present-day Sophia was still a very handsome woman. No, the difference was in the very essence of her spirit, which I could feel even through the filter of memories. The younger Sophia's power signature felt fresh, confident, and vibrant, like strawberries in early July—sweetly half-ripe but with a good amount of crispness.

The adult Gregory was keeping his eyes anywhere except on the mother and child, his jaw locked and his expression grim. This must be hard for him to watch, the innocence on his younger self's face before the world turned cruel. He'd tensed up ever since we got here, and I bet that if he could escape anywhere, he would. But since I'd already picked this memory, we would have to see it through. I remembered well what he said about how exiting a damaged memory might also cause it harm.

And I couldn't do this alone. He was the one who'd experienced the actual event, so he knew better than me what had been tampered with and what hadn't.

"Well, time to sleep, young man. We'll finish the story tomorrow night." Sophia took the book away from the younger Gregory, kissed his forehead, and got up.

"Mommy, can you tell me about Father again?" Young Gregory's voice was full of eager anticipation. There was not a hint of the bitterness and contempt that Adult Gregory would associate with his biological father.

The child's question seemed to be their nightly ritual, as Sophia smiled and settled right back onto the chair.

Her face took on a dreamy expression. "Your father and I met when I went to college. We knew right away that we are each other's *solus iungere*."

"What's that?" Young Gregory had a look that told me he already knew the answer to that question, but he simply wanted his mom to say it again night after night.

"That means soul mates for our people." Sophia ruffled her son's hair with great affection. "Your daddy and I love each other, and we both love you very much. He can't be here all the time, but he wants to. He's a very powerful vengeance demon, and he does very important, grown-up stuff for the Council."

"What kind of stuff?" Young Gregory asked, his expression avid.

"Stuff that helps a lot of people."

"Does he help kids, too?"

"Especially kids." Sophia winked.

"Is that why he can't come to read me bedtime stories? Because he has to help all those people and all those kids?" Young Gregory asked, surprisingly not out of bitter disappointment, but rather, fierce pride. It was there in the gleam in his eyes—the kid was so proud of his father. Hero-worshipping, even.

I stole a furtive glance at the stony expression on Adult Gregory. They said parents existed to disappoint their children so the latter could surpass them, but this was quite the whopper. Ouch, the more we build up our heroes, the farther they fall. No wonder the Gregory I knew harbored such animosity toward the old man.

"That's right, pumpkin." Sophia tucked a lock of hair behind her son's ears with great affection. "So many people in the Cosmic Balance are relying on your father to deliver justice for them. He has to travel to a great many planes. A lot of worlds you've never even heard of before."

"Across the *whole* Cosmic Balance?" Young Gregory flung his blanket aside and spread his arms wide, clearly excited by the idea.

"Yes, across the whole Cosmic Balance," Sophia confirmed with a laugh as she tugged her son's arms back into the blanket.

Young Gregory flashed his mother such a brilliant smile, the nightlight paled in comparison. "When is he coming to see us again?"

Sophia's face dimmed, but she quickly hid it. "Very soon, dear. Very soon."

"When?" Young Gregory persisted.

"He has one more assignment to do. After that he should be free."

"But that's what you said last week."

"It'll be soon, dear. And you know that even when he's away, he's always thinking of you. Do you like the gift he sent you?"

"Yeah." Young Gregory looked excited at the mention of it.

In a clear attempt to distract her son from further questioning along such a sensitive topic, Sophia got up and took a vengeance practice doll from a nearby shelf. It was a popular toy for both male and female vengeance younglings. The doll was enchanted to behave like a real target when vengeance was performed on it, with the appropriate screaming, cursing, and struggling. The perfect gift for a future punishment giver.

Like everything else in this room, the doll was above the pay grade of an average vengeance demon. The skin texture appeared more realistic, the outfit better tailored, and there were three different volume settings to the screaming, giving the player a better idea of the degree of force to use when applying vengeance. The practice target would even go as far as struggling to get away. I knew all this because one of my richer classmates in kindergarten had gotten one and paraded it around class. The endless bragging had only come to an end when the doll successfully escaped up the water pipes, but got permanently lodged there.

Young Gregory squeezed the ankle of the doll, and it cursed, "You rolled my ankle, you vengeance brat!"

At least they kept the cursing PG.

Delighted, the brat in question squeezed harder.

"Ouch, now you gone and twisted it, you demon!"

Young Gregory giggled, hugged the doll to himself, and started to drift to sleep.

Sophia sang him a lullaby until his breathing became even, then tugged at his blanket one last time and started to leave the room.

"Mommy?" Young Gregory's drowsy voice came right before Sophia closed the door behind her.

"Yes, sweetie?"

"When I grow up, I'm going to be a vengeance demon just like Father."

"I think he'll like that very much." Sophia chuckled and closed the door.

That was the end of the memory.

A long pause as Gregory and I stood against the frozen backdrop of the bedroom, his face as hard as granite. Wow, how drastically different had my mercenary partner's life turned out to be, and how deeply disappointed he would have to be over his biological father in time.

I hesitated. What should I say to him now? If I overdosed on kindness, it would come across as pity, and that would be the last thing he wanted from me.

In the end, I fell back on pure facts and what common knowledge there was regarding memories.

"What we just saw now is a core memory, isn't it?" I commented.

A pause, then Gregory cleared his throat. "I suspect as much, but how did you know?"

"It's just the way this memory feels to me. Look at the details of this room. Every train on those stickers is detailed to a tee, from the tiny insignia that are painted on the engine to the complex way the set of wheels work together to take the train across the room. This memory has been visited over and over again by your mother, tended with a great deal of care."

Core memories never fade, because they are the cornerstones in the foundation of a person's very being.

"Did you feel any negative vibes?" he asked, looking around the room with a frown.

"No. I have been wondering about that. It didn't feel like the memory has been tempered with at all."

He shook his head. "No, it hasn't been. But you chose it for a reason, right?"

Granted, I picked this one out of pure randomness, but I was choosing it out of all the places I thought Vera's footprint had been.

I paced around the room. "Vera has been here. I'm sure of that. Yet she hadn't done any damage. Why?"

How were we to exorcise something that couldn't be detected?

"Let's go to another memory," Gregory suggested. "Maybe that'll give us some answers."

"You want to pick this time?" I asked.

He sighed. "No. Sorry I sounded like I was doubting you. I still think out of the two of us you're the best person to pick."

And so I did.

I closed my eyes, visualizing the memory nodes again.

There was a corrupted memory that seemed to entangle with this one more so than any other, creating what would be a knitter's nightmare if they were balls of yarns. Out of pure instinct, I jumped right into the other thread.

I opened my eyes and found that Gregory and I were in a very cramped apartment that had chipped plastic tiles for flooring, and a tiny kitchen with an ancient fridge and almost no counter space. There was a small area off the kitchen that served as both dining room and living room. The yellowed wallpaper was peeling, and the muffled argument from a neighboring couple could be heard. With all the curtains drawn, I had no idea whether it was day or night.

What a contrast it was from the last memory's surrounding.

There was an oppressiveness in the air, and it had nothing to do with the closed curtains or the tight living quarters. With a sour energy signature of expired milk and unwashed socks, it was the rancid stink of hardship, disappointment, layered on with a thick coat of shame.

Gregory's mother, a decade older if not in physical appearance then in the essence of her spirit, was at a work desk squeezed between the wall and the two-seated dining table. She was designing a logo on an old computer, using enchantments to refine the image instead of Photoshop. The logo, which appeared to be for a perfume brand, was given a supernatural twist so that a burst of floral fragrance would hit the viewers every five seconds. His mom was really quite talented, as the fragrance was also accompanied by a mental image of rolling on a sun-filled meadow in a lazy afternoon, which was exactly the sentiment that the brand was trying to capitalize on.

Gregory tensed as he watched an early-teen version of himself walk out of his bedroom with his head downcast, a dirty-looking schoolbag over his gangly shoulder. This younger Gregory was beginning to resemble the one I knew, his cheekbones sculpted after the baby fat melt away, and his eyes took on the hardness of someone who'd grew up a little too fast.

"Mom, I'm going to school," he muttered.

At the sound of her son's voice, Sophia looked up, her tired face brightening. "Don't forget to come straight home right after, sweetie. I can't wait to celebrate your birthday. I'm making roast pork tenderloin tonight."

Young Gregory looked away. "Actually I think I'm just going to hang around at the Field and grab a slice of pizza on my way home. Don't wait up. I might be late."

The Field was basically like a basketball court in low-income human neighborhoods, except rather than basketball, the supernatural kids hang out there to practice magic. And they were known to play rough with each other.

Sophia frowned. "But...but it's your birthday and we have to celebrate. You only turn twelve once. I already ordered a cake from the bakery. It's strawberry mousse. You love strawberry mousse cake, remember?" Sophia tried to keep her tone enticing, but inside she had begun to panic. I didn't have to read her face or body language to know—the atmosphere surrounding the memory took on a pulsing in both lighting and sound, like a heartbeat that sped up in urgency with every breath she took.

"That was my favorite when I was five. I'm not five anymore," Young Gregory said with a weariness that was jarring given his age.

"But it's not safe at the Field after dark." Sophia wrung her hands together, whispering, "I heard they have mercenaries practicing there."

"It's fine, Mom. They've been nice to me." I got a feeling his unspoken words were, *unlike everyone else*.

"But you have to be home for your birthday—"

"Why, Mom? Tell me why I should be home." Young Gregory glared at his mother, daring her to continue.

"Because your father might be here." Sophia swallowed. "And you're going to miss seeing him. How's he going to feel if he shows up and you're not here?"

"He's not going to show up." Young Gregory's eyes flashed, and his wings came out involuntarily.

The poor kid looked so annoyed and embarrassed by the display of his lack of control, it only made him madder.

"He's not going to show up," he repeated to his mother. "He's not, alright? He hasn't been here for the last three years, and I don't want to spend another birthday waiting for him. He abandoned us a long time ago, why can't you accept that? Look around us."

Young Gregory's hands gestured all over their humble surroundings, from the yellowed wallpaper to the crack tiles.

"He hasn't abandoned us." Tears started filling Sophia's eyes. "He's just too—"

"Busy. Yeah, I know," Young Gregory bit back. "And do you know what he's busy with? My *friends* at school so helpfully informed me while they stomped me onto the ground yesterday. Dear Dad is on an official visit to the witches' plane as a newly elected Council member, with his *real family*. You know, his real wife and kids? We're nothing to him. Why can't you see that?"

"We're *not* nothing to him. We *are* his real family. I'm his *solus*—"

"No, you're not. They taught us these things in school. A soul mate is someone who's your one and only. Once you meet that person, that is *it*. No one else matters. But Dad is doing just fine without you, isn't he? He didn't feel compelled to marry you, did he? That means his wife is his true *solus iungere*, not you. You're his former mistress, and I'm his bastard."

"No, no, that's not true. Your father and I love each other and we're meant to be together, I swear." Her voice distressed, a single tear fell down Sophia's face.

"Stop lying! Thanks to you, I'll never belong!" Young Gregory bawled.

As he stormed off, Sophia fell to the ground, dissolving in tears.

And that was the end of the memory.

I looked over at the Present-Day Gregory, who had tears streaking down his own cheeks. I'd never even imagined that he *could* cry. He was always so...collected. A part of me marveled at this new facet of his personality, while the other ached for the boy he had been. "I regret saying those cruel words to her now. She was young and trusting when she met my dad, and she fell for his lies. But that's no excuse for how *I* treated her. I was all she had. I should've been nicer to her. She tried so hard to be good to me. She could barely afford the pork tenderloin and the strawberry mousse cake, and I wouldn't even show up to enjoy them."

"You were, like, twelve. Give yourself a break." I kept my voice gentle.

I stayed quiet while he wiped the tears away with his sleeve. When he looked like he was more composed, I asked, "So which part of this memory is damaged?"

Gregory shook his head. "It's perfectly intact, just like the last one. But I think I know now what Vera is trying to do. It's not about destroying my mother's memory—it's about connecting and building up the bad ones, and trapping her spirit in an avalanche of pain, while taunting me about my role in it."

"Give me some more context here," I hated to ask that of Gregory, but I couldn't help if I didn't have all the information. "So your biological father was more or less in the picture for the first few years, then he bailed on the two of you, and then he came back after you left home for booty calls with your mom?"

"He left us around the same time he married his current wife and got the seat at the Council." Gregory's hands formed fists at his side. "My mother is from a middle-class family, and he belongs to one of the first families of vengeance. She was only eighteen when they met, but he was already an arch-vengeance-demon-in-training. I guess he's taken a more political career path since then."

"And after he left, he stopped supporting you and your mom financially?" I took it that Sophia couldn't have afforded those pretty things from the first memory herself.

"It was far worse than that. My mother has always been an amazing graphic artist. It's not a common career path for vengeance demons, but she's truly talented. Both my maternal grandparents were also artists. By all rights Mom should be working for some huge advertising firm and have a bright future. But her past with my biological father made sure that no one wanted to hire her. You know how our culture is. Everyone saw her as being tainted and dishonored. So she was forced to take on low-paying freelance gigs in order to support us."

"Dishonored, huh? I guess they never bothered to blame the guy." I scoffed.

The double standards in polite vengeance society always drove me crazy. I swear, in this aspect they were forever stuck in the fifties. The man stood proud and still got accepted into the most elite social circles, while the woman got blackballed professionally for having the audacity to mistake lust for love and have a child out of wedlock. And the child was ganged up on in school simply for being born. No wonder Gregory dropped out eventually.

"Mom never recovered from my biological father's leaving, and she took him right back in such a shameful capacity once he wagged his finger at her," Gregory sighed. "All my life, she never looked at another guy with any amount of interest, insisting that she's already met her soul mate. She allowed him to diminish and vanquish her."

I knew I should concentrate on the matter at hand, but this glimpse into Gregory's background was putting my personal experience and interaction with him into perspective.

No wonder he ran off after our little kiss. Even if we were true soul mates, how the hell was he supposed to have faith in that, with that term being used as a crutch for so much shame through the years?

And how the hell was I supposed to feel about it? Joy that he just might not have turned me down flat as I thought, or sad that the romance department with him would always be an uphill battle, with his parents' entanglement lurking in the shadow of his mind?

Lots to digest.

"This is also a core memory," I said softly. "But you already know that, don't you?"

Gregory nodded. "This was a turning point in my relationship with Mom. It was the first time I ever spoke my mind about her and my biological father. I hurt her deeply. In a way, we were never truly the same after that argument. As an adult, I visit her every now and then. I settled her into a house and I fixed her sink. Every year, I bake her a cake for her birthday. But there was an unspoken barrier between us that we never dared to break down. And now she's trapped here."

He looked so mad at himself that I wanted nothing but to reach out and smooth the scowl from his brow, but I knew he would not welcome the comfort. And I had my own emotional turmoil to sort through.

So I gave him what we both needed, or rather, what he needed and as much as I could manage at this point.

I kicked his shin for the second time this morning, making him wince no less than when I did it in the physical world.

"Will you stop kicking me?" He rubbed the unfortunate spot again.

"Will you stop being so hard on your younger self?" I snorted. "That kid's had enough shit from life without you piling more on him."

After a long pause, Gregory smiled. He actually smiled, even if a bit ruefully. After the disastrous reliving of the second memory, it was progress. And if I had to go a bit dominatrix on him to get that out of him, then it was well worth it. He shook his head. "Oh, Megan. What am I going to do with you?"

I took a deep breath and refused to let my mind wander where it wanted to. "You can start by forgiving yourself. As I said before, you were very young."

His face turned serious again. "Old enough to have met my future business associates already. My friends at the Field are the ones who started me in the mercenary business."

Everything made sense now. How the son of a Council member ended up attending a school at a poor neighborhood and became a mercenary before the age of eighteen.

Anger at Minister Sumpsi, Gregory's father, threatened to boil over. It didn't matter whether or not Sophia was his true soul mate, a child was created out of that liaison and the mother and child should've been better cared for. If I, a hybrid who had a father who *remained* in the picture had had it bad, Gregory's experience had to be even worse.

And yet, without that experience to set Gregory on the mercenary path, we would've never met and he wouldn't have played such an instrumental role in the would-be changeling war. And I wouldn't have had a job to go to, a way to stay away from the Council's influence upon my exit from Demon U. Funny how things worked out.

"Alright." I flexed my fingers. "Let's just concentrate on freeing Sophia's spirit. What's the game plan?"

Gregory narrowed his eyes in concentration. "We have to find the pattern behind Vera's attacks. Individually, all of these memories are not any more hurtful than they had been originally. But added together they are far more than their parts. If we could find the pattern, that would be the first step of freeing mom and finding Vera."

I straightened. A pattern. That made me think of something.

When I was a child, I got into trouble with my parents once, and my punishment was to weed their lawn without the use of magic. I dug up a whole yard full of weeds before I figured out that every single one of them, big and small, was the offspring of a major mother lode. It was kinda freaky how far its roots extended, and how every weed was actually connected. In fact, I came to suspect that every weed in the entire neighborhood was joined to each other.

"I want to take a look at the big picture again. Come with me," I said excitedly and closed my eyes, visualizing the memory nodes again. I could feel Gregory's consciousness next to mine as I took everything in.

Now that I had in mind to search for the memory version of a mother lode, I could see that all of Sophia's core memories, one way or another, tied back to one major node—like, a core memory of all core memories. It formed the basis of every single one of Sophia's decisions almost since the beginning of adulthood. It was a part of her very identity.

Before Gregory's birth. Before Sophia mastered her graphic design skills. Before she was even a college senior.

I opened my eyes, and Gregory and I were standing

outside Eumenides Hall. The student resident was one of the two at Demon U that housed mostly first years. It wasn't the one I stayed at when I was a freshman there, but I'd attended lectures around the area and knew it well enough.

Gregory looked around us questioningly. I shrugged. "Let's just see where this leads."

It was a fall evening, and the pavement was wet from a recent drizzle. Leaves, which were dried and had fallen onto the ground, got re-hydrated and stuck on the concrete in a bright display of yellow and brown.

A couple was a few feet in the front with their backs to us. The girl's laughter, as lyrical as bells, was audible even through the sound of cars traveling on wet roads.

"So how did I start out going to a party with your brother, and end up having you walking me home?" the girl teased. I almost didn't recognize it as Sophia's voice. She sounded young, carefree, and flirtatious.

The guy turned his head toward her and smirked. "Because I'm the superior brother, in case you're interested in Louis."

Once his face was visible to me, there was no question in my mind that this guy was the younger version of Gregory's father. Macallister Sebastian Sumpsi, who appeared to be in his early thirties, was a spitting image of his future son.

The younger Macallister was cocky, with a matching power signature that reminded me of smooth brandy. He was definitely no college student. Then I remembered what Gregory had said about him being an arch-vengeance-demon-in-training. If so, that must've been some major career fast tracking. My own daddy wasn't in that position until his late-thirties, and from what I heard he was considered fairly young for the job.

"It's not like that with Louis." Sophia shook her head, casting a drying spell on the step at the front entrance of the residence and sitting down on it. The guy followed suit. "We went to the party as friends. But do tell me, why do you think *you're* the superior brother?"

"Well, for one, I'm older." Macallister chuckled.

"Uh-huh." Sophia didn't sound convinced, her eyes dancing with mockery and challenge. It was shocking to see how she held her own with Gregory's father at their initial meeting, when later on in their relationship he seemed to be the one holding all the cards. It really made me wonder just what the hell had happened to cause such a shift in the power dynamic. It couldn't be just because she had gotten pregnant, could it?

"For two," Macallister counted the second point with his finger, "my little brother is hoping to get a VBA, while I already graduated from vengeance co-op. A long time ago."

VBA stood for Vengeance Business Application. It was like a MBA for vengeance demons. Not a surprising academic path, as the younger brother was groomed to join the family business while the older one was expected to take over the political mantle.

"Yeah, Louis has told me all about how your parents play you against each other. So what, Mr. Big Shot, you're going to try to be the youngest arch vengeance demon that ever existed or something?" Sophia rolled her eyes and didn't appear terribly impressed.

"Oh, I plan to be a lot more than that." Sophia's attitude seemed to have the effect of challenging Macallister to reveal what he normally wouldn't to complete strangers.

"Really?" Sophia rose her eyebrow.

"I'm going to be the youngest Council member ever."

"Isn't there anything else you would rather do?" She frowned. "Some *other* dream? Must be pretty boring having your whole life planned ahead of you by someone else."

"But I happen to *like* that plan. I'm not my brother."

Macallister's charming tone took on an edge of annoyance. "Always dreaming up ways to create new products rather than sticking to what works. People want more of the same thing. They don't need soaps that could store up to ten different kinds of scent—the rotating three would do just fine."

Sophia laughed. "Well, you can keep your ambition and lack of creativity. All I want is to make designs that'll make people *think*."

"Think, huh?" Macallister leaned closer and lifted Sophia's chin with his fingertips. He seemed to have done it at least partly out of a desire to shut her up about questioning his choices in life. "What are you thinking about right now?"

Sophia breathed in his scent and suddenly she became perfectly still, like a deer caught in the headlights. She didn't answer him, her early self-assurance gone from her face, replaced by surprise. And a hint of wonder.

That was weird. Was he casting some sort of stun spell on her? I sensed the air around them and detected no sign of magic, though. What the heck was going on?

"Well?" Macallister leaned even closer so that he was practically breathing on Sophia's lips; satisfaction radiated from him for finally having things on his own terms.

"Wh-what?" she stuttered.

"I asked what are you thinking right now," he whispered.

"I...I..." she whispered back, "Macallister, I—"

"Call me Mac."

Macallister pulled Sophia closer and she started closing her eyes.

"Stop!" Gregory roared half a second before his parents' lips touched. I started, so focused on the couple that I almost forgot about Gregory's presence. Abruptly, he turned his back on the scene with a disgusted grunt.

I wasn't even aware that one could stop a memory from progressing while in another's mind, but upon Gregory's protest, Macallister and Sophia became frozen, their lips less than an inch away from each other.

Even in the healthiest of circumstances, children were never keen on watching their parents smooch. Given what Gregory knew of what came after the start of that intimacy, I couldn't blame him for not wanting to witness it.

"Let's skip to the next memory." Gregory growled. "Now. There's nothing here to see."

"No." My voice came out firmer than I expected, but I realized that I meant it. Yes, I could hear the begging beneath Gregory's harsh words, and it almost made me give in to his request. But there was a reason why this memory trumped all memories, and I wasn't convinced it was all about the head rush of young love. I wouldn't have done right by Gregory if I let his misgiving prevent us from seeing the whole story.

"But—"

"Why don't you wait here?" I walked up to Sophia. "I won't be long."

Without waiting for his reply, I took a deep breath, repressed the ick factor of what was to come, and squeezed Sophia's hand.

The memory was progressing forward again, and I was in Sophia's head, experiencing it in her place. *I* was kissing Macallister Sebastian Sumpsi, the guy my business partner and maybe-soul-mate despised. I, as Megan, found it disgusting and felt like I was betraying Gregory on more level than one.

On the other hand, I, as Sophia, thought that I was in heaven.

I knew it! I knew it once he got close enough for me to really *smell him.*

I, as Megan, tapped into Sophia's senses.

Macallister's scent was like an expensive Cuban cigar to

her. Rich, intoxicating, and from a world so different from hers. As he kissed her, a warm fire spread to her insides, like a hot toddy with the perfect balance of honey and spices. Burning yet achingly sweet at the same time.

Adventurous yet anchoring.

Ever and always.

I will help him find his dreams, and he will cheer me on as I chase after mine. I'll follow him to the ends of the world, because nothing and nobody matters anymore, except this man who's holding me in his arms.

I, Megan, reached out with my senses again. Nope, there was no magical disturbance here. Nothing to indicate that Sophia's reaction was a result of any kind of enchantment.

Then Macallister pulled away from the kiss suddenly, his lips disengaging from Sophia's with a loud smack. With his eyes narrowed, shock, annoyance, and bitter anger chased across his face in quick succession.

What's happening? He's looking at me as if he hates me. Why? This is a joyful occasion. We're so lucky to have found each other.

Macallister held onto Sophia's shoulders, keeping her at bay yet not letting go. He closed his eyes and took a few deep breaths. When he opened them again, the hostility in his gaze was gone. In its place was a deliberate playfulness. His lips twisted into a sexy smirk that bordered on cruelty. He winked. "Well, gorgeous, you're quite the kisser, aren't you?"

Something's wrong. He's making a monumental moment of our lives out to be something entirely too light-hearted and casual. But maybe he just needs some time to adjust. I'll be patient. I'm his now.

Ever and always.

I pulled out of Sophia's mind and stumbled back, landing on my ass. I welcomed the pain. Anything but that raw vulnerability and utter confusion I'd already experienced personally once before, after Gregory pulled away from our kiss in an all-too-similar fashion.

The couple in the memory froze as they had done when Gregory yelled in anguish. I wasn't surprised because the emotions going through me right now were no less strong.

"Megan, are you alright?" Gregory asked.

I allowed him to help me up, my body shaking. Then, couldn't help myself, I hugged him fiercely and let out a shivered breath.

"She never lied to you," I whispered into his ears. "She's been telling the truth the whole time."

"What are you talking about?" Gregory asked, his voice sounding utterly confused.

"Sophia. She's been telling you the truth all your life. She *is* your father's *solus iungere*."

❧ 9 ❧

CHOICES

SOPHIA'S INABILITY to date anyone else...her steady insistence that she and Gregory's father were meant to be together...it wasn't the talk of someone who was obsessed with the idea of love—she felt the truth in her guts when no one else can.

And no one believed her, not even her own son. It must've bothered her deeply, to have felt what she did and for it to be considered nothing but cheap and stupid by her own flesh and blood, not to mention the very man she was tied to. Was that why she went from an independent, spirited woman to a broken, defeated shell that was only a shadow of her former self? Was she driven mad by the *why*?

She wanted to help her mate with his dreams, and he crushed hers.

"So how does that work?" I paced around, or whatever walking back and forth inside someone's head could be called. "I'd always been taught that there was a *solus iungere* out there for everyone. I mean, sometime he or she never showed. Maybe like, they got stepped on by a mad ogre five years before the couple was supposed to meet or something. And people could definitely be mistaken in these things—my dad and his first wife being a case in point. But I'd never heard of anyone actively walking away from a true mate before."

It would be a sacrilege of the highest order, going against one of the most fundamental values that a vengeance demon was raised in.

"And you're sure they're true mates?" Gregory asked, skeptical.

"Yes."

"How do you know?"

I gave him a look, and murmured, "The same way I thought I was sure before."

That earned me a guilty look from him, so I hurriedly moved on. One true mate debate at a time. Besides, in the rush of all these rescues we hadn't even resolved our fight regarding Candy and the Internet attempt yet.

"So from what we're told, when a vengeance demon meets his or her soul mate, they go bat-shit crazy and start wearing bright pink and doing other out-of-character goofy stuff. That reaction should've been completely involuntary. But your dad went on his merry way and started a whole new family. How the hell did that happen?"

This was once again a time when I really wished I could have Grandma's counsel. What was common sense was obviously not true in this matter, and she always seems to know what was beneath the surface more than anyone else.

"I'm not sure. I never considered the possibility that what she was saying might be the truth," Gregory admitted with a low voice. "I thought she was mistaken and foolish."

Now that I did have the truth, a few pieces of the puzzles had started to fit together, making a sick kind of sense.

...the younger brother was groomed to join the family business while the older one was expected to take over the political mantle.

"But I so happen to like *that plan...I'm going to be the youngest*

Council member ever."

"He left us around the same time he married his current wife and got the seat at the Council..."

"It's not like there's a test they could run to make sure all the engaged couples are true solus iungere to each other."

"Both my maternal grandparents were also artists."

"Gregory," I said in a strangled voice, feeling ill, "what if a soul mate is not an absolute path like they say it is, but rather just a really nice option? What if your dad made the choice to pick a wife who's not his true mate, in order to advance his political career?"

It was the only thing that made sense in the absence of magical influence. After all, Macallister's seat in the Council came right after his marriage. Gregory's mother was a free-spirited artist from a family of artists, a political nobody, and Macallister needed a Jacqueline Kennedy to fit into the plans he had for his life.

Gregory's eyes flashed, and he kicked at the ground. "Son of a bitch! If that's the case, then he condemned my mother to a lifetime of misery."

Now was probably not the time to point out the hypocrisy of that statement, since that was the same fate Gregory pretty much condemned me to if he ignored the possibility that we were true mates. Except...

It did sound like there *was* a choice, when it came down to it. It wasn't an I-absolutely-couldn't-live-without-you thing. It was comforting and alarming at the same time. The idea of having choices made things both easier and harder. I basically found out that he had a good motivation for denying what was between us, at around the same time I realized that what we had didn't necessarily have to define us. We could walk away if we want to.

Something to think about.

I wondered how Gregory's life would've been different, if

his father had followed his heart rather than his ambition. Would Macallister have found other dreams and had other adventures? Would Gregory have grown up as a happy child, basking in his parents' love?

Who knows? That was the essence of uncertainties that came with choices.

"She never wavered, yet still I doubted her. I assumed my father simply grew tired of her and threw her away like a candy wrapper, only to be picked up later when he felt like it. I was too busy being ashamed of her to really hear her out." Gregory's eyes were downcast. He ran his fingers through his hair and pulled at his scalp.

"What were you supposed to think?" I pointed out. "Your mom moped around like she had a decades-long hangover from cheap love potions, while your dad seemed perfectly happy being the asshole that he is."

"Do you know what this means?" Gregory's anger was starting to turn outward. "My dad turned what should've been genuine and beautiful into something that's debasing. He made a whore out of his true mate, and when he saw her in trouble this morning, he shrunk away from his responsibility of saving her. The *bastard*!"

I had no words left to comfort him, so I simply stood by in silence while he let it all sink in. He would deal with Minister Sumpsi in his own time. Of that I was absolutely certain. Right now we had to focus on Sophia. Vera had obviously used this master core memory as a springboard to connect all the dots that would amplify Sophia's pain, and there was only so much of this a person could take before permanent damage to the spirit set in.

Eventually, Gregory's breathing became more even, and he spoke in a much calmer voice. "Now the question is, how do we go about freeing my mom from this?"

How, indeed? In Rosemary's case, we just had to get rid of

one single menacing presence which was Vera. In Sophia's case, we had a whole web of pain to detangle.

Once again I found myself wishing that Grandma was here.

Then thinking of my gran gave me an idea.

I turned to Gregory. "The memories that got connected together go from the initial meeting with your biological father, to your disbelief of her claim. What's hurting her is that not only is her love not taking her seriously, but even her own flesh and blood thought she's just a floozy." I saw Gregory's wince and said hurriedly, "Sorry. Not trying to put salt on the wound here. I'm just trying to point out that if your lack of trust hurt her, then by the same logic your faith could heal and free her."

Gregory went perfectly still. "Elaborate, please."

"The battle in Rosemary's mind was won because of her optimism. We can't give Sophia your dad, but we could give her your trust and love. Trust me, it could work."

"How do you know?"

"I spent my whole life thinking Gran didn't care." I stared at my feet, remembering all those anguished years. Then I looked up at Gregory. "But when Enid tried to kill me, Gran came to my aid. Then she re-synced our memories so that I could see that she'd been there for me all along. Every major event in my life took on a whole new meaning once I realized Gran was a part of it."

"So it's all about context," Gregory guessed.

"Yep," I confirmed. "What we need to do is add a different context to all the affected memories."

I took Gregory to the second memory, the one where he had that ugly fight with Sophia. Gregory's face was hesitant when he realized where we were.

"Can't we start with something a little less challenging?" he asked, his voice more anxious than I'd ever heard it.

The Gregory I knew was no coward. This really showed how uncomfortable he was with what we were about to do.

"This is the one you're most ashamed of," I said. "Think of it as ripping off a Band-aid."

We got to the part where Young Gregory was telling his mother exactly why Minister Sumpsi wasn't around anymore.

"...do you know what he's busy with? My *friends* at school so helpfully informed me while they stomped me onto the ground yesterday. Dear Dad is on an official visit to the witches' plane..."

Gregory stopped the progression of the memory—knowing what to expect, he was able to do it without roaring like the last time—just when Sophia flinched from her son's words. With infinite gentleness he touched Sophia's shoulders. "Mom, can you hear me? Please come."

He was pleading for his mother's spirit to manifest itself in this memory. But unlike with Rosemary, our surrounding didn't get any less gloomy. But eventually a second Sophia did appear. Semi-transparent and looking like a gust of wind could blow her away, she swayed and Gregory immediately shielded her with his arms and his protective magic. I poured my strength to join his in an effort to prevent her from fading away.

"Mom, stay with me," Gregory pleaded.

"I'm so sorry, sweetheart. I had no idea how much you're suffering in school. I'll go talk to your teacher. Or maybe the school principal. I'm so, so sorry. Hades forgive me, are you hurt? My sweet, sweet baby..." Sophia cried, struggling against Gregory blindly, not seeing him for what he really was—the present-day counterpart of her child in the memory.

A person's spirit should be omnipresent in all the memories, yet not entangled by any individual ones. Sounded like Sophia's spirit was so immersed in the pain and anguish of the memory web Vera had woven that she wasn't independent from it. The segregation between mind, body, and spirit was at the essence of a person's well-being. Blurring those lines meant Sophia could very well be on her way to insanity.

"Mom!" Gregory's voice took on a fearful note, no doubt arriving at the same conclusion as I did. He shook his mother's shoulders slightly. "Look at me."

Sophia blinked, and for the first time really looked at her son.

"It's me. Today's me. I'm no longer a kid. I'm no longer weak." Gregory kept his voice firm for his mother's sake. "And even back then, it wasn't too bad. What I didn't tell you in the memory is that after they jumped me I got right back up and gave back more than I got. I'm okay, Mom. Really. I didn't get hurt that badly at all."

Sophia lifted her hand and stroked Gregory's hair. "I'm so sorry, dear."

"Don't worry about it. Just stay focused. We're a team, and..." He swallowed. "I love you."

I got a feeling that Gregory as an adult had hardly been this open to his mother, and Sophia seemed pleased, if a little shocked.

With his arms wrapped around his mother's shoulders, Gregory walked through the memory with her. I trailed behind. He was the one who loved her and knew her best, so I would just stand back and let him do his job.

And so he continued to add new context to the old memory.

When Young Gregory said to his mother, "We're nothing to him. Why can't you see that?" Adult Gregory assured his mother that he didn't hate her and never would—he simply hated what his father had put her through. He believed all along that his mom was the only parent he'd ever needed. All he wanted to do was for them to stick together, and to take care of her always.

When they went backward in the memory to the point when Young Gregory was talking about his newfound friends at the Field, Adult Gregory explained to his mother that seeing the mercenaries there made him wonder if their path would be a way out for him, a way to make money so that he could give her a better life.

"I dreamed of giving you a nice big house one day," he admitted with a wistful expression I could imagine his younger self had.

"And so you did," Sophia said, then sadness filled her eyes. "But it came with the price of never becoming licensed like your father."

Gregory shook his head with zero regret in his eyes. "That was never my path."

"But the risk with this kind of life—" The corners of her mouth turned down in dismay.

"I've been very careful. We vet all our clients even more so than the licensed ones do."

"Still, it's not the life I wanted for you. Nothing in life makes sense." Sophia lowered her head.

Gregory dipped his head so to be at her eye level again, "It doesn't because his behavior didn't. He didn't act like a soul mate should. I understand that now. I'm so sorry to have doubted you. Please, Mom, believe me."

Sophia paused, then a look of peace and serenity crossed her face. "I do. Thank you for telling me this."

This time, when the image of Sophia shimmered, then faded away, I knew she was still here—but with her spirit free and unencumbered from the memory now.

I closed my eyes and visualized the overall picture of her mind again. With the core of the mother-child estrangement resolved, let's hope that the memories heal themselves in a dominos effect.

It didn't.

Yes, all the angry red colors that represented the infected memories had lightened to a salmon pink, but the ties that bind them together seemed stronger than ever. I directed my magic to try to poke around, and the bonds refused to give, flexible like some sort of industrial-strength polymer elastic band.

Gregory joined me in the overview. I felt his confusion and fear over what was in front of us. There was still something we needed to do. But what?

I took a more careful look at the bonds. The networks, so like octopus tentacles, were not solidly white as I'd originally thought. They contained tiny, clear bubbles of jelly inclusions, and the latter weren't stationary. They flew through the bonds like blood through the veins. Acting as some sort of information transmitters, perhaps?

When my magical reach brushed over some of the jelly inclusions, they changed color to white, then clear again.

"Megan," Gregory's voice came through a bit slurry in this state, but his cautiousness was evident nevertheless. "Are those inclusions some kind of weapon?"

"If it's a booby trap, I'd already have triggered it." I brushed my magic over the inclusions again, and it changed color once more. I poked at them, hard, but nothing happened.

Out of impulse, I reached out with my bare hands instead of my magic. Immediately, Gregory and I got pulled into yet another memory.

"Where are we?" I asked Gregory when I found us in the living room of yet another apartment. This one had bright open windows and a couple of wall-to-ceiling bookshelves full of board games, Pathfinder books, and fantasy novels. An old mutt was sleeping on a large rug under the coffee table, and the whiffs of something spicy and wonderful was coming from the kitchen off the right side. The apartment was as crammed as the one from Sophia's memory, but contained the signature of fresh lemon cream pies—a strong sense of joy, hope, and looking forward to the future.

"This is not from my mother's memories," Gregory puzzled. "We never lived in a place like this before."

I was slightly disappointed. It would've been really cool if he was a closet nerd. "Then who's place is this?"

There was the sound of keys jingling on the other side of the front door, then it was opened. A woman in a waitress uniform entered the living room carrying a white plastic bag. She dropped the keys into a bowl and said, "Hon, I'm home!"

The old mutt lifted his head in greeting, then settled back down to continue his nap.

A man of medium height and built in an oversize apron came out of the kitchen, a wooden spoon still in his hand. He pulled the woman in for a hug and a kiss.

Gregory shook his head in puzzlement, not appearing to know this couple at all. I had no idea what we could possibly get out of viewing this little domestic scene, or how a memory that Gregory didn't recognize would be hidden in his mother's mind. The inclusions I touched seemed to have been some sort of an Easter egg—hidden message within a video game that popped up when a certain level was achieved or a specific sequence of actions was implemented by the player. But Vera had left it there for a reason, and it would be wise to see it through.

"Welcome back," the man said to the woman when their lips finally parted. "The spaghetti is almost ready."

"And I got us dessert from work." She grinned, lifting the plastic bag, which contained two small take-out containers.

"Why don't you go change into something more comfortable, and I'll start serving?" the man suggested. "The show's starting in a few minutes."

They parted for their respective designations, and

moments later the man carried two plates back to the living room laden with spaghetti and meatballs, and laid it on the coffee table. Then he went into the kitchen again and came back with two glasses of orange juice. He had just sat on the couch with the TV remote in hand when the woman joined him, having changed into comfortable yoga shirt and pants.

They ate in companionable silence while watching a documentary about the navigation skills of birds. The mutt jumped onto the couch and settled onto the man's lap. He reached down and patted the animal now and then.

During the commercial the woman asked the man, "How did the job interview go?"

The man's hand tensed on the dinner plate he was holding, "It went well until they asked me the standard background questions, when they heard I had a record it kinda cooled down from there."

The woman took his plate and placed it on the coffee table along with hers. Then she leaned into the man's arms, her voice full of faith. "You'll find something. I'm sure of it."

The man planted a kiss on the woman's forehead, "I'll keep trying. I want to make some money and marry my girl, you know."

"You better try," the woman teased, "or else who's going to watch good old boring docs with you."

The couple laughed and went back to watching TV.

Well, it wasn't exactly a scene of grand romance, but there was something really sweet about the way they were taking simple joys in each other's company, sharing a meal and some television entertainment together. Not sure how this tied to our current dilemma with Gregory's mom, though.

Wait, did the guy say he had a record and couldn't get a job because of it?

Once I thought of that, the couple's image blurred and morphed, until the man's oversize apron, which he'd never bothered to take off, filled out and stretched to accommodate a large and muscular body with tattoos covering his biceps. A scar cut a path from his forehead to his cheek, edging nauseatingly close to his left eye.

The woman's yoga outfit could barely conceal her voluptuous figure. She, too, had tattoos, a pattern of blood-red roses and thorns peeking out of the collar of her shirt. She shifted her position on the couch slightly, tugging in her tail as she snuggled up with her man.

We were looking at Boyce and Vera. A hardened criminal and a kidnapper, watching a documentary about how birds managed to fly around the globe with their internal guidance system.

Gregory and I looked at each other. Just what the hack was Vera trying to do here?

A second Vera appeared in front of us, this one in a black polyester bodysuit like the one we'd seen before, with her arms crossed over her chest. "That was Boyce and I, before the false murder charges ruined our lives. Did you find your perception changed once you realized whom the memory is really about?"

"You!" I pointed at her. "You tricked us into accessing this memory."

Usually, a memory was downloaded into a USB, reconfigured, and cleaned up by vetting software before they were viewed. In Rosemary and Sophia's cases, we had no choice but to dive in. But at least they were people Gregory and I each cared about in real life. Being tricked into viewing a memory of unfamiliar people was forcing us to see things from their perspective whether we liked it or not. And hiding their true identity during the viewing process was even more disrespectful.

And yet I had to admit, when that memory was observed without all the preset prejudices, it felt rather authentic.

Well, maybe not the physical appearances of the couple, but the feelings they had for each other and Boyce's desire to find work. It was forcing me to think of him not just as a case file, forgotten as soon as our bounty was collected.

Sneaky shade.

"Look here," I pointed out. "If you're trying to get us to see things from your side, kidnapping our loved ones is a bad way of going about it."

Long pause. Then Vera's nose flared as if she was sensing something we couldn't. Her eyes widened. "You're right. Come back to the physical world and we shall talk."

She faded away, and so did the Easter-egg memory, and once again Gregory and I were at the overview of Sophia's brain. Before our eyes, the bonds that were tying her negative memories together dissolved, and the memories turned from salmon pink to a healthy, cool blue. Sophia should be able to make a full recovery.

Looked like this was an olive branch from Vera. Problem was, we couldn't exactly afford the price she would once again demand.

Gregory let out a deep breath, relieved at the state of his mom's mind.

"Ready to go?" I asked.

He gave everything a final inspection, then nodded with grim satisfaction.

We exited Sophia's mind. This time, the return to the physical world was faster than with Rosemary. We soon knew why when we saw Sassy and Vera sitting on opposite sides of my bed, and the latter seemed to have helped her brethren in the task of pulling Gregory and I back.

Sassy gave Vera a look that said *I didn't ask for your help*, while Vera simply grinned back.

Gregory immediately went to my bed and took hold of Sophia's hand. "Mom, please wake up."

Knowing his mother's mind had healed was one thing, seeing her coming out of her coma was another. I know that Gregory wouldn't relax until he saw that for himself.

I glanced at Vera. It didn't look like she was interested in going anywhere.

Sophia opened her eyes tentatively.

"My son, was it all a dream?" she whispered.

"No, I *was* in your mind," Gregory answered. "And I meant everything I said. We should've had a talk about all this a long time ago."

"I'm glad we did."

With his face more relaxed and carefree than I'd ever seen him, Gregory straightened up and said to Vera, "I suppose in a way I owe you a thank you."

After working with him all these months, I understood Gregory enough to know why he offered gratitude to Vera. It wasn't because he was acknowledging that her action would earn her any brownie points in our upcoming discussion, but because he was a man who lived by his own code of ethics, and he believed in giving thanks when thanks were deserved.

But that didn't mean he would be any more likely to give into her demand. And neither would I.

And yet...

Boyce did seem pretty genuine in his desire to begin a new life with Vera. Was that the behavior of someone willing to commit mass murders at the risk of putting that new life in jeopardy? The Book of Life and Death was supposedly never wrong. The Council could corrupt, but the Book should be above politics, as dependable as the fact that all vengeance demons were born with wings.

But it would just be the story of my life to be the exception of the exception.

❧ 10 ❧

THE FELON'S GIRLFRIEND

GREGORY, Vera, and I excused ourselves from Sophia's presence and went downstairs. Sassy followed suit. She didn't trust Vera, and I couldn't blame her. Vera could get nasty, fast, if she didn't get what she wanted.

Once we reached the living room, Vera got right to it.

"I have something that might interest you, Megan," she said. "For a trade, of course."

"What trade?" I blew out a breath in frustration. "Over-looking the fact that you just offered me something right in front of my partner, I can't help your boyfriend break out of Hell. You know that. And I don't have an in with Lucifer, despite what the flowers suggested."

"Well, duh, I know *all that*." She waved her hand at me.

"You knew? Then why the heck did you make that demand?" I threw my hands up.

"Just to see how far I could push you. I was so angry at you. When they took Boyce away, I thought I'd never see him again. Having him escape and return to me felt like a gift beyond measure. It's not easy for a shade to form relationships but once we do, it's for life. All I wanted to do was for us to lay low and move to a far off plane as soon as I could secure passage. Then I found out you arrested him and sent him back, and I got so mad."

"Wait, you said you were angry. You're not anymore?" I asked.

"After viewing my memory with Boyce, I sensed something from both of you. And it changed my mind," Vera admitted.

"What is it?" Gregory asked curiously.

"Your conditional sympathy," Vera said.

"What the heck is that?" I asked. I had never heard of the words "conditional" and "sympathy" being put together in such a manner. From the look on his face, neither had Gregory.

"As in, provided that I'm telling the truth, you both feel sympathy for the situation Boyce and I are in. I realized then you're my best chance. You both know how it feels to want to be more than what the rest of the world thinks you could ever be. My Boyce worked so hard trying to go legit. And he really took care of me. I even stopped most of my shade activities after I met him. That's why I took that waitress job. I know no other vengeance demons who would root for us the way you would, if only you know he's truly innocent. All I'm asking for is a fair, independent investigation into the murders that my man is accused of, to prove that he really didn't do it."

"An investigation. That's it?" I asked with suspicion. "No insistence on suicidal jail breaks?"

"No," Vera's insisted. "That's because I know that when you realize that I'm telling the truth, you'll have no choice but to break him out of Hell, even if it's suicidal. I know your vengeance nature would demand it."

She was confident, I would give her that. It made me a little queasy. What if she was right about Boyce? And she hit the nail on the head when it came to predicting my reaction in the event that he was indeed innocent. My inherent sense of right and wrong would demand that I help him, even at great cost to myself.

Even against Lucifer.

"And you *will* get something out of it if you agree, Megan," Vera added.

I had no idea what the shade thought I would need from her. But whatever it was, if it only benefited me and not Gregory, it wasn't something I would want to consider.

Then Vera dropped the bombshell.

"I could take you to the Internet," she announced. "I'm the missing piece you need. The Lies and Illusions half of the equation."

My jaw sagged, and I felt like all the oxygen had been sucked out of the room.

"How did you know I've been trying to go there?" I demanded.

Who else knew? Oh no, was the Council aware of Grandma's whereabouts, and my attempt to get her back? I thought all who were in the know were keeping it hush-hush, but somebody must've talked. Grandma was someone who, shall we say, knew where all the bodies were buried, and her return to the physical realm could really bite the Council in the ass. If they knew I was trying to bring her back, then they would try to stop me.

Vera rolled her eyes. "I know because I'm a shade. We are always in the shadows, witnessing your every desire and misdeed. There isn't much that escapes the attention of my kind."

"If you're so powerful, why not help your lover yourself?" Gregory pointed out, speaking for the first time since Vera offered a deal that would benefit me but not him. I resisted the urge to look at his expression.

"Many of the places my Boyce was processed through—the police station, the court—are shade-proofed through blanket safeguards erected when the existence of my kind was still common knowledge. I couldn't get to the information I need on my own."

"And now you conveniently have exactly what I need. How unsuspicious." I placed my hands on my hips.

"You want to go searching for your grandmother yourself, don't you? I can help you get into the Internet so you can search it to your heart's desire," Vera purred. "It's a good deal. Think about it. If my man is innocent, you're honor-bound to confirm that anyway. If he's guilty, you'll get a free ride into the Internet for your trouble."

When she put it that way, it was an easy offer to accept. That was, if she was capable of doing what she claims she could.

"How do I know you really could guide me and not trap me there?" I narrowed my eyes.

"To answer question number one: the Internet is nothing but an illusion, a place where people go to pretend to be something they're not. Photoshopped profile pictures, images of big happy families, inflation of one's popularity... It's the perfect nurturing ground for my kind, and we've been there ever since its inception. It's like a built-in web of lies, ready for us to play in. We do our *R* and *R* and even nurse our younglings there. So believe me when I say I could take care of the Lies and Illusions component. I might've stopped doing shade activities when I met Boyce, but I'm perfectly capable of doing it again to get him back. As for the second question, my kind, like you mercenaries, have our own rules of conduct. If I give you my word, I'll follow it through and won't trick you. Isn't that right, little sister?" The last sentence was addressed to Sassy.

Sassy gave a little nod, however disgruntled she seemed at having to back up Vera's words.

Wait a minute.

"Hey, have you been able to get me into the Internet yourself all this time?" I scowled at my cat.

"No, she can't." Vera laughed. "It's a *Wild Wild Web* out there. As I said, your pet has been domesticated for far too long. Lies and illusions don't become her anymore."

ANOTHER CRISIS

I ASKED Vera to give me some privacy to talk to Gregory. She disappeared to wherever shades disappeared to when they get gone, leaving Gregory and I in the living room. Sassy watched us with unblinking eyes.

If Vera was eavesdropping, there was nothing I could do about it—I knew next to nothing about shade-proofing. Here was to hoping the rules of conduct she claimed would apply here.

I had to talk to Gregory privately because Vera's offer only benefited me, but Gregory and I were business partners. The decision to help Vera involved actions that might lead to pissing off our biggest and most dangerous client, aka Lucifer, the Lord of Hell himself. And oh, to top it off, we'll be working with someone who had just caused his mother a great deal of pain and distress.

I would never have considered it had it not be what was at stake.

"The Book of Life and Death is never wrong," Gregory began.

"I know." I sighed. "But—"

"However—" Gregory held up a hand. "We are obliged to do at least a cursory investigation if a complaint is made. That is the mercenary code we must follow. Any personal benefit you happen to gain from this is your own business."

I stared at Gregory. Did he just give me his blessing and support in going ahead with helping Vera? Despite his claim that it was all business, that was only half true. I was perfectly aware that he was taking on the risk of irking Lucifer because he knew that finding Grandma was important to me.

"Thank you," I said gratefully.

"Don't mention it." He shook his head.

"All right then." I started making a mental summon to Vera so we could give her our decision, but Gregory opened his mouth, looking like he had something else to say. So I stopped the call, looking at him expectedly.

Then he didn't say anything. So I started the summon again, only to see Gregory wanting to speak again. After it happened for the third time, he just sighed and pulled me into his arms altogether.

Oh.

The unexpected embrace was nice. Very nice. He was solid and warm, such a contrast from the memory world we'd been venturing in. He kissed the hair around my temple, then pulled away from me slightly so he could see my face.

"Megan"—Gregory looked me right in the eye—"before we go into another crisis, as there always seems to be *another crisis* when it comes to you and me, I want to take a pause and ask you, formally, if you would like to go on a date with me."

"A...a date?" I stammered.

"Yes." His eyes glinted with determination. "It's about time."

Whoa, that was unexpected. After what happened inside Sophia's mind, I assumed we were going to go through at least another month of song and dance—or as Gregory put it, a few more crises—before we deal with the whole soul-mate business. Things between us had gone the way of molasses in January for a long time now, and a part of me was a little afraid of moving forward in regular speed.

Would I dare to explore a possible relationship with Gregory? He'd been running away from me for months. Now that we found out we have the free will to *not* be together, he wanted to give it a go?

On the other hand, it was pretty amazing that despite how the idea of soul mate was perverted by his father, Gregory still wanted to try exploring it with me. If he was willing to do that, how could I back away?

Gregory was looking at me expectantly, and I realized that I'd remained silent long enough to borderline on insulting. "Er..." Looking at Gregory, his face open and his eyes reflecting a hint of fear and vulnerability that I knew I probably shared in my own, I heard myself say, "Sure."

In the end, it was no tough decision at all. I wanted to see this through, even if we ended up crashing and burning.

But there were a few things I wanted out in the open. I told Gregory about how I came to have Lucifer's flowers in my bedroom, and his bizarre invitation.

"I did nothing to attract his attention, I swear," I told Gregory.

Silence.

"I know that," he said eventually. "You've never even met him. Neither have I, for that matter. You did a good job with declining it. Keep it ambiguous and not too hardline."

"Thank you." The compliment meant a lot to me, since I wasn't sure if I was doing it right. But what was I missing? "So what's the problem?"

"The problem is not with you." Gregory grunted. "The problem is with him. How dare he come near my—"

He paused, looking a little embarrassed at himself, "Er, you."

I guess neither of us were ready to say the words *solus iungere* out loud. Fine by me. One date at a time.

"What does it mean working with him going forward, though?" I asked, keeping to a more neutral line of conversation.

Gregory gave me a look. "Let's just see where we stand after this investigation is over, shall we?"

Right, one issue at a time.

"And about Candy." I made a face. "I should've checked with you and Mel before trying anything with her."

"I know how persistent that little rascal can be." Gregory smiled ruefully. "I'm afraid I was rather harsh with you."

That was very understanding of him. I doubt I would be as reasonable if our roles were switched, but I was grateful of the olive branch.

"Well, I'm just glad nothing bad happened." I said, "I mean, permanently."

"Me, too," he agreed. "And Megan, I might be assessing the situation with Lucifer clinically, but make no mistake that I am very glad that you're showing no romantic interest in him."

"Oh please." I rolled my eyes. "It'll take a lot more than that to sway me. He didn't even send chocolate. So, how do you feel about shawarmas?"

That got a chuckle from him. "Shawarmas, for our first official date?"

"Yeah," I replied, deadpan. "They got the freshest veggies."

"Don't you want to go somewhere more romantic, like an Italian restaurant or something?"

Gregory looked so confused, it was my turn to laugh. "Actually, French restaurants are more romantic." Plus I'd always been curious about frog legs and escargots. A person should try anything once, right?

"I don't get it. Why a shawarma place then?"

I turned serious. "Because there's one on every street corner. It's inexpensive and accessible. Given our lifestyle and how things have a tendency to get blown to shit and back, it's the best way to make sure our date will even happen, and happen soon."

"But we've eaten at places like that before, as business partners."

"I'll *know* that it's different this time."

And it would be enough.

I didn't want to put this date on some kind of pedestal. I already felt like I'd spent a long time waiting for it to happen. Besides, shawarmas was what was in my head right before Gregory kissed me for the first time. I would take that as a good luck charm.

"And, oh—" I winked. "I'm holding you to the French cuisine for the second date if we make it through the first one. Hold onto your credit cards."

Even if we liked each other enough on the first date for the second one to happen, it would probably be, like, another five crises later. He would have plenty of time to save up for the big meal.

Such was my life.

❧ II ❧
THE INVESTIGATION

❧ 12 ❧

THE HEART OF VENGEANCE

To MAKE sure that both Sophia and Rosemary got the proper rest after their ordeal, Gregory and I gave them herbs that would make them sleep for three days straight. While there didn't seem to be any long-term damage to their minds, the extra healing time would make absolutely sure of it.

I re-arranged Rosemary's schedule around, telling everyone she had a bad flu, then built in a charm to discourage visitors, even her boyfriend, Jordon. People would be concerned about Rosemary upon hearing about her condition, but then they would put any desire to visit her out of their mind the minute it popped in.

Gregory did the same for Sophia when it came to her business clients, but said his mother didn't have any close personal friends that needed notifying of her sudden absence.

Note to self: never get so busy with love that there was no time left for friendship.

Sassy was assigned the task of watching over the ladies while they stayed in their healing state. My feline shade would much rather stick with me to make sure that Vera wasn't up to any funny business, rules of ethics or not, but somebody had to stay behind and it couldn't be helped.

So she settled with glaring and dirty looks as we teleported away. Poor kitty.

We had to gather as much information as we could about the multiple murders that Boyce Armstrong was convicted of. Our work order from Hell didn't give us much. All it said was it was a robbery gone wrong involving the death of four people.

Before we started digging, though, we went to Vera's home to pick up a key piece of evidence she claimed would prove that Boyce was otherwise engaged during the time of the murders.

The apartment seemed pretty much the same as in the memory, except the coffee table was covered with empty take-out boxes. Looked like someone did a bit of emotional eating before setting out to hunt the loved ones of Gregory and mine down.

Vera reached into the bookshelves containing the fantasy novels and Pathfinder books, and pulled out an oversize booklet about an inch thick. She waved it at us triumphantly.

"What is that?" Gregory asked, his voice sharing the same puzzlement I was feeling.

"It's a syllabus for the London Kiwanis Music Festival. It takes place every year in London, Ontario. On the vengeance plane."

"Okay, but what does this have to do with Boyce?" I asked.

Vera flipped the syllabus to a section she already earmarked and pointed at it with a wealth of pride in her voice. "There."

Under *Class ST22-04 – Male Voices – Classical Opera – Adult Under 35*, there was Boyce's name as a contestant.

"He entered with *Nessun Dorma*," Vera explained. "That's

his favorite aria. Not even the death of his pet parrot could drag him away from this competition. It's what he's been working on for months, the one thing that gives him joy and peace while trying to make a new life as an ex-con. Why would my baby drop out just to rob a bank?"

The guy had a pet parrot? Never mind.

"So let me get this straight—Boyce couldn't have committed the crime because he was at an amateur opera-singing competition?" I asked incredulously.

"Yes," Vera said with a straight face.

So the seven-foot dwarf-giant thug with the tattooed arms and facial scars couldn't possibly have killed four people, because he was busy killing the high C at a local music festival?

Gregory and I exchanged a look, wondering if Vera was playing us.

And yet, it was so ludicrous, it was almost believable.

"Why would they even welcome him?" I asked. "I thought that kind of festival is known for its snobbishness."

I knew a thing or two about snobbishness of the vengeance society. One look at Boyce and they would've disqualified him.

"He's a tenor," Vera replied, as if that ought to explain everything.

The annual festival, ran by a group of society ladies and catered to people who could afford private music lessons, was the last place I would expect the former convict to be. The competition was closed to the public, with no official recording of it, making the only witnesses to support Boyce's claim being the judges themselves and the other competitors. Since Boyce's supposed participation was early in the game, and he was only in Hell for a short time before the prison break, the three-week long festival wasn't over yet. In fact, tonight they had the trophy final for the voice category.

I had to admit, with the evidence of his entry the judge assigned to his case should've at least asked for a more thorough investigation before convicting him for murder. Huh.

"So you were at the competition with him?" I asked.

"Yes, but being his girlfriend, my words aren't considered evidence." She sighed. "Conflict of interest, they said."

For the first time, there was evidence staring at me in the form of the syllabus, pointing to the possibility that Vera might be telling the truth. Being in the apartment she was sharing with Boyce, having the sofa they'd spent tender times together on in full view, was hitting home to me the stake in this investigation—not just the potential fall out with Lucifer, but the fact that I, Megan Aequitas, might've inadvertently had a hand in sending an innocent man to be tortured by Hell.

And the torturing was still happening right this moment.

Like any other vengeance demons, mercenary or otherwise, the very idea that my own action might've ironically caused injustices was horrid to me.

Boyce looked like a criminal, he'd fought us like a criminal, and we'd sent him back to Hell like a criminal. Vera was right. I went into the whole thing with preset prejudices. I would do well to remember not to do that again.

The trophy final wasn't until tonight, and it wasn't even noon yet. We had some homework to do in the meanwhile.

"Gregory"—I turned to him—"is it alright if we go to Mel's?"

We went to Mel's whenever we needed information gathering for our business. But after what happened with Candy, I wasn't sure if that was a foregone conclusion for this case.

Gregory sighed. "Of course. We need him for more than just information. Vera might be holding the Lies and Illusions key, but Mel is holding the Hardware and Facts. We need both to access the Internet when the time comes."

We teleported to a discounted supermarket on the human plane and went straight to the deli section. Staff waved at us along the way, with built-in perception filter to see us as regular customers picking up our staple milk and cereal. We pushed open the vertical plastic strips covering the entrance next to the deli counter and headed in.

We crossed a small tiled area to another door, which opened into a dark hallway. Judging from the echoing siren music and the overpowering incense, Mel must be in session. The new-age-y crap upon entry was only for show.

At the end of the hallway, a fire demon stood at the entrance to Mel's office, carrying a whip that sizzled at the tip. The female demon wore the outfit of a belly dancer, with a deep red skirt lined with silver metal coins that jingled when she moved. Her exposed navel was covered in grey cluster of asbestos ash, and so were her collarbones and ankles.

Her stance was formidable, and when she saw us, she ran toward us immediately.

And morphed into an elementary-school-aged girl along the way. As she ran, the siren music stopped and the incense smell cleared from the air.

It was Candy.

Though it had been barely half a day since I'd last seen her, it felt longer. Remembering how shaken she was the last time I saw her, I was relieved to see her being so lively and well. Oh, the resiliency of children.

"Pete and Megan!" The little girl hit Gregory's middle with the force of a miniature cannon ball, her blond curls flying everywhere. Then she somehow found the momentum to bounce herself onto me, only to go right back to Gregory with a carefree laugh.

"Hey, little brat." Gregory picked her up affectionately

and swung her around, much to Candy's delight. "I see you're feeling better."

Like everyone else in the mercenary world except me, she referred to him by the moniker "Pete." I just couldn't get into it. To me, he would always be Gregory, a guy who was born into the shadow of a prestigious family, but became so much more on his own.

While Gregory was busy listening to a chatty Candy update him about her day so far, I turned to Vera. "I saw that."

Her expression was blank. "I don't know what you're talking about."

"When you saw the fire demon rushing toward us, your first instinct was to pull ice magic around yourself, the same kind of cold power that your boyfriend used when he tried to run from us. You taught him that, didn't you?"

Her lips curved into a smirk. "Of course. I told him he should never rely on brunt force only. That's what people would expect of him."

"Well, if he could sing, that would be the ultimate definition of defying expectations," I muttered.

"Oh, he can sing alright, trust me. Maybe I'll be able to get him to add some singing into his fighting repertoire." She giggled. "That oughta surprise his opponents, don't you think?"

Ever since Gregory and I came on board, Vera took on a more optimistic demeanor. Maybe a little too optimistic. She was talking as if it was a given that she would be seeing her boyfriend again very soon. It was disconcerting, seeing her complete faith that her love would get out of Hell. That was a lot to bet on his innocence.

And the investigative ability of Gregory and me.

After Gregory put Candy back onto the ground, she

turned to me, biting her lower lip. "Megan, sorry for getting you into trouble last night."

I smiled ruefully. "Don't worry about it. I'm just glad we're all okay."

I didn't bother hiding the conversation from Vera. As a shade, she most likely knew about the ordeal last night already, especially since she would've wanted to know as much about Gregory and me as possible before grabbing our loved ones. There was no hiding secrets from a shade—only the management of it. I just prayed that the rules of conducts governing her kind were just as ethical and restrictive as the ones for vengeance mercenaries.

"Everyone was mad at me. I was mad, too," Candy said. "But then mom cried. So I told her I'm sorry."

"Good show." I looked at Gregory over the little girl's head and mouthed *I'm sorry* to him. He mouthed back *I'm sorry, too*.

I asked Candy, "So, Mel is in session, huh?"

"He should be done soon. Mum's in there helping with the paperwork, so I'm manning the fort for a while."

Candy's expert illusion of the adult fire demon was a pretty intimidating front for Mel's oracle business, and apparently, a little terror in the night and sleep deficit didn't detour her from her duty.

The little girl turned to Vera and squinted, paying attention to the latter for the first time. "Oh, a shade. Am I supposed to pretend you're not here?"

Candy's tone was conversational, as if she was asking Vera if she would like a pen to fill out her first-time client application form. I wondered if she'd encountered other shades before. Hopefully not from the attack that drove her family into hiding in the first place.

Vera huffed. "If you have to ask, then you're already not doing it, kiddo."

Candy grinned. "Must be important, for you to come see an oracle."

Vera just pursed her lips, ignoring Candy.

I wondered what that was all about.

As per Candy's instruction, we waited at the back office while Mel finished up his appointment. Then we waited some more as we knew the guy kept impeccable record of all his clients and liked to spend a few minutes after each session to make notes for himself. I sometimes wonder if he kept any files on me and Gregory. We weren't his clients, but Mel seemed the sort to keep a file on everyone.

Ever since working with Mel a few months ago, I'd come to respect his skills as an oracle, not to mention the fact that he'd taken Candy and her family in during their time of need. I was beginning to think of him as an extended family member of sorts, though in truth I knew close to nothing about him, not even what supernatural race he was born into. Like warlock and witches, oracles were identified not based on species, but the nature of their power. Candy, for one was born a human. In my quiet moments, I sometimes wondered why even Gregory didn't know what Mel was.

Candy poked her head into the back office. "Mel can see you now, and Mum is making lunch. It'll be ready in less than an hour. She said you're not allowed to leave until you eat."

I snorted. "Yeah, like I'll pass up a free meal."

Sarah, Candy's mom, was a really good cook. I got to eat healthy without breaking a sweat. What was not to like?

Candy laughed at me. "I think Mum is feeling competitive, with you eating so well with your roommate."

"Hey, there's enough of my tummy to go around. What are we having?" I asked, my mouth already watering. Sarah worked for a catering company before going on the run with Candy and her little brother, so freshness and creativity was always guaranteed.

Maybe gluttony was already a sin I had down in the Book of Life and Death. Or would that be sloth for not wanting to make what I craved myself?

Candy grinned. "Green apple pecan salad, butter chicken sandwich, and Greek yogurt parfait for dessert."

"Can't wait!" I said wholeheartedly.

We all got up and walked toward Mel's office, with Candy carrying her highly powerful laptop with her. Gregory's brows creased, clearly uneasy that she was acting like she was part of the upcoming session, but he said nothing. I got a feeling whatever misgiving he had, he was saving it for when he saw Mel.

As we got near Mel's office, a sense of anticipation filled me. I couldn't help but wonder what the office would look like today. Mel liked to magically transform his workspace to fit whatever mood he was in that day. So far I'd seen everything from the bridge of the original *Star Trek*, to the T.A.R.D.I.S of *Doctor Who*, to Camelot's round table, to all things LEGO.

Today, Mel again didn't disappoint. We opened the door to find the office being turned into the set of *Charlie and the Chocolate Factory*. The cheery and campy seventies version, not the one with Johnny Depp.

There was a canal made of liquid chocolate, giant gummy bear balloons, and oversize lollipops that was quite obviously made of foam. The smaller candies hanging on the trees, though, looked like the real deal. My fingers itched to pluck one off, if only to see if the enchantment would hold if I put it in my mouth.

Yeah, sure, that was the only reason why I wanted to grab one.

Standing on a boat in the chocolate canal was Mel, dressed in a purple suit and top hat. As always, he seemed ageless. He could be anything from middle-age to elderly, and he could alter his appearance at will just like Vera.

Today, Mel was a human male of medium height and darker blond hair, his face round and friendly.

"Hello, Megan and Gregory," he greeted us.

"Hey, Mel," I replied. "Cool set."

"Why, thank you." Mel grinned. "I knew you'd get a kick out of it."

"So where are the Oompa Loompas?" I asked, looking around. He wasn't the type who would leave such important characters out of his transformation.

"Maybe you're volunteering to be one, since you're the one who's got a perfect puzzle for me." Mel narrowed his eyes on Vera. "Let me ask you: what is a shade doing at my place of business?"

I looked from Mel to Vera, and found the two of them glaring at each other. "Um, do you two know each other?"

"No," Mel said after a while, seemingly having collected himself, "not her in particular, but her kind. You can say that they're an oracle's natural enemy. They're always hiding in the shadow of the Cosmic Balance, giving me false readings when I try to gauge its temperature. It's like having gremlins in your car engine. Most annoying."

"And you oracles are the most irresponsible." Vera spat. "After you take your reading, do you bother to return darkness to where you shed light? Many of my brethren got forever trapped in the eternal sunny spots in the Cosmic Balance because of you lot. A lifetime of cat videos, the horror."

"Vera." Gregory cleared his throat. "We're not here to trash Mel's professions or his colleagues. We're here because I think Mel could help us with Boyce."

Being reminded of the goal of the visit seemed to have

calmed down Vera. She said no more, and simply looked at Mel.

Gregory turned to his mentor and said formally, "Mel, this shade has accused us of carrying out an injustice toward her intended in the course of our mercenary work. I'm honor bound to look into the matter and would like to ask for your help."

Mel opened his palms in a welcoming gesture. "Of course, son."

"How is he going to help?" Vera asked.

"You mentioned that Boyce was arrested, tried, and promptly sent to Hell within a week. That music festival syllabus with his name on it should've warranted at least a more thorough investigation. We have to find out why it didn't, and what happened in that court proceeding. Unlike the music competition, there has to be an official court record somewhere."

"I wasn't allowed into the proceeding," Vera explained. "Shade-blocking safeguards are embedded right into the very insignia of the Council, and that bloody symbol is in every official government office including the courts. I can't get access to those records."

I had to say, it was rather comforting that there was some limitation to Vera's power, given how omnipresent she was capable of being. I made a mental note to get my hands on a few copies of the Council's insignia to put around the house and on my person—provided there was a way to make an exception for Sassy.

"You can't, but Mel can," Gregory assured Vera.

"And I'll help, too," Candy chimed in as she made her way toward the boat to join Mel.

"No, you won't." Gregory blocked her path and turned to Mel, "She can't. Not after what almost happened."

Gregory's tight face shown just how much the attack on Candy had shaken him.

"It'll be okay, I'm only helping as a hacker this time," Candy explained.

"Even on the off chance that her signature shows through, I'll be shielding it anyway," Mel said. "I promise you, no harm will come to her. This is not like last night."

"Why are you allowing this? You're rewarding bad behavior," Gregory said accusingly.

"No, I'm not. You were the one who encouraged her rebellion in the first place by not wanting her to learn astral projection. Trust me, Gregory, it's safe."

Gregory looked like he wanted to argue. Then he sighed and moved out of Candy's way. The little girl gave him a quick hug and bounced onto the boat with a happy grin.

Vera asked Mel, "Can you really help my Boyce?"

"Well, hop onto the boat and find out." Mel gestured the rest of us to join him.

"Is this one going to get dizzy like that one in the movies?" I asked worriedly.

"My dear, has your life ever been smooth sailing?" Mel snorted.

He had a point.

With everyone getting onto the boat and settling down, Mel waved in the air until a transparent bubble was formed. I'd worked with him long enough to know that the bubble was his mental representation of the Cosmic Balance.

"So," Mel said, "tell me everything you know."

Gregory started speaking, with Vera providing extra details such as the exact time, place, and dates of the legal proceeding and the crimes in question. As Mel "fed" the information into the bubble by tapping on its surface with his fingertips, it became cloudy with white vapors, like having droplets of milk falling into a glass of water.

Mel studied the pattern of the vapors thoughtfully. The ever-shifting cloud was mostly pure white, with wisps of brown shading the edges, lending it a more three-dimensional look.

Mel tapped on the bubble some more, making the milky vapor disappear. The remaining brown shade now looked almost black.

The bubble should've returned to its initial clear color if all was as it should be, but it didn't.

"Boyce's judgment doesn't have the Ring of Vengeance." Mel leaned back on his seat after a long while and whistled. The Ring of Vengeance was the instinctive knowledge that tells a vengeance demon whether justice was truly served. It was like the ring of truth for humans. Not always obvious, but never failed if one pay attention to it. "Mind you, the case gave a very good impression of having the Ring, but not quite so."

"A false Ring?" I asked, frowning. I'd never thought of such a thing before.

"Looks like it. A rare thing. Usually either the Ring was there, or not."

A look of vindication crossed over Vera's face, "*Now* will you believe me?"

"Not so fast, young lady," Mel cautioned. "Let me look into this further. You yourself admitted you weren't physically there to listen to what was presented against your man in court."

"Who's the judge residing over this?" Gregory asked Vera.

"Judge Montgomery Remington Tabella."

I'd never heard of him before, but then it wasn't surprising. His last name, which meant "record" in Latin, wasn't one of the old vengeance families. Ancient houses like mine, Serafina's, and Gregory's—not that he was officially a part of it, and neither was I in a sense—all had family names that were rooted in justice-related words. One ought to think that in this day and age the appointment of High Court judges wouldn't be so nepotistic, but there it was. Judge Tabella, by the virtue of his last name, resided over the lowlier Civil Court.

"I know Judge Tabella by reputation," Mel said. "He's said to be tough but fair. He doesn't seem the sort who'd be dirty."

"And with the death of four people, shouldn't this have been tried at a higher court?" I asked. The Civil Court was a place for cases deemed not unique, or serious enough, to qualify for a more personalized brand of vengeance.

"Let's find out what really happened there." Mel waved at the almost black vapor until the bubble was clear once again. He stared at it, reading the transparent space in a way only he could, his gaze a million miles away. I did my best not to fidget as we waited for him to do whatever it was that he was doing. Unlike the boat scene in the movies, waiting for Mel during this part of the process was always far from excitement. It usually only lasted minutes, but there were a few times when he had Gregory and I sit for well over an hour.

Focus on the upcoming lunch. And the Greek yogurt parfait, with drizzles of honey over crunchy granola and summer berries...

Alright, that's enough. Do you want your stomach to rumble so loud that everyone hears?

As time passed, a crease began to form between Mel's brows. Then he said, "I might have to take my word back. The Ring might be real, after all. The judge had based his decision on evidence pointing at Boyce losing his cool while exiting the scene of the robbery. Once the first person was shot, he seemed to have killed the others for the sport of it."

"Wait," I puzzled, "so first the Ring looks real, but it's not, and now it looks real again?"

"A mystery," Mel admitted.

Was it my imagination, or was there a trace of unease in

Mel's voice? A slight tremor passed through me. Being an oracle, and an expert reader of the Cosmic Balance itself, Mel wasn't the type that got fazed easily. The fact that he was concerned was making *me* concerned.

"Candy, can you access the testimony from the law officer?" Mel asked.

Candy nodded—not that Mel could tear his eyes away from the bubble to see it—and made a few taps on her laptop. "Already got it."

Her young voice sounded even more high-pitched than the last time she'd spoken. She, too, must've picked up on Mel's anxious vibe.

Mel lifted his fingers toward Candy's direction, and vapor, moss green this time, oozed out of Candy's laptop and entered the bubble.

Mel did his waving thing, and once again the bubble became clear after a while.

"Well, there you have it." Mel leaned back onto his chair. "A Ring of Vengeance. But not."

"How could it be possible?" Gregory shook his head. "Like Megan said, the Ring should either be there, or not."

Mel said thoughtfully, "The lead investigator *believes* that he got the right man. The judge *believes* that he was convicting a guilty person. Yet they weren't."

Gregory drew in a sharp breath. "They were enchanted."

"See, I told you he's been framed!" Vera pumped her fist in the air victoriously.

"But I thought vengeance cops and judges are incorruptible and charm-proof." At least that was what I had been told all my life. First the Book of Life and Death, now this?

"You've been told a very convenient lie, Megan. They're charm-*protected*, not charm-*proofed*," Gregory said. "I've enchanted a cop or two to look the other way in my day. How do you think I managed to avoid trouble with the authorities all this time?"

Gregory and I looked at each other, letting the realization that we really did send someone innocent back to Hell sink in. It was a sobering moment, with every fiber in my being hating it.

But we couldn't stay in limbo forever. Boyce was *still* there. We had to help get him out. Vera was right. Now that we knew we couldn't help but want to help. Our conscience demanded it, in fact.

"But if we suspect that both the investigator and the judge have been enchanted"—I cleared my throat—"that's even more serious than if they'd been bribed. We need to see the hard evidence."

"It's gone," Candy said.

"*Gone?*" Gregory asked sharply.

"The robbery was captured on closed circuit camera and was submitted as evidence in court. It's now missing," Candy explained.

"Well, that sucks." I punched the edge of the boat in frustration, causing it to sway left and right.

Whoever was framing Boyce for the multiple murders must be powerful *and* connected. It was the only way to explain their ability to remove crucial evidence straight out of a courtroom, on top of beguiling the officials involved.

"The only evidence that wasn't stolen," I reasoned, "would be the ones that weren't submitted to the court at all."

"His alibi at the music festival," Gregory said, coming to the same conclusion I did.

"Well, we got the trophy final tonight," I said excitedly.

"That's tougher to get into than you think," Vera warned. "At this point in the competition, the festival judges are very well-guarded—you would not believe the stupid stunts people pull in order to sway the judges. And Boyce's fellow participants aren't exactly a friendly bunch."

Well, let's see if we could get them to sing then, so to speak.

But not before having lunch. A girl's gotta fuel up, you know.

❧ 13 ❧

AFTER A FULFILLING LUNCH with great company at Mel's, Gregory and I parted with Vera and went back to the duplex to check on Rosemary and his mother. Vera agreed to meet us in front of the recital hall for the trophy final that evening at six.

Upon entering the house, we found an energetic Sassy bounding down the stairs to greet us. Her eagerness was partly due to the fact that she was glad to see me, but partly due to the doggy bag in my hand.

No, it wasn't the butter chicken sandwich that attracted her.

The bag contained the broken pieces of bad guys' souls that Mel picked up during his visit to the Cosmic Balance. When he came across morsels like that, he packed it up and saved it for my Sassy. It was good for the overall health of the Cosmic Balance and good for my feline shade, who was a devourer of evil souls.

With her teeth, Sassy grabbed the treat out of my hand before I could even offer it to her, and took off to wherever feline shades went when they enjoyed a snack of pure evil. I guess upon my return she assumed she was officially off babysitting duty for now.

Rosemary and Sophia were still sleeping in their respective rooms and appeared to be well. I felt like taking a nap myself, to be frank.

And why not? It would be hours before our meeting with Vera. I would need some rest if I was to bring my A game to tonight's event.

Catching Gregory yawning behind his hand discreetly, I bet he was feeling the same way.

"Nap?" I asked.

"Oh yes," he said with feeling.

Gregory settled in the living room armchair while I curled up on the futon after pulling it out. Exhaustion and stress from the previous night soon caught up with us. Before I drifted off, I thought I heard his thought brush against my consciousness.

Rest well, sweetheart.

———

I was woken by the sound of Vera's voice. No, that was not the accurate description. It was more like Vera was whispering over the landscape of my mind. "Hey, Megan, wake up!"

"What?" I sat up from the futon and checked my phone, seeing Gregory jumping to his feet. I guess Vera must've got to him, too. "Am I late—oh, it's only four forty-five. Why are you here? We're meeting at six. At the recital hall."

Vera looked down at her feet. "I just...want to make sure you're not going to be late."

I caught what she didn't want to admit. She was scared and excited over tonight, and the waiting was getting to be too much. She didn't want to be alone right now. And she wanted to double check that we were still going to honor our deal. "Well, we should be getting up anyways." Then I turned to Gregory, "You want to grab an early dinner?"

His eyes widened. "We just had lunch."

"It was light." I shrugged. Truth be told, my trickster genes made my metabolism work faster than the average vengeance demon. Plus I was a bit nervous about tonight as well, more so than any regular assignment we normally took on. So maybe I was trying to emotional eat a little.

My cell rang. Not Marv, but my personal phone. A quick glance at the call display showed that it was from Esme, and I answered right away. Maybe she had some news regarding Grandma.

"Hey, sis," I said into the phone.

"Megan, I believe I received a message from Gran," Esme said.

I barely stopped myself from squealing. "What did it say?"

"It's rather...cryptic." Esme hesitated. "I was inside the Internet with Mother when it came. Just an impression of a few words over and over again. The power signature behind the message definitely felt like Gran, though."

"What did it say?" I asked impatiently.

"Two words: rain raw."

"Rain wha?" What the hell of a message was that? Cryptic indeed.

"I don't know." Frustration seeped into my half-sister's voice. "Maybe it's a code. Mother and I are going back in an hour or so to see if we could hear it again."

"Is there anything you need?" I asked.

"No. I just wanted to call and give you an update. I'll call again when I have more."

"Good luck."

As I hung up I was feeling oddly optimistic. Two leads in one day. After months of impasse. Not bad at all.

Gregory, Vera and I took off, leaving Sassy, who had just come back from her evil-soul snacking, in charge again.

We only had around an hour, so we teleported to a street near the recital hall that was lined with shops, hoping to grab something quick.

And of course, there was a shawarma place right there. The irony was not lost on me that had Vera not been around, this could well be my first official date with Gregory.

The corners of Gregory's mouth lifted ruefully. Seemed like he was thinking along the same line.

"Just pretend I'm not here," Vera suggested, reading our minds. "I lurk in the shadow all the time anyways."

"Yeah, except this time around I *know* you're there," I pointed out.

"Fine," Vera snapped. "I'll leave you alone. Make sure to be there by six."

She faded away. Gregory chuckled. "She could still be here, you know."

I let out an exasperated sigh, "Don't I know it."

Gregory ordered a gyro sandwich, salad, and soft drink. I ordered a beef shawarma sandwich, guava juice, and a healthy helping of baklava. Yes, that was my second dessert of the day. Bad, bad, Megan. But wait, this was for celebrating Esme's finding. Yeah, that was totally what it was. We got to celebrate the small wins in life while we could.

We sat down at the back of the restaurant and dug in. But as I chewed, my mind was somewhere else. Thinking about Esme's call got me thinking about that weird message again. Rain raw, as in raining raw food? Or like, raining in such a heavy way that it felt raw on the skin? I'd never heard those two words used in combination by Grandma before, so if it was a code, it was nothing I'd ever been privy to.

"You'll figure it out," Gregory said, guessing where my thoughts had turned to. With supernatural hearing, he didn't need to have his ear pressed right next to the phone to catch the other side of my conversation with Esme.

"Thanks," I murmured, grateful at his faith in me, which I wasn't exactly feeling right now.

Suddenly, I realized that now that there were only the two of us, this could technically be counted as a first date. I had no idea what to say to him, so I ate some more, buying myself a bit of time.

The thing was, had we gone on this date soon after we met like most vengeance couples did, there would've been a lot more Q&A opportunities to fill the time.

I couldn't ask him what it was that he did for a living, because I was already his business partner. I couldn't be horrified by his mercenary lifestyle. Been there, done that, and became one of them. I couldn't ask him about his parents because I'd already met them, under rather unique circumstances to boot.

Heck, I couldn't even ask him about the nature of his magical power, because I'd already figured out how to complement his with mine to work as one well-oiled machine.

So we just kept eating in companionable silence, like we did during our many business dinners before, often for the purpose of being at the right place to punish a target.

Maybe it was a bit *too* companionable. Weren't first dates supposed to be all about angst and foot-in-the-mouth moments?

Here went nothing.

"Er, so," I began, "the payment from Leonard already cleared my account. Did it clear yours yet?"

I winced. What the heck of a date-like question was that? Asking about money transfer into a guy's bank account?

Gregory cleared his throat. "I haven't had a chance to check yet. But I'm sure it did."

Pause.

"Yeah, 'cause it's, you know, never late," I mumbled.

Pause.

"So, have you ever had frog legs?" I had no idea why those words popped into my head, but as soon as they left my mouth, I kicked myself. We talked about going to French cuisine for the second date. Now the first date had barely started, and it sounded like I was already angling for a second one.

Desperate, much?

"No, I haven't," Gregory said between bites. "It sounds interesting, though."

Interesting? That was the go-to word to use when something was totally not.

You're doing great, Megan. Just great.

"Are you into bondage?" I blurted out.

Gregory's eyes widened and he choked on the end bit of his sandwich. You know, the part with folded pita and plenty of dry bread to lodge in one's throat. He quickly took a few large gulps from his drink. "What are you talking about?"

I shrugged. "I suck at this first-date conversation business anyway, why not embarrass the hell out of myself and see if I come out the other end?"

Gregory laughed. "Would you be offended if I give it a try?"

"Sure." I grunted.

"So what got you interested in the human pop culture in the first place?" he asked.

I admit, that was a pretty good conversation topic. "It started from a pretty young age. I think it comforted me that there's this race of beings out there who has no magic in them whatsoever, yet manage to survive just fine. It made my hybrid issue seem smaller, somehow. I mean, I might be of two bloods, but at least they're both of magic, right? These humans have neither."

He folded the tinfoil sandwich wrappings neatly into an ever-smaller triangle as he contemplated my words. "I admit. I do admire them. They now have stuff that's even more effective than what the supernaturals can do."

"And you know what I also find fascinating?" Warming up to the topic, I added, "The lack of magic doesn't stop people from doing bad things. The percentage of humans ending up in Hell is on par with every other race from the Cosmic Balance. It really comes down to personal choices."

"To choices." Gregory lifted his soft drink cup, and his eyes told me he was talking about more than the choice to sin.

"To choices." I lifted my guava juice.

After talking about the human pop culture, we moved onto the human geek culture, and to my surprise Gregory was quite familiar with it. An old client of his, a comic book artist, was famous for drawing very life-like female monsters that were both intimidating and sexy. Turned out his secret weapon was the essence from real monsters that Gregory smuggled to him for use in his ink.

"When you say essence..." I let my voice trailed off.

"Saliva." He gave me a sheepish look. "Don't ask for details. I was young, desperate, and stupid."

I bit back a laugh. "Did you kiss she-demons in order to collect—"

"—I'll say no more." He promptly pushed the plate of baklava in front of me, distracting me.

Bastard.

———

When we came out of the shawarma place, it was ten before

six, and the summer sun was still pretty high in the sky. The recital hall was just off the side street ahead, so we had plenty of time to make it.

As we walked past a closed hardware shop, Gregory pulled me right next to its front window.

"What are we doing here?" I asked.

He pulled out a packet that was similar in size to the ones containing sugar in coffee shops, opened it, and sprinkled a golden brown fairy dust all over us. Instantly it was as if I'd put on a pair of ultra-dark sunglasses, and the surrounding area looked like it was nighttime.

"What is this?" I looked around me. There were people on the street, but they didn't appear to notice the switch to nighttime. In fact, they acted like Gregory and I were invisible, as one middle-aged woman nearly bumped into my shoulder as she passed by.

"We're hidden from them." Gregory smiled. "And we see everything in semi-darkness. The powder is one of your brother's more obscure products. Believe it or not, they're building up a side business for the romantically inclined."

I understood now. Gregory was buying us some privacy complete with mood lighting.

Ever so gently, Gregory took me into his arms. He made sure our eyes were locked, wanting me to know that he knew perfectly well what he was getting himself into. He pulled me close so our faces were inches from each other.

I nervously licked my lips, knowing he was going to kiss me.

Granted, we'd kissed before. But this felt like the first time we should've had. Without the shadow of his parents' entanglement, and his fear of it, encumbering us.

Gregory caressed the spot my tongue had moistened with his fingertip. Then he lowered his head.

Our lips met. His unique brand of clean citrus body scent

and Earl Grey tea power signature enveloped me in a protective haven of warmth and hope. I ran my hands over his broad shoulders, then his chest. His torso was clothed now, but I'd seen it bare, with intricate patterns of tattoos telling the story of a noble house he would never be a part of. It didn't matter to me. I accepted all of him. His origin. The innocent boy that he was. The angry adolescent who nevertheless loved his mother. The mercenary adult that he became.

Ever and always.

After a long time, we broke off the kiss and I raised an eyebrow at him. "So, you just happened to have this fairy dust on your person this whole time?"

"I kept it around as a talisman." Gregory shrugged. "A guy could hope."

❈ 14 ❈

THE MOST UNWILLING ALIBIS

THE RECITAL HALL for the music festival was on the vengeance plane of downtown London, Ontario. I was sure that on the human side, the large stone building with steep steps would've been an old church. But on the vengeance side the structure was simply a community hall that people rented for everything from wedding receptions to line dancing classes.

Yes, vengeance demons were into line dancing, too. The older ones, at least.

The wooden front doors of the hall were wide open, and a reception table was placed right inside the entrance. Men and women in handsome clothes were making their way there, accompanied by kids who resembled miniature adults with their formal wear. Most of the kids looked bored. And who could blame them? Classical music was an acquired taste.

Vera was already waiting for us on the steps. With her default cat suit and tattooed arms, she fitted in with the recital crowd like a snake blended in with a pack of bunnies.

"What the hell took you so long?" Vera got up and demanded as soon as Gregory and I were in hearing range. A few people turned and looked at her, frowning at her uncultured manners.

I checked my cell phone. "What are you talking about? We're right on time."

I guess I should be glad it at least didn't sound like she'd witnessed my kiss with Gregory.

"Let's go. Let's go." She hurried up the steps and gestured us to follow suit. "Every minute we're *not* getting to my man is like a year in Hell's time."

"Have you checked that it's safe for you to enter?" Gregory asked Vera.

Sometimes the insignia of the Council got displayed in major sporting and musical events. We needed Vera to guide us through the festival, and the last thing we wanted was for her to be barred from the premises.

"I'm good," Vera assured us. "I checked already."

According to the syllabus, tonight's trophy final was for all of the voice categories, adult or otherwise. I had no idea what to expect from such a competition. Music education had never been a big part of my upbringing, because there was always more than enough to deal with thanks to my dual background. Like learning how *not* to get tricked by my half-brother, Fir, into singing during a math test as if I was in the shower.

We approached the reception table and there were two girls there.

"Do you have tickets for tonight?" one girl asked. She was giving our everyday clothes the once over with a distasteful look. Well, what did I expect? This was an event for both vengeance demons and classical music lovers, it didn't get more snobbish than that.

I guess I should've put on an expensive dress. Too late now.

"No, we don't have tickets. Can we buy them here?" Gregory inquired.

"Do you have a festival membership?" The other girl asked, her eyes flickered to Vera's sexy getup. Was that disgust, or envy in her gaze?

"No," I replied. "Can we buy *that*?"

"Were you members in the past?" the first girl asked.

"No," I bit out, trying to keep my frustration in check. I had to really watch myself here. There might be some powerful vengeance demons in the proximity, as there was a high correlation between people who came from old families and those who enjoyed classical music. We were supposed to be doing this on the down low, especially if it involved Hell. Last thing we needed was an incident worthy of the local paper.

"Then no," the second girl said with glee. "Not on the spot. The application process is six months long. Through regular mail. It has to go through the board, you see."

"But—" I started to argue.

"Who is your superior?" Gregory placed a hand on my shoulder and interjected in a voice that allowed no horsing around. I took a deep breath. He sounded intimidating to my ears, and I wasn't even the ones he was trying to intimidate.

Like a deer caught in the headlights, the girls lifted their fingers and pointed at a figure in the main lobby, a middle-aged woman with glasses and a clipboard greeting guests as they went in.

Gregory sailed passed the reception table and pulled the lady aside, whispering into her ear. Then he showed her something on his cell. Her spine straightened, she stalked toward the entrance with Gregory following close by.

"Beatrice, Victoria, please issue this gentleman and his friends tickets for tonight."

"But they don't have—" the first girl, Beatrice, protested.

"Just do it." The middle-aged lady snapped. Then she turned back to Gregory, beamed at him, and said in a much nicer tone, "Please forgive us. I'm Patricia Annabella Cantabo, the organizer of the festival. Come find me after you're done and I'll introduce you to a few people."

She went back inside.

I leaned closer to Gregory as the girls quickly got to work, creating temporary entry badges for us. They kept stealing glances at Gregory, probably wondering who he was to get that kind of reception from their superior. "What did you do? What kind of enchantment did you put on that poor woman? She's practically putty in your hand."

Not that I was complaining. Just curious.

"I put no spell on her," Gregory claimed, straight-faced.

I narrowed my eyes. "Then how?"

"I gave her an incentive."

"Like, what?"

"Of the monetary type." He smiled. "I just made a generous donation to the festival and showed her the e-transfer record for it. I haven't blown through all the money I made from rescuing the kidnapped children from the changelings yet, you know."

I laughed. Whoever said that vengeance demons couldn't be bought? Then I turned serious. "I should share half of that cost."

"Don't worry about it." Gregory shook his head. "You handed that profit to me to begin with."

Still, I was touched. I made that offer with him in exchange for his help when the changeling war seemed imminent. He'd won it fair and square. And now he was spending a part of that money not only for the benefit of our business, but for me, so ultimately I could have a chance to find Grandma.

All right, so maybe I, too, can be bribed as well.

Inside the building, there was a lobby, and beyond that, an auditorium with a large center stage that I assumed was for the performances. The auditorium was only half full, with people who weren't ready to be seated yet milling around in the lobby, enjoying refreshments and checking out the silent auction table. There were items to bid on from a night of dinner and show in town, to master piano classes. An oversize trophy in the shape of a harp, about five feet high, graced the center of the room in all its golden glory. There were four alcoves spread out across the space, lined with shimmering brownish gold satin curtains and providing little nooks for groups of people to hang out and chat with each other over wine and hors d'oeuvres.

Patricia turned out to be quite helpful. She showed us around the lobby and explained that while the trophy final tonight was for all adult and children vocal categories, it was really only for solos and duets because otherwise the program would be so long as to be unmanageable.

I'd always thought that singing was just singing, but the sub-categories were super diversified. Just under Classical Style, there was Art Song, Canadian Art Song, English Art Song, and French Art Song. Then there was Opera Aria, Folk Song, Jazz or Blues, Musical Theatre, etc.

And here I was, thinking that the whole thing would be over in, like, an hour. Boyce's category, *Male Voices – Classical Opera – Adult Under 35*, was nestled between the female voices in the same age group and the male voices in the next one, and it wasn't until the second half of a four-hour program.

Seeing how more and more guests were heading toward the auditorium, I better hurry things along if I hoped to have the opportunity to question Boyce's witnesses without having to last through until the intermission to do so. The early shawarmas dinner wasn't going to last me that long.

"So"—I made a casual gesture of flipping through

tonight's program, and asked Patricia—"I suppose all the participants are already here, huh?"

"Of course, it's considered polite for them to stay for the entire duration of the final. We strongly discouraged diva behavior." She smoothly removed a piece of lint from her dress suit.

"Do you think we can meet some of these participants? Say"—I pretended to point at a random spot on the program —"the male opera finalists under thirty-five?"

"They're right over there." Patricia pointed at a small alcove on the left side of the lobby where three young men were standing together. "Funny you should pick that category to ask. My son, Theodore, is the youngest finalist there. Forgive a mother's gushing, but I think he's going to go far. He already started getting callbacks from the London Opera House. Twice. Isn't it marvelous? Let me introduce you."

As we got closer, I could see that Theodore was about nineteen. He was too old to be grouped with the teens, and too young to compete with everyone under thirty-five in a fair manner. He must be pretty good to be a finalist then.

Vera elbowed me and whispered in my mind. *The top three participants in every sub-category advance to the final.*

Ouch, I'd almost forgotten that she could speak directly into my mind like that. It was creepy. From the grimace on Gregory's face, she must be doing the same to him.

Vera continued, *But for this group there were ever only four participants to begin with. With my Boyce not able to be here, these three automatically advanced. My man had been kicking their asses in every contest from here to North Bay. He would've won tonight if he was here.*

So Theodore might not be that good, after all. I should've known to never underestimate a mother's ability to praise her own child and gloss over reality.

But if the advancement is automatic, then why even bother with the final? I asked Vera with my mind. *It would be like being in the Olympics with a metal guaranteed. What's the challenge?*

Because technically they can still put it on their resume and brag that they're finalists of this festival, Vera replied. *Unless someone bothered to check the syllabus from that particular year, who's to know?*

Wow, talk about the ultimate delusion of glory.

We reached Theodore and his friends, and Patricia introduced them proudly. "This is my son, Theodore Owen Cantabo. And these are his friends Amos Dominick Carminis and Jackson Quintus Theatrum. All three of them are baritones."

The guys' lips thinned once they caught sight of Vera, but they didn't say anything to Patricia. Interesting. I guess Patricia either didn't recognize Vera, or the shade did something to disguise herself from the mother of her lover's competitor. Come to think of it, she'd probably put a perception filter over her own clothes just for Patricia, as the dignified organizer never frown once at Vera's sexy get up.

Gregory smiled at Patricia. "I've taken up enough of your precious time, my dear Mrs. Cantabo. Why don't you go greet other guests while I get to know Theodore a bit more?"

"That's so considerate of you, dear. I do have to go. We'll have to tell everyone to go to their seats very soon."

Once Patricia left, Gregory rounded on the three guys. "I understand you know Boyce Armstrong?"

Theodore exchanged glances with his friends, then crossed his arms. "What about him?"

"Did you see him during the qualifying round? He would've been singing 'Nessun Dorma.' I heard that he'd done quite well."

Theodore replied "no," and after an elbow to the rib at Jackson, the latter said the same. But Amos snorted. "Oh, please. He'd done *quite well* according to whom? His little girlfriend here? That oaf did *not* do 'Nessun Dorma' justice at all."

Theodore and Jackson both gave Amos looks that said "shut up" loud and clear. Amos seemed too mad or arrogant, or both, to care.

"So you *had* seen him at the qualifying." Gregory's voice took on a smooth, velvety tone. The hair at the back of my neck stood. I always like this part, the calm before he tore his opponents apart.

Vera rolled her eyes. *Please don't tell me you're getting turned on by that. We're here to help my man, not to have you pant after yours.*

Stay. Out. Of. My. Freaking. Head!

Can't help it. I'm a shade. Nooks and crannies of the mind is where I go, she replied smugly.

I ignored Vera and focused on the byplay between Gregory and the three finalists.

"Cantabo, Carminis, and Theatrum." Gregory rolled their last names around his tongue as if they were secret codes to decipher. "You're all from old performing arts families. You're expected to win in these events. This is no hobby for you. These festivals are launch pads for your careers."

"So what?" Theodore shrugged dismissively. "It's no secret that we're taking this very seriously, unlike all the amateurs here."

"Serious enough to prevent someone from staying in the competition? Good tenors are hard to find, and judges are known to favor them. You're all baritones, and less experienced than Boyce Armstrong. You know in your hearts that he was going to win the top prize tonight if he'd been allowed to compete."

Huh. I never knew that about tenors—I guess as a veteran mercenary, Gregory came across all sorts of information. That was what Vera meant when she was confident of Boyce's welcome at the music festival. Nothing like an imbalanced supply and demand to make people overlook a few tattoos.

"What does it matter? He's *not* here." Theodore sneered. "He never had any business being here. My mother should've never allowed that...that thug to join us. Look what he's in trouble for now."

Vera snarled and started toward Theodore. "Why you little—"

I grabbed Vera. *Don't. Can't you see what just happened? Gregory got them. Theodore had just tipped his hand.*

Gregory gave Theodore a cold smile. "So you *are* aware of Boyce Armstrong currently being in Hell, and what he's there for. Then you must also know that he couldn't have robbed that bank because you were with him at the time."

A muscle jumped on Theodore's face. "I admit to no such thing. I didn't see him at the qualifying round. Did you?"

He turned to his friends.

"Nope. Too crowded. Might've missed him," Jackson replied.

The angrier Amos seemed to have gotten onto the program. "Yeah, what they said."

"Come on. You guys didn't see him because it was *too crowded?* There were only four competitors," Vera said incredulously. I tightened my hold on her.

Gregory stared hard at the three guys until one by one they bowed their heads, refusing to meet his eyes. Even the more hardline Amos looked contrite as he stared down at his shoes. "I know you're under a lot of pressure to succeed. It doesn't matter that you're all over eighteen and ought to be making your own decisions by now—you've been groomed all your life to follow the path that your families had set out for you. But are you really willing to make someone suffer in Hell just to keep him out of the competition? Think of what you're condemning him to. You're vengeance demons first, musicians and family legacies second."

The three stole glances at each other, pride, guilt, and doubt warring on their faces. Then I saw it—deep down they were decent guys. They were placed in a cutthroat environment at a young age and forced to compete to secure their self-identity. I, of all people, should understand the struggle to find one's path.

Suddenly there was loud mechanical feedback, then Patricia's voice came through the intercom. "Ladies and gentleman, the vocal trophy final will be starting momentarily. Please take your seats. The silent auction will be re-opened during intermission and…"

It was as if a spell had been broken. With his mother's voice droning on over the air, Theodore blinked and shook his head.

"If you'll excuse me," he murmured and fled, his friends following suit.

"Cowards," Vera yelled after them, drawing a few startled glances from the other festival guests.

Damn. Looked like we had to stay for the show, after all.

❧ 15 ❧

AN HOUR LATER, I was ready to claw my ears off just to not have to listen to another screechy high C. My knowledge of classical music might be limited compared to other vengeance demons from old families, but even I could tell when someone was forcing a high note.

Hate to agree with Theodore, but most of the contestants were indeed amateurs. I bet everyone in the audience was there because a family member was performing. The auditorium, with its soaring ceiling and open space, was built to amplify sound in the most acoustical way possible, which totally worked against my poor, long-suffering ears.

At long last, we got to the last performance before the intermission. I checked the program, and the song was called "The Cat Duet."

I knew this song because Mom loved it. No need to learn any foreign language, the only word in the entire song was "meow." The duet was usually performed with two females, with plenty of snarls and mock scratching to keep the catfight entertaining.

I suppose when the human contestants sing this song,

they do so with cat masks and imitate feline behaviors. But of course, the supernatural version went a step further. The two contestants stepping onto the stage had enchanted themselves to resemble real cats. Two reddish orange tabbies standing upright.

Then they began singing, and everyone started laughing.

The two contestants were males, performing the song in falsetto. But what was really funny was that as the song went on, their body forms changed, from slim form to potbellied, from gorgeous mane to balding. They took turns batting around a can of tuna, only to slip and lose their grip on it before they were able to open it.

Instead of a couple of dignified divas, we got two fat and clumsy tomcats fighting over food. It was a rather ingenious twist of expectations, and definitely amusing.

Wait, there was something recognizable about that protruding belly and reddish hair. No, it couldn't be...

"Aren't those your half-brothers?" Gregory leaned toward me and whispered.

Yep, that was Fir and Clef.

❧ 16 ❧

BREAK

I DIDN'T REALIZE that when intermission finally came, I would have such a hard time deciding whom to talk to first. I wanted to go to Boyce's unwilling alibis, but I also want to throttle my half-brothers. The boys were supposed to be at the United Sneakworkers Annual Expo, where they were going to make contacts and spread the word about the Greys. And here they were, pulling a prank instead.

Though if that performance was a prank, I wasn't sure what purpose it achieved other than a few laughs.

"Go to your brothers," Gregory suggested. "Theodore and his friends aren't going anywhere—they haven't performed yet."

I went after Fir and Clef, who were at the backstage high-fiving each other.

"Good work, bro," Clef said to Fir.

"Likewise," Fir replied.

"Fir! Clef!" I called out to them.

My half-brothers jumped collectively. Feeling guilty, perhaps?

"What the hell are you doing here?" I asked accusingly. "I thought you guys were at the expo?"

Fir put his hands up defensively. "We were. We just sneaked out for a little break, that's all."

"Initially we'd considered skipping the competition altogether, but figured we'd come this far," Clef added. "Besides, it's fun and relaxing. We can't always be all doom and gloom, you know? It ain't healthy."

"Alright," I conceded. Maybe I overreacted a bit. Seeing my half-brothers here was a shock. "So what's the trick of the night? I'm here on a mission. Please, please don't tell me you already rigged this whole place with vampiric flying monkeys. I have a few people I have to get co-operation from, and I can't have them running away from this building screaming."

"Actually," Fir said sheepishly, shuffling his feet. "There is no trick."

"Excuse me." I put my hand behind my ear, not believing what it was telling me. "There's no what?"

"No trickery," Fir insisted. "We're taking a break by going straight. That comedic duet was the farthest we're going to go tonight."

"Wait." A light bulb turned on in my head. "You...you guys actually *like* singing?"

My half-brothers blushed, which was a rare sight.

"We do," Fir admitted. "It's not a trickster's calling, but at least we made the piece funny and entertaining, not like the rest of them."

Wow. How could I have lived under the same roof with these two for almost twenty years and never realized they had any passions other than trickery?

"Well, now that you're here, you might as well help me." I told my half-brothers what was happening with Theodore and his friends.

The naughty gleam in Fir's eyes told me trickery would always be his first love. "Let's go and say hello then, shall we?"

I didn't know until that point just how much I'd missed my half-brothers. The last few months had been so hectic, with everyone in my life fighting the Council in their own ways. I missed the simpler times when the only thing giving me pause about an impromptu family vacation was whether I would have enough time to study.

After regrouping with Gregory and Vera and briefly introducing my half-brothers to the shade, we went in search of the three little weasels.

Then I saw a pair of vengeance demons across the lobby that stopped me in my tracks.

The woman was Madeleine Abrianna Lex, the bully and bane of existence in my former life at Demon U. She was in the company of a slightly older, male version of herself. He was her brother, but I'd only known his face around the campus and not his name. He dressed like he was here as a competitor, in an expensive, tailored tux. Both were dressed in black, as customary of our race.

Two mercenaries, a couple of tricksters, and a sexpot shade, we really didn't need the attention of the Lexes, who were from one of the oldest vengeance families and the embodiment of everything that we tried to stay under the radar from.

I cast a trickster spell called the Hide N Seek, which would prevent us from being seen by the Lexes to a certain extent. I'd only started to master the enchantment, and there were so many of us I had to cover. Here's to hoping it would hold.

Now even more motivated to get the whole business over and done with, we cornered our three witnesses by the fruit punch fountain.

"Go away. We can't talk to you right now." Theodore's jaw

squared upon seeing us, he stood a little taller. "We're up right after the intermission and you're going to throw us off our game."

"Tell it to someone who cares," I muttered.

Gregory took out a USB drive and simply pressed it into Theodore's palm. "No more games. Just do the right thing."

The teens' focus of tonight was winning the trophy. We couldn't openly drag them out of the recital hall, kicking and screaming, and get them in front of Judge Tabella. We were not vengeance cops and we had to keep a low profile.

But we could get them to provide us with a copy of their memory of competing with Boyce at the time of the murder. Supernaturals had the ability to make a duplicate of their memory strand and, with a modern twist, place it on a regular USB drive. The combination of the memories from three individuals should make adequate statements to sway the judge. That was probably as much as we could get from these guys anyway.

Theodore pushed the USB drive back toward Gregory as if it burned him. "No. At least, not until after the final is over tonight."

Amos coughed. "There's the North Bay Music Festival next week."

"Right," Theodore corrected. "After North Bay next week. And the big one in Toronto the week after. Then the festival season will be over."

Vera bared her teeth. "You selfish assholes. Every second we wait is another eternity of pain for my man. You guys want to win every trophy of the season in Boyce's absence before saving him?"

Theodore nodded and his friends followed suit. "Take it or leave it, witch."

Then suddenly Theodore, Amos, and Jackson's eyes

glossed over, and Theodore wordlessly took the USB drive from Gregory.

Theodore concentrated until the light on the drive flashed green, indicating the receipt of a new memory strand. Then he passed the drive to Amos. The latter took it, his eyebrows burrowed as he started the same process of memory duplication. Then it was Jackson's turn, and he, too, did so with minimal fuss.

I could barely stop myself from doing a little happy dance. Judging from the boys' wooden movement, it was obvious that they were enchanted by a trickster spell called Drink the Kool-Aid, a blind obedience spell that was responsible for cults and mass hysteria alike. I grinned at Fir and Clef, and they smiled back.

But when I looked back at Jackson, the USB was gone from his hand.

"Did you truly believe your little trickster spell is going to shield you from us?" said a voice to our right. It was Madeleine Abrianna Lex's brother. He stared at me and his lips pulled back from his teeth, disapproval radiated from every pore of his body. I might not know him beyond his face, but he seemed to know my reputation well. A lot of vengeance demons did, and they had plenty of opinions about Megan-the-Hybrid-Turned-Mercenary.

Madeleine was standing behind her brother. She frowned as he pulled the USB out of his pocket with the showmanship of a magician and toyed around with it. She refused to meet my eyes. "I wonder what you have just stolen."

"Excuse me"—Patricia had made her way to us—"is there a problem?"

I realized then the people around us had stopped talking amongst themselves and were staring at us. They must've sense the tension in the air, or maybe caught wind of the word "stolen."

"These are mercenaries," Madeleine's brother told the organizer.

With that announcement, everyone in the lobby was pointing and staring at my group. Up until now, though dressed differently, we had managed to move through the festival rather inconspicuously. Not anymore.

Well, we didn't want the attention, but that was exactly what we'd gotten.

A look of horror crossed Patricia's face, and she gestured two burly security staff to come to her. Theodore and his friends, on the other hand, had managed to shake off my half-brothers' enchantment, and were now looking at us gleefully from behind Patricia.

"I'm afraid you're going to have to leave," she told us. "Right now. Or I'll call the authorities."

I got a feeling the only reason she hadn't done that yet was because she didn't want to attract the attention of the media. Mercenaries seen at local festival wouldn't exactly raise the event's profile. Get us out fast enough, and they could get on with the second half of the evening without fuss.

With a signal from Patricia, her guards got into our faces, not so subtly started "guiding" us toward the entrance. Gregory, Fir, and Clef weren't happy with the turn of events, but after everything we'd been through, we all knew it was time to retreat.

I glanced at Madeleine, who stared straight ahead with no hint of recognition. Truth be told, I was a little taken aback by her cold attitude. It wasn't like we were friends or anything like that, but after what happened a few months back with the satyr and his adopted nymphs, and Madeleine's role in rescuing the girls, I thought we'd come to some sort of an understanding. Though she hadn't say a single word tonight, her silent backing of her brother spoke volumes.

I admit, it hurt a little.

Vera hissed out of pure rage. She was staring at the USB on Madeleine's brother's palm. With the means to save her man just a few feet away, she was too close to her goal to give up. She made the motion toward him.

No, I told her.

The USB—

Leave it. Look, these aren't your run-of-the-mill rent-a-cops. I tilted my chin toward the silver armbands on the guards. *These are Ares's henchmen making a little money on the side between wars. You might be able to evade them in your non-corporeal form, but then you can't take the USB with you. Either way, you'd lose. At least they aren't servants of Hell, or word would really be getting around to exactly where we don't want it to get around. Do you want to endanger Boyce further?*

Vera gave me a murderous look, but made no further move toward Madeleine's brother.

Listen, I told her. *We'll get the statement from those guys another time. We know where they'll be next week, remember?*

My Boyce can't wait another week!

We can't afford to make a scene. Well, a bigger scene than it already is. Believe me when I say it's not going to help your cause.

Because of the Council? Her eyes glinted dangerously. *Is that why you're so damn careful?*

I looked at her. I shouldn't have been surprised. The shade could get into my head and access my memories, after all. She would know the reasoning behind my call for self-restraint.

Why, oh why, did I recruit help from people who had even more restrictions than me? she lamented.

Walking away from good, solid evidence when we were that close to obtaining it was hard. The humiliating tread to the door, being escorted out while everyone was staring openly, didn't improve the experience.

And I feared what just might get back to the Council about tonight.

Forcing my spine to stay straight, I stalked out, trying not to let my worries and embarrassment get the better of me. The heat of a great many eyes burned holes into my back, and my cheeks flushed despite my effort to act cool.

Then I felt Gregory's hand on my lower back, his warmth permeated the fabric. I relaxed into his strength, and felt just a bit taller and stronger.

❧ 17 ❧

THE BOOK CLUB

"I'm sorry about the competition," I told Fir and Clef as we headed toward the side street beside the recital hall, where we would teleport the hack out of this place.

Fir shrugged. "Don't worry about it. The judges are old school geezers that have no appreciation for humor. They wouldn't have given us the first place anyway."

"For what it's worth I thought it was really good," I said.

"Thanks, sis."

My half-brothers left, with the promise to update me once the expo came to a close. It might be a while before I could see them again, especially given the current situation with Vera. My heart ached as they teleported out of sight.

Then it was Gregory's, Vera's, and my turn.

"Wait!" The *click, click* sound of heels rapidly approaching came from behind us.

I recognized that voice. It belonged to Madeleine. I turned abruptly and snapped, "We're going, okay? Leave us alone."

"Look, I had to play along, alright?" she tried to explain. "Once my brother saw you, it was over already."

"Whatever." I tried to inject a sense of casualness in my voice, but there was a tremor there that I hated. I wished I had better luck finding allies. If that was the case, then I wouldn't have deluded myself into thinking that Madeleine could be one of them. So on top of feeling hurt, I was also embarrassed by my own wishful thinking. "It didn't change the result, did it?"

"Yes, it did. I got this back for you." In Madeleine's offered hand was the USB drive that we'd lost.

Gregory took the drive and closed his eyes briefly, concentrating. "This is the real thing."

"Of course it is. I conjured a decoy for my brother to take home," Madeleine replied.

A cry of joy tore from Vera. She grabbed the USB from Gregory and pressed it right next to her heart.

Okay, my night just got a little brighter.

"Now can we talk?" Madeleine asked. Her image blurred, and I blinked. While before her dress was tight and black, she now stood before me in a loose, white lace number with embroidery of bluebells all over that matched her eyes. She looked softer than I'd ever seen her. Sexier, in a sensual kind of way.

The standard black color of vengeance she had on inside the recital hall was just a glamor. She even let loose her blond hair, a riot of curls falling all over her face as she talked. She looked less like a vengeance demon and more like the part-nymph that she was.

Up to now, the privileged girl from one of the oldest vengeance families had always been careful to hide her nymph blood. I only found out about her secret accidentally. It was so out of character for her to be in anything but black, never mind the flying blond curls and vibrant bluebells embroidery.

She must've been skipping out on Monk Leeches, the black market self-meditation that kept her nympho energy in check and helped her stay cold and hard. Did that mean she was more embracing of her nymph nature, now that she'd allowed herself to care for her own kind?

"What's going on?" I asked her. I had to say, the gifting of the USB drive had earned her considerable brownie points.

"I need your help. All of your help." Madeleine turned to Vera. "I've seen you around the Book Club and you were there this afternoon. I heard you mentioning going after evidence, so I put two and two together when I saw you tonight."

Vera's eyes widened. "You were there at the Club, too? But that would mean—"

"Yes."

"And yours is also—"

"Yes."

Gregory shot me a look, his eyes reflecting the puzzlement that I was feeling.

"Will the both of you stop being so cryptic? What the hell is happening?" I asked impatiently.

"Hell is happening," Madeleine replied. "To our loved ones."

———

We made our way around the inside of the Robarts Library, the largest library of the University of Toronto on the human plane. The building was shaped like a concrete peacock on the outside and was a bit of a maze on the upper floors. There were student bulletin boards lining the hallway, advertising essay writing help and used textbooks sales.

"Let me get this straight. Your 'Book Club,'" I put air quote around my last two words. "Is like Alcoholics Anonymous, except it's a support group for women addicted to falling for men serving in Hell?"

So while Gregory and I were napping after lunch, Vera was at this support group we were making our way to right now.

"No," Vera corrected, irritation apparent in her voice. "AA would imply this is some kind of habit I have to break out of. It's not. I love Boyce, I'm proud of it, and I'm never going to stop."

"And we didn't all joined because of our lovers. I went because of Rhys, my cousin," Madeleine added.

"Your cousin?" Gregory asked as we rounded yet another non-descriptive hallway.

"Younger cousin, twice removed. We shared the same great-grandparents. But on Rhys's side they kept marrying full-blooded nymphs."

"So there's much more nymph in him than in you," I concluded. "A conveniently forgotten part of the exalted Lex family tree, I assume?"

Madeleine gave me a glare and said nothing. That was as close to admitting I was right that she was going to get.

"I don't understand." Gregory frowned, his voice puzzled. "He's your second cousin. It's not like you guys are closely related. Why attend this group at all and risk exposure of what you are?"

He'd learned enough about Madeleine from me to follow the conversation, and he had a good point.

"Rhys is not the only one," Madeleine explained. "He's the second male in my extended nymph family who got wrongfully condemned to Hell in the last three months. There are rumors flying around that the same is happening to other nymphs all over. My grandmother wanted me to look into it. She's very close to that side of the family. In secret, of course."

Ahhh, so my former tormentor was playing nice because she was on a mission. A part of me, though, wondered if it went beyond that. Maybe responding to the pleas of her kidnapped brethren months ago had made her embrace her nymph heritage more.

Thinking about Madeleine taking orders from her grandmother was making me miss my own gran. I thought of her constantly, but most of the time I was able to compartmentalize it in a small corner of my mind. I had to, or else I'd go comatose with worry. But sometimes the barriers got knocked down when I least expected it and losing her felt like a fresh twist of a knife in my heart.

"So the matriarch of your family sent you," Gregory said thoughtfully, "but what about the patriarch? He served on the Council before his son took over, didn't he? How does he feel about all this?"

Madeleine swallowed. "He doesn't know. None of the men did, including my own brother. Look, in diluted form, the effect of nymph blood is only felt by the female descendants. For the males, it's just a recessive gene with some heightened supernatural sensitivities. My brother never even questioned why he was able to break free of your trickster spell and see you so easily. Since the men experience none of the discomfort that come with the nymph heritage, the women in my family had long decided that in all fairness they aren't privileged to the very existence of that heritage, either."

"Why are you telling us all this?" I asked.

"Because I need your help. *We* need your help," Madeleine replied, gesturing to Vera.

I glanced at Vera's closed face, noting she didn't exactly jump in to lend support to Madeleine's announcement. So while she had been leaning on the support group for strength, it looked like she wasn't thrilled by the idea of sharing her resources with the class.

"Vera, when were you going to tell me you suspected that what happened to your boyfriend might not have been an isolated incident?" I demanded. One single case was a mix-up, multiple cases was a conspiracy. I was in a business where I couldn't afford to get dragged into something like that blind. "You do realize that if you'd told Mel about this connection, he might've been able to get more information about Boyce's case?"

"Yeah, and in doing so, compromised his safety," Vera shot back, unrepentant. "I know how things would've gone if he's just one of many. You lot would've planned, plotted, and moved so very carefully that he would have to suffer a lot longer before you'll get to him."

I hate to admit it, but that was exactly how we would've acted if we realized the scope of the issue. We would've researched the hell out of the whole thing before making a single move.

"I always intended to tell you about the support group," Vera's voice gentled, "when my Boyce was free and clear. I don't want anything to jeopardize that."

"Well, too bad," Madeleine said. "You have a responsibility to the Club to make these mercenaries aware of us right away. We supported you through the darkest time in your life, after all."

Vera didn't have a retort to that, so Madeleine turned to Gregory and me. "I don't know what kind of deal you made with this shade, but you are morally obligated to see this through for all of us. I assume this is not the first guy you've returned to Hell for profit? And yes, I'm aware that you're bound by your own codes."

I gritted my teeth and exchanged a glance with Gregory. She was right. Since my start in the mercenary life we'd sent back plenty of people. They all protested their innocence, of course. How the heck would I know some of them might actually be telling the truth? As annoying as it was that

Madeleine knew more about the mercenary codes that I did before I became a mercenary, she was right.

The part of me that wanted to do the right thing warred with the part of me that just wanted Vera to get her man back so she would take me to the Internet to find Grandma as promised. I understood Vera's selfishness when it came to putting her needs over her fellow support group members, because I so wanted to be selfish, too.

And yet Grandma, while substance-less, wasn't in pain as far as I could tell from Esme's mom. But for the people I sent to Hell, who might or might not be guilty, every second of torture was an eternity. Damn Madeleine, but she was right. I needed to investigate the matter further. A glance at Gregory's grim face suggested he was thinking along the same line.

Vera, however, didn't think she owed the support group anything.

"Suppose I just take this and run?" Vera stopped walking and flashed Madeleine the drive. The rest of us halted in our steps as well. "Get the court to order my man's release while you sort everything else out?"

Madeleine was unfazed. "Remember who secured the drive for you. I can get it for you, and I can take it away. Come with me. Allow the mercenaries to learn about the victims through their partners. You know it's the right thing to do."

Vera growled at Madeleine, then resumed walking, teeth baring. The group moved forward again.

After half a minute of awkward silence and another two turns, Madeleine and Vera stopped before a door. From the ones we'd passed before, they tended to open to classrooms or study areas of various sizes.

Vera beat Madeleine to tapping on the door. I got a feeling it had less to do about wanting to go in and more about having one up on the other girl.

"Knock, knock!" Vera said.

It must be some sort of secret code, because a muffled sound from the other side asked, "Who's there?"

"Your worst nightmare."

"My what?"

"That's right. You won't even remember it."

That must've been the right code, or the right code for Vera anyway, because the door swung open, revealing a female fire demon—the type that was the disguise of choice for Candy. This one was the real deal, though. She moved out of the way and allowed Vera to enter. Madeleine leaned close to the fire demon and whispered, "Gilda, these are mercenaries and they're here to help."

Gilda looked Gregory and I up and down. "What's your name?"

"Megan and Pete," Gregory replied, using his professional name.

"Alright, but keep it on the low down. I don't want to get the girls' hopes up until there's a good reason to."

"Of course," Madeleine agreed.

We followed Madeleine into the room, which was about the size of a large classroom. All the tables were heaped haphazardly to one side, forming a clearing in the middle with a dozen chairs circling it. Over a dozen women and a few men were already seated, chatting amongst themselves. They were a diversified bunch, with supernaturals ranging from goblins, chess fairies, trolls, dark elves, ogres, and firbolgs.

"You came at the right time," Gilda said, "we're just about to start."

Every seat was taken save for one. I assumed that was Gilda's. Madeleine grabbed a folding chair close to the wall and Gregory and I did the same. There were the sounds of chair legs shuffling on the floor as people moved to incorporate us into the circle. They were looking at us with open curiosity.

Madeleine said to the group, "These are friends of mine, Megan and Pete. Please make them feel welcome."

"Hi, Megan! Hi, Pete!" Everyone greeted.

"Let's start the meeting like we usually do. That'll give the newcomers a sense of what to expect." Gilda gave Gregory and I a meaningful look, telling us to play along.

A lithe shapeshifter, probably one that could turn into either a lion or a leopard, stood. "Hi, I'm Kat. I've been without my man for one month, five days, and eleven hours."

"Hi, Kat," the group chorused.

Yeah, not an AA meeting, my ass.

As everyone introduced themselves, I met the lovers of magical enforcers, fairy dust smugglers, and crooks who sold the Purgatory Bridge to unsuspecting tourists. All of them had one thing in common—they had done only small-time stuff until they were arrested, charged, and quickly sentenced to Hell over offenses that were a heck of a lot more violent and serious in nature.

Most of the convicted had been taken to Hell, or escaped and returned to Hell, in the last three months. In two cases, Gregory and I were the ones who handled the, er, logistics of that retrieval. Just like how we'd done with Boyce.

Awkward. If only these attendees had known.

The emerging pattern of mass miscarriage of justice was disturbing. Could all of those prisoners have been patsies? With their past record, they could fit into that type of role and no one would worry about their innocence overly much. But if so, where the heck did the real bad guys go? It would take deception on a major scale to pull it off. We were talking about enchanting supposedly incorruptible police officers and judges, the disappearance of official court evidence, and doing that a dozen times or more over.

It was in the last three months that Hell started hiring lots of freelancers to deal with their little problem of jail-breaks. I thought back on the assortment of supposed wrong-doers that Gregory and I had sent back, creatures that span from a wide variety of races very much like the support group had. Like Boyce, they had loved ones who missed them, and life plans that were ruined.

I did a mental face palm. What if Lucifer was the one behind all this? The Lord of Hell would definitely be capable of this massive switcheroo. It was hard to imagine him spending all this money to control, or to contain, these prisoners if he wasn't in on the deception.

And then there was that blasted note from him, asking me to visit him, offering to take my troubles away. What if that was really an invitation to be a part of his conspiracy? It was way more convincing than an out-of-nowhere romantic interest.

Could it be that every fear that I'd had about dealing with Lucifer was coming to fruition? Just what kind of entanglement were we in for? What kind of wrong had Gregory and I helped perpetuate?

But perhaps I was getting ahead of myself. So far, there was only solid evidence of a single case of wrongful conviction—Boyce's. I needed to find a way to either prove or disprove this theory about a massive number of innocents being trapped in Hell.

We needed to talk to Mel again.

❦ 18 ❦

PROTECTIVE STREAK

AFTER THE SESSION, I was giving Madeleine instructions on how to teleport to Mel's place when Gregory coughed.

"Megan, can we have a private word?" he asked.

"Sure." We walked into an empty classroom nearby. "What is it?"

There was hesitation on Gregory's face. "Do you think we could do this one on our own?"

"You mean, without the girls?" I puzzled. "I thought they could be useful."

"No, not the girls." Gregory's lips thinned. "I mean I wonder if we could do this without going to Mel's."

"Because of Candy?" I guessed.

Gregory exhaled. "You must've come to the same conclusion as I did that Lucifer might be involved in all this."

"Yeah, well, that's not exactly big leap."

"If Lucifer *is* involved, I don't want Candy anywhere near this mess. And that means we can't go to Mel, either."

I sighed. Gregory's protective streak would've been super sexy if he wasn't throwing such a huge monkey wrench into the whole operation. If we were to investigate over a dozen potential victims, we had to do a lot of research, and Mel's resources and foresight were second to none.

But I could see where Gregory was coming from. Candy might be a prodigy, but she was still a very young child. And dammit, I was fond of the little girl, too. Who knew what the consequences were if she was to attract Lucifer's attention? I grit my teeth. "Fine. We'll do it your way."

"No, you won't," Candy said a few feet from me. I had no idea when she got there, but there she was, standing in front of the professor's table. She told Gregory smugly, "Mel had an unusually clear reading on your findings tonight, and he'd foreseen your pigheadedness and told me to come get you. Seriously, Pete, you have to trust Mel. I'm safe."

Gregory glared at the little girl. "Isn't this past your bedtime?"

"Not for a witch." She smiled. "Witching hour is not even here yet."

Yeah, that witching hour had already gotten me into enough trouble as it was. I wasn't going to comment on that.

————

Candy's mom, Sarah, was at reception when we showed up at Mel's. Madeleine looked around the office with undisguised mistrust, her eyes darting everywhere, expecting a trap to spring at any time.

And who could blame her? This was, after all, the head-quarters of Gregory's and my business. Maybe not officially, but it was the heart of it. Vengeance demons like Madeleine —and me, for that matter—were weaned on the notion that mercenaries were all unethical opportunists. I mean, I didn't know any better until I became one of them.

I almost laughed at the puzzled frown Madeleine kept

sending Candy's way, clearly unsure how a child fit into all this.

Vera, on the other hand, was just brooding that she'd returned here at all, with her prize already in hand.

"Mel said to go right in." Sarah waved us through. Candy walked ahead and led the way.

Madeleine lifted her eyebrow and said nothing.

Mel's office had morphed into the precinct of the TV show *Castle*. Was it just a coincidence that like the characters in the show, we, too, were on an investigation? In a typical episode, there was always a point when more questions were presented than answers. I felt like we were in that exact position right now.

At least we still had Mel's help. Heck, he and Candy pretty much insisted on it. Was I a bad person for being relieved that they'd made the choice for me?

I noticed the glare Gregory shot Mel's way, but the latter simply smiled serenely.

Mel had been busy since we last met. Instead of facial recognition software running through faces and profiles on the computer screen like they did in the cop shows, mug shot after mug shot of mean-looking supernatural thugs flashed across Mel's ceiling.

"What is this?" I asked.

"A little bit of magic, and a little bit of technology," Mel replied. "I'd collected all the rumored disappearances from the Internet forums that the likes of the Book Club members frequented. They're mostly written in codenames. I've been trying to match the codenames with profiles and updates of supernaturals from Facebook, Twitter, Pinterest, Instagram, and even Linkedin. We're looking at a hundred or so codenames, and counting."

Yep, supernaturals all over the Cosmic Balance used the same social media platforms as humans. When someone online said LMAO, there was always a chance that they really could detach their bottoms when they laughed too hard.

Then I realized what was wrong with Mel's words.

"What do you mean, you've been *trying* to match them?"

Mel was like Yoda. There was no "try" with this guy.

Madeleine, on the other hand, looked pretty freaked out by what he could do as it was. She narrowed her eyes at Mel with suspicion and a hint of fear. "How could you have known about the missing men if you weren't at the Book Club tonight?"

Vera rolled her eyes at Madeleine. "That's the essence of being an oracle, isn't it?" Then, to all of us, "Hey, why am I even here? I've done my duty to the support group and I'm going to repay Megan later. Right now, I gotta go get to my Boyce."

"You can't," Mel stated.

"Why not?" Vera demanded.

"The same reason I'm having a hard time getting an idea of the real scope of this matter. Something is blocking me from finding out the truth, possibly some kind of blanket distortion spells that make me unable to connect all the dots together. But I can tell you this much, young lady. This is far, far bigger than a hundred or so ex-cons getting throw into the pit of Hell for no good reason. This is about who they're made to replace, and why. This is a cover up of something more sinister than you and I could imagine. Until we figure it all out, do you really want to draw attention to your man and risk having him get wiped out of existence for our nosing around? Hard as it is to believe, he might be safer staying put and facing the standard torment for now."

Vera pulled her lips back from her teeth, but said nothing. That was probably as much a concession as we were ever going to get from her.

Damn, I hated the idea that Mel's skills might have

reached their limit. On my way here, I was so glad that we could have his two cents on things, after all. Now it would seem that he, too, was stumped.

"Mel, Megan and I think that Lucifer might be behind all this," Gregory said, earning gasps from both Madeleine and Vera.

"I suspect as much," Mel admitted. "He would certainly be powerful enough to be behind all this."

"What do we do?" Gregory asked softly.

"If I could get around the blanket distortion spell"—Mel looked at the ever-shifting profiles and pursed his lips—"I can discover the true identities of the missing. With that, I can discern a pattern that could link them together and get an idea of what the conspiracy might be."

"How do we break the distortion spell?" I asked.

"By going straight into the Internet."

✿ 19 ✿

IN A CASE OF SERENDIPITY, or whatever it could be called given the Three Fates were retired already, I ended up going to exactly where I'd wanted to go when I first made my deal with Vera. These kind of coincidences hardly ever worked in my favor, so when it did, it was absolutely wonderful and surreal. I had to suppress my joy at the prospect of possibly seeing Grandma again and listen to what Mel was saying instead.

"Between me and Vera, we have the components needed to help you enter the Net. She holds the key to Lies and Illusions, while I control the Hardware and Facts element. She'll be your guide, manipulating whatever data needed to navigate around the virtual landscape, and I'll stay here and interpret the information with Candy."

Gregory's shoulders relaxed visibly at Mel's words, relieved that Candy would be safe in the physical world.

"I managed to match the codenames and identities of a few people. The more connections we could make between codenames and identities, and between the identities themselves, the more strain we put on the blanket distortion to bring it down. Once it comes down, Candy will download the list of all the wrongfully accused for further analysis." Mel continued, "Interestingly, those few I identified are all linked to one single person, and her name is Ginny Smith. It is from Ginny's site that we'll enter the web."

"It's like the Six Degrees of Separation," I commented. "With Ginny being Kevin Bacon."

A room of confused faces looked back at me.

"He's a human actor," I explained. "The idea is that everyone in Hollywood is tied to each other, and their connection could all be traced back to within six or fewer acquaintance links apart from this guy."

"I suspect in both cases the congregation is organically-formed. Nature has a way of grouping things together." Mel's jaw hardened. "Even under a distortion spell."

Before we began, I dialed Esme's number, hoping to connect with her and her mom before we headed into the Net. Perhaps they'd gotten another message from Grandma, or could tell me how to receive such a message myself once I got in. Maybe we could even, I don't know, meet up in there or something. But no one answered the call, suggesting that the mother and daughter team hadn't returned to the physical world yet. So I left a detailed message hoping they would get it in time and come after us. As it was, I didn't even know how one went about meeting inside the web. Was it like trying to find someone at Time Square on New Year's Eve, or worse?

By the time I pocketed my cell, everyone had gathered around Mel, staring at a mirror he'd conjured. It was about five feet tall, hovering just above ground.

"Here," Mel said. "The official website of Ginny Smith."

I squinted. The large mirror was acting like a monitor, except it was just a bright, white screen.

"Er, it's blank," I pointed out.

"Just wait for it," Candy said. "It takes a while to load up."

"Why?" Gregory asked.

Candy shuddered. "This is one of the old ones from Web 1.0."

When the site finally finished loading, the first thing that popped out were an array of ads that covered the website on four sides. An assault of bright colors in highlighter red, orange, and green formed large, pixelated shapes that flashed in a seizure-inducing frequency. The real content of the site, if you could get past the ads at all, was filled with graphics that weren't size-adjusted and jerky videos that started without permission. The fonts were jumbled, overlarge and bold in one area, and tiny in another, and the layout looked like it was thrown together by a four-year-old.

It was an over-the-top hot mess.

"Now all we have to do is find the right balance between Hardware and Facts, and Lies and Illusions, and the mirror will become a portal," Mel said as he gestured Vera to place her hand on the frame of the mirror like he did on the other side.

"The right balance?" Madeleine asked.

"It's a complicated calculation with many variables, such as the level of integrity of the facts on the site, the believ-ability of its lies, the percentage mix of the two, etc. Even a little off, and the portal won't open, or it'll drive you insane"—Mel shot Candy a glance—"or it opens but you can't leave your corporeal body behind to enter it, and monsters come to you instead."

Candy shifted her weight uncomfortably, a sheepish expression on her face.

Ouch. Was I glad we got Mel on board this time around. Then I thought of Cynthia, Esme's mother, and how she'd managed to do all that calculations on her own and command the different components. Never did I appreciate the skills involved in such a feat until now.

"So the right combination is like the address used in dialing a stargate then," I commented.

Gregory laughed. "Oh, Megan, you and your nerdy references."

I grinned, then a solemn thought came to me. I turned to Mel. "If the wrong combo means no-open, insanity, or a visit from the scary guys," I counted the consequences with my fingers. "What about once we're in there? What risk do we run into?"

"You just might stay lost," Mel said simply. "So get the job done and come back quickly."

He proceeded to work out the various calculations and incantation with Vera, and the mirror took on different hues of colors with the addition of a little data here, and the pulling of a little illusion there. Mel and Vera might as well be speaking French for what they were talking about, so after a while I tuned it out and focused on the site itself.

Looked like Ginny Smith, like Kevin Bacon, was a human actor, but a little-known one at that. I might not have been a performing artist, but even I could tell that her acting credentials were heavily inflated. The resume listed credits from so-called feature film I'd never heard of before, and one of the two demo reels was really a homemade video of Ginny dressed up as a princess at a kid's birthday party.

The second demo reel was a grainy video where the actress was an audience member of a daytime talk show, and her participation was being touted as being a co-host.

Then right at the bottom of the actress's resume, without so much as a page break, the narrative changed to that of a broken-hearted girl blogging about her breakup with some guy called Frank, bemoaning about how much she missed him, and how much she resented his new girlfriend. Huh, I guess that was the days before they encouraged people to have a unified theme for their online platform.

There was a ripple effect on the mirror, and Mel announced, "The calibration is now done."

Gregory, Madeleine, Vera, and I looked at each other and nodded. We were as ready as we would ever be.

"Let's go before I run for the hills." I took a deep breath, then hesitated. "Do I just step through the mirror?"

"No, your spirit has to go through it. The easiest way is to think of one of the seven deadly sins that could be applicable to this site," Vera replied. "Then I'll direct the mirror to pull you in."

I rubbed my fingers under my chin, looking at the actress's resume again. "There's a great deal of illusion of grandeur there. So I'll say pride."

"Pride it is." Vera smiled. "Now keep thinking that word over and over again. It should go smoothly, unless you get caught in one of the system glitches and get trapped there forever."

"What—" I couldn't get more than that one single word out before a force pulled my spirit into the mirror. Great, the risk of being lost on top of the risk of being lost.

I was flying through a sea of ads in a dark background. It was like zooming by Las Vegas Strip while hanging onto a hover car by the fingernails, with banners for weight loss, college diplomas, hair loss, work-from-home-for-a-hundred-dollars-an-hour, and sexual enhancement drugs coming at me at a thousand miles an hour.

Observing the flashy ads as a flat image, from the comfort of Mel's office, was bad enough. Going through them was migraine inducing.

Then a pixelated dragon lifted itself from its rectangular confines and started chasing after me.

It had a rudimental construct, with a red "S" for a body, orange triangles for wings, and a jaw that huffed out a tiny fireball whenever it opened. It seemed to have been programmed to detect motion, likely one of those annoying early ads that forced visitors to click on it whether they liked it or not.

I tried to get away, but I wasn't in control of my forward motion.

As the dragon closed in, other ads joined in the chase. A pill bottle, either containing a supposed cure for weight loss or sexual malfunction, opened and closed its white lids like the dragon's jaw, shooting missiles of pills at me. Then came the college diplomas, trying to wrap their parchments onto my feet like shackles. I had to balance between avoiding contact with them, and not looking at the highlighter-colored shapes too closely.

Then I crashed landed onto something.

I opened my eyes and found myself within one of the video clips on Ginny's site, sprawling over the seat beside her in the audience section of a daytime talk show. The video wasn't of the best quality, and my surroundings reflected that. The wall at the back of the studio was a little bit warped, and everything from the dated clothing of the audience members to the plastic chairs lack details, making them one dimensional and surreal.

The ads were nowhere to be found, and neither were Gregory, Madeleine, and Vera. Or did they land in a different area of the site altogether? How do I get out of here and find them?

"So, our question of today is—" The host, a blonde woman with her hair in a bun, smiled. "Would you sell a friend out for a box of chocolates?"

The host put her mic in front of Ginny, who said, "Yes, definitely, because—"

The host took the mic away and moved onto an audience member in the row in front of Ginny. "What about you, dear?"

With her mouth still gapping, Ginny tried to stick her head between people's shoulders in a futile attempt to keep herself in the camera's frame for as long as possible.

How was that for pathetic?

Gregory and Madeleine dropped from the sky, arms flailing as if trying to fend something off.

"I guess you guys had trouble with the ads, too, heh?" I asked, relieved at seeing them. The less time we had to spend finding each other, the faster we do what we had to do and get out of here. Being on the Internet, especially such an ancient part of it, was making me uneasy, like I was inside a building designated for demolition or something.

"It was horrible." Madeleine adjusted her boots, one of which was half pulled off her foot. "The ads *attacked* us. Who did that just for a sale?"

"That's why they call them spams," I muttered.

Vera landed gracefully next to me, unfazed and looking right at home. "Ready for the main site?"

"Oh yeah," I said fervently. Who knew when the video would start getting choppy and freeze up altogether? Best to get out while we could. "But next time do give me some warning before—"

I shot up into the air and started flying again, landing right at the tiny empty space between the end of the actors resume—"principle musical lead" of a caroling troupe for a local mall—and the first heartbreak entry—"It's over. Even after the restraining order, I really thought we still had a chance..."

Gregory, Madeleine, and Vera soon joined me.

Gregory looked around him. "Now that we're in the main

page, should we be able to see the blanket distortion? I can't feel the spell."

"Me, either." Madeleine's brow ceased.

Like them, I hadn't detected the existence of any enchantment. How could we break a spell if we couldn't tell if it was there in the first place?

"Right at the edges, where the white space of the site meets the black edge of the screen in the physical world." Vera pointed. "See that thin strip of grey wrapping all over? That's the blanket distortion. There's one surrounding every site on the Internet, controlling how information is linked to one another."

Talk about hidden in plain sight. I didn't even recognize the border to the physical world for what it was until Vera pointed it out. Now I felt like a character inside a TV set.

After reading through the desperate breakup text, Gregory shook his head with the general horror males had over crazy ex-girlfriends.

Madeleine looked confused. "I don't understand. How does Ginny connect with so many of the wrongfully accused? She's just an average, weepy human."

"She's more than that," I pointed out. "Not every girl gets a restraining order from her ex."

Madeleine huffed. "I could never understand the concept of a restraining order. If someone unwelcome gets too close, why not just zap off his balls? Why depend on a piece of paper for protection?"

I laughed. "Humans can't exactly do that."

It took me a moment to realize what was odd about Madeleine's words. The old her would never use the word *balls*, as dignified as she was trying to be. This really was a brand-new Madeleine in front of me.

"Ginny connected to the wrongfully accused through a

case of pure coincidence," Vera answered. "Eventually she quit acting, got over Frank, and married a guy who runs a temp agency. One of the candidates in his database is a supernatural ex-con who was trying to go straight by blending in with humans. One of his buddies is currently serving in Hell. We could link to his info from here. Or, one of the girls Ginny worked with as an extra ended up supplementing her income with some stripping on the side. The girl's friend at the club is really a succubus, who got sent to Hell for killing a long-term customer whom she'd never had any problems with. There's also a third connection involving Ginny's old makeup artist and her troll boyfriend. Whichever way, Ginny is going to lead us to one of the wrongfully convicted we're looking into."

"And once we establish enough links, the distortion spell will just break?" Madeleine asked, hope presence in her voice.

"Yep," Vera confirmed. "I suggest that we start with the temp agency. With any luck, there might be other supernatural ex-con connections there."

Vera started "walking" down the page. It was more like the page scrolled down while she placed her feet one after the other on the same spot over and over again, and we moved down with her. At the bottom of the page she took out a small, portable keyboard.

I raised my eyebrow. "Really? Shouldn't you be using something a bit more magical? This is like what any geek would use sitting in front of a monitor."

"Sometimes the simplest method is the most effective one," she said, her index finger pressing three keys on the keyboard.

And just like that, our surrounding changed to that of the landing page of a tradespeople's temp agency, presumably the one run by Ginny's husband. I could tell immediately that it was a modern site, with a professional layout, fast loading time, and clean fonts. There were no flashy ads, and the color theme was a soothing palette of cream and light brown. After the jarring train wreck that was Ginny's website, my eyes and brain thanked me for the relief.

"How did you do that?" Madeleine asked Vera, struggling to keep the sense of awe from her voice. "It should've taken us just as much time getting into that arcane site as it is to get out of it, yet here we are."

"Shift, number sign, and nine." Vera smirked, waving her mini keyboard. "A lot of primitive sites have a built-in code for programmers to access the stuff behind the scene. Makes for a quick getaway or work around. Nobody use that standard code anymore, since everyone fancies themselves a hacker these days."

Gregory pointed at a tab on the upper right corner labeled *Meet Our Candidates*. "Is that where we could find the supernatural ex-con?"

Vera nodded. "That's where he is. All we have to do is link that tab to Ginny's site."

"Just the tab?" Madeleine asked, "We don't have to get in there and view all the candidate profiles one by one and find the one belonging to the ex-con?"

Vera shook her head and took out a red silk scarf, ripped off a thread, and tied it over the tab like one would wrap trimming over a Christmas tree. A very thin trimming.

"Just the tab is fine. My silk threads are spun in the darkest corners of the Internet, and they are as tenacious as the deepest root system. The end that latched onto that tab will seek out all the online records of the ex-con and his buddy in Hell—every bit of information helps solidify the thread's hold on the men's identities. The thread could stretch to infinity in the virtual world, across all websites no matter the programming quality or encryption technology. We bring the other end back to Ginny's site, and this piece of connection is complete. Solid information on the wrongfully accused is the antithesis of the distortion spell, and every connection would put extra stress on it."

I was glad we didn't have to go through the profile one by one—it saved us tons of time. We went back to Ginny's website, the wide flashes of colors took some very painful re-adjustment after the serenity of the newer site. Vera used one of the letter "J"s in the overblown text as a hook, and tied the other end of the silk thread there.

Next, we went to the site of the strip club that Ginny's fellow actor worked at. Once again Vera pulled out a silk thread and tagged the tab, which was called *Meet the Girls*. By the same logic, the thread would seek out information on the fellow actor's succubus friend, weaving itself tightly into the fabric of her identity.

Then Vera did the same with Ginny's old makeup artist and her troll boyfriend.

Through all that work, I came to realize my naivety in thinking that being in the Internet meant I would somehow miraculously run into Grandma or have a message from her delivering right to me. I had envisioned the digital world as a large lecture hall, when it was more like a series of intercon-nected classrooms. It would be a lot easier to spot someone in a lecture hall, but looking classroom by classroom was an entirely different story. No wonder it was taking Esme and her mom so long to search for Grandma or get anything close to a manner of communication from her.

We stood in front of the letter "J" in Ginny's site, which by now had the ends of three threads tied to its curved lower section. Vera started pulling and releasing on the threads like one would to manipulate the movement of multiple kites.

"I'm commanding the thread to lose their elasticity," Vera explained. "So the tension of pulling on them will break the distortion spell."

The air thickened. Actually, I wasn't sure if *air* would be the right word, since we were only here as spirits. Regardless of how it should be called, as Vera kept up with her pulling-and-releasing motion on the threads, pressure continued to build around us, pulling at the thin grey strip at the border of the site that was the blanket distortion, twisting and reshaping it.

I held a hand to my temple. Corporeal or not, the pressure was giving me a hell of a headache. Fear slammed into my heart, and I was convinced that any moment now the strain would become so intense that everything would collapse onto us.

Without a word Gregory took me into his arms and held me close. His support warmed my insides, making my headache lessened. I took a few deep breaths—or whatever gulping at vacuum air was called—and my panic receded.

Eventually, the grey strip got stretched and pulled to the breaking point and beyond. One moment it was there, the next it was gone. Utterly disintegrated. The distortion spell broke, and in its place was a sharp, contrasting divide between the black edge of the computer screen and the white space of the website.

Almost immediately, Vera threw her silk scarf into the air, and all of its threads broke free and shot out in all directions, until there was no more fabric left in her hands.

"What was that?" Madeleine asked.

"I'm sending the rest of my threads out into the Internet. Thousands of them," Vera replied. "Seeking out as many wrongfully convicted as possible."

"So they're like, mini heat-guided missiles?" I looked up from Gregory's arms, feeling loads better now that the pressure was gone.

"Yes, and your little monkey is already following up. Look." Vera pointed at multiple strands of yellow light, with the power signature of scented bubblegum and orange-favored popsicles, entering the web from the physical world and rushing after the silk threads. That must be Candy trying to record all of Vera's findings.

Suddenly, Vera started clawing at her throat as if an invisible hand was tightening around it. Then to my horror, the threads she sent out were coming back to her, their soft bodies turned rigid and straight.

Thousands of sharp arrows headed our way.

"Watch out!" Gregory cried out, conjuring a shield to block the incoming attack. I came up with a magically reinforced umbrella at the same time Madeleine pulled another shield out of thin air. We all ran toward Vera and covered her, seeing how she had fallen to the ground and was unable to fend for herself. Together we hunkered down and bore the brunt of the assault. The red threads bounced off our defenses and fell to the ground, becoming limp and harmless again.

Well, at least our magic still worked in this digital world. And who would've thought I'd be huddling down with Madeleine, of all people, in a bid to survive?

"What the hell was that?" I asked.

"Whoever...is behind the switcheroo plot...found out we're here and shut us down." Vera, struggling to catch her breath, pointed at the grey strip that had appeared once more. "The blanket distortion is back up."

I hoped against hope that in the brief moment that it was down, Candy was able to download some names of the wrongfully convicted.

Just to prove that things could always get worse, Ginny's site was growing dim, as if someone had adjusted the brightness setting on the screen.

"Flaming sunshine," Vera cursed. "They're shutting the

site down. If we're still here when that happens we'll be stuck on this web page forever."

"Then let's get us out of here," Gregory barked.

Vera concentrated, but nothing happened. "I...I can't."

Her voice was full of disbelief and fear.

"What do you mean, you can't? Didn't you and Mel already work out the exit combination?" Madeleine demanded.

"Yes, we did, but it's not working!"

At least the site was taking its time shutting down, dimming by what felt like one pixel at a time. Could the slowness be attributed to the site being so old? Was this an unexpected side benefit of the process being bogged down by redundant programming codes?

But there was no doubt that it was only a matter of time before the site got completely shut down, and a great sense of lethargy had already started to envelop me. It had happened so slowly, like boiling a frog in a pot, that I hardly recognized it for what it was at the start. But I could feel myself relaxing, and escape just seemed like such a big hassle.

Yet for some reason, those around me seem to have a lot more fight left in them. Madeleine started gathering her energy, trying to brighten up the site with the sheer power of her magic. Vera typed into her keyboard frantically, in a bid to counter the shut down, I assume. Gregory struck the blanket distortion with one attack spell after another, many I never even knew he could do, all to no avail.

Even in my stupor, I asked myself, why was this affecting me more so than those surrounding me? Why did I just want to lay down and let it all go?

Suddenly Vera narrowed her eyes on me, noticing my lethargy. She dropped her keyboard and stalked toward me. She yanked at my arm, turning the upper side around for all to see.

Everyone gasped at the tip of a small red arrow protruding from my arm. I couldn't even work up the energy to be alarmed, though Gregory was doing the gasping for the both of us.

"This thread is anchoring her to this site." Vera cursed profusely as I slumped against her. "That's what's stopping us from leaving here. We come as a group, and we must leave as a group. That's how the combination was programmed. Every variable is calculated and non-negotiable. If she's stuck here, then we're stuck here with her."

Gregory pulled me into his arms and tried to pull the arrow out of me. It refused to come out even an inch. My eyelids fluttered. They felt so heavy. Maybe I'll just take a nap...

"Megan, don't you dare fall asleep on me. You still owe me a second date," Gregory commanded. "Come on, think of all those frog legs."

He was trying to keep his voice coercing, but I heard the underlying panic in it.

"I dunno, maybe it'll just taste...like...chicken." It took too much work to talk, so I stopped. I closed my eyes, but Gregory shook me vigorously.

"Ouch," I complained. "My neck."

"Stay awake, damn you!" Gregory growled.

Madeleine, ever so practical, conjured a nasty-looking sword and came toward me with a determined glint in her eyes. I guess she figured if my arm got chopped off, then we'd all be free. I mean, maybe the combination didn't say we have to have all our limbs intact to get out of here. I wished I could work up the energy to freak out, but I was barely hanging onto my consciousness as it was.

Gregory lowered my body onto the ground—if it could be called ground—and stood to his full height, blocking Madeleine's path. "Knock it off!"

"Move away, mercenary!" Madeleine yelled, banishing her sword. "We're going to die here thanks to her."

There was a scuffle, and that was when I slipped into unconsciousness. I was kinda sure that it wasn't because Madeleine had cut my arm off, but I was too out of it to be sure.

❧ III ❧

FRIENDS & FOES

❧ 20 ❧

THE PIT

IF I WAS DREAMING—COULD I even dream here?—then I was more clearheaded than before losing consciousness.

I blinked, trying to adjust to the semi-darkness surrounding me. I was at the bottom of a deep, dim pit, next to its side. The pit was around the size of a baseball field, carved right out of the earth at least twenty feet deep. There was a clear space in the middle, with gym mats covering half the area, and office furniture such as desks, chairs, and lamps dominating the rest. It was such a weird combination, and in such a strange setting, that I had no idea what to make of it.

And there were plenty of people here. Bulky men and women engaging in all kinds of physical combat on the gym mats, and, on the other side, nerdy-looking supernaturals sitting in front of office desks, seemingly lost in their own world in a variety of activities.

Fearful of being discovered, I dove behind a trio of large, towering utilitarian shelves positioned by the wall that stored all manner of practice weapons on its upper half, and paper supplies on its lower half.

I half-expected to be spotted, but after a long while, when

no one came after me, I carefully took a peek out. The shelves, located right by the dividing line between the two crowds, gave me an excellent vantage point to observe both of them discreetly.

I had never seen a group of brains and brawn coexisting with each other without one side trying to intimidate the other with their muscles and the other side twitching their nose at the smell of sweat and unwashed gym clothes. Yet these two groups just minded their own business as if the other didn't exist.

In the brawny group, there were firbolgs, trolls, ogres, and dwarf-giants. I saw tattoos, scars, and some kind of brand on the forearm of everyone that looked like an upside-down octopus with a spike through its middle. Like a Hail Hydra gone wrong, with the octopus being served like a delicacy on toothpicks. I smelled the stink of pent up sexual frustration, which explained the brute force and ferociousness each man and women brought to their matches.

But it was the sight of the geeks that bothered me the most. Well, "geeks" was an overly-general term. I just meant everyone who weren't actively fighting. There was a broad range of supernaturals in this group, including two guys working on some kind of computer programming, and an oracle-like creature waving prediction bubbles with skills that rivaled Mel's. And then there was a chess fairy contemplating the game that made his race famous, a shapeshifter who was practicing his transition from man to feline, a dark elf polishing his bow, and a goblin drawing up a design for a new dagger.

Every member of this group wore long sleeves, but I had a feeling if they were to roll them up, each of them would have that same upside-down octopus brand on their forearm.

Then I saw the nymph. A male. Unlike the female-only race usually found in human fantasy literature, real nymphs had two sexes, though the females still tended to outnumber the males.

I almost missed him as he was leaning over a table in the corner—if one could call anywhere in the opal-shaped pit a corner. He was a year or two younger than me, his face as beguiling as his kind would be. He was—was he for real?—performing some sort of erotic massage on a female mannequin lying on the table, applying oil on the her inner thighs with practiced hands. The mannequin, obviously enchanted to respond to his every touch, moaned as he intensified the pressure. Thanks to her skimpy outfit, I could see her privates had begun to dampen.

Great, a lustful nymph out for his own pleasure was one thing, a lustful nymph who was honed in the act of providing pleasure was practically a weapon.

"They all are, Megan." An achingly familiar voice said from behind me. "In their own way, everyone here is a weapon."

There was only one person in the world who could read my mind almost word for word.

I spun around, staring at Grandma disbelievingly. She was standing with her back to the wall, dressed in a low-key, plum-colored designer suit that she favored. She appeared healthy, not a hair strayed from her bun.

With a strangled cry I ran into her arms, and she cradled my head on her shoulder, her hold surprisingly solid. I sniffled, taking in a whiff of her Chanel perfume. She looked and smelled so normal that I was almost tempted to convince myself that the last few months didn't happen, and that she was never lost to me.

"But oh, I was, my child." Grandma pulled me away from her and shook her index finger at me with a non-nonsense attitude. "I *am* still lost to the Internet, but then so are you. For now, anyway."

"How...how have you been?" I swallowed. I mentally kicked myself. What a silly thing to ask someone who was injured and was forced to flee into a place that disconnected her from everyone she loved?

Grandma merely smiled. "I'm not in pain. At least that's something."

"What corner of the Net have you been in? Esme and Cynthia have been looking for you."

Grandma sighed. "I know. I'd been trying to reach them, to send a message. I'm afraid it came out rather distorted. I've been investigating this pit. When I sensed that you were inside the Net and were getting close to the truth, I brought you here to show you what I'd found. A vision within the land of illusions, so to speak. I'm becoming rather adept in manipulating space, time, and location within the boundary of the Internet."

"The truth? What truth? What *is* this pit, anyway? And what are these guys doing here?"

"You already have all the information to answer those questions. Think," Grandma encouraged, as if this was nothing but one of our mentoring sessions.

Yes, as varied as the creatures in front of us were, and despite the contrast that divided them, I had seen this grouping of supernaturals before—most of them anyway, except the oracle and the computer programmers.

I knew them through the poor souls who'd taken their places in Hell, if the switcheroo was matched by species.

"Do you see the pattern?" Grandma asked. "Do you know what you're looking at now?"

"This is an army." I breathed.

Shit, shit, shit! Could Lucifer really be behind all this, and was his plan to raise an army to take over the Cosmic Balance? What better way to do recruitment than to offer wrongdoers a way out of eternal torment? It was an offer most would find impossible to refuse. And what a pool of diverse talent the Lord of Hell could choose from, with so many arrivals landing on his doorstep every day?

It all made a sick kind of sense.

"An army, indeed." Grandma nodded in confirmation. "The first group is all about the muscles—firbolgs, trolls, ogres, and dwarf-giants. But what makes this army especially dangerous is the second group. Dark elves for their precision use of bows, shapeshifters for infiltration, chess fairies for strategy, goblins for weapon forging, and nymphs and succubi for the art of seduction."

"And oracles for predictions, and programmers for hacking?" I guessed.

"Not just any programmers, dear. Tell me, what species are they?" Grandma gestured at the pair who were still poring over their computer codes.

I sent my senses out. Now that I was focusing on just those two, I realized what was missing about them. They had no supernatural signatures. My breath caught. "They're humans."

That means they weren't just the regular, run-of-the-mill computer programmers. They were Geekomages, human geeks who garnered supernatural power through an overdose of comic books, D&D, video games, and *The Big Bang Theory*.

"Before coming here, one was designing drone prototypes for the human military, while the other was the owner of a new social media platform that promised to become as big as Twitter and Facebook," Grandma added.

Those who controlled these guys, controlled the development of the human world and beyond.

That meant Lucifer was dead serious about taking over permanently. He understood that it took more than muscles to win for good, and he had the resources to cover every aspect of the fight in both long-term and short-term, from active combat to intelligence gathering.

I mean, don't get me wrong, I wasn't entirely thrilled with the Council, aka the Greys, but that didn't mean I wanted Lucifer to rule. And to think that I might have played a role in his plan—I hate the idea of it. I hated myself more for not listening to my initial mistrust of him.

I turned to Grandma. "Your message, *rain raw*, what did it mean?"

"I had to send the message character by character and some got dropped in the distortion. I meant to say *brains and brawn*, hoping to give you a hint of what you're dealing with. From this end, I could see and hear a lot from the physical world, but to help and guide was another matter altogether."

I barely got the chance to be truly horrified before my body felt lighter, as if I could be blown away with a gust of wind.

"Your friends are calling you back. They managed to remove the arrow," Grandma said gently. "Go back to them before Ginny Smith's site shuts down and you're even more lost than I am."

"Come back with me," I pleaded.

Regret filled Grandma's eyes. "I can't."

No, I refused to believe that. I had to try. "If you won't leave with me now, at least tell me which website you hang out at, and I'll come get you. I know people who can get me the right combination now."

"You don't understand. I cannot leave with you even if you can find me again. When you and your friends came to the Internet, you left your body back at the physical world. You were able to properly split your body and soul because they were both healthy and whole. In my case, I had to leap in here while my body was severely damaged, to go back now might just send me crossing over to the afterlife altogether."

"Does that mean you're stuck here forever?" I bit back the sob that threatened to escape from my throat.

"I don't know, dear." Grandma's usually severe face softened. "But I do know that I'm not leaving here today."

"Should I go get your body when I get back? Would it help?" I asked desperately. She couldn't be trapped here for all time. I wouldn't have it.

"It should've healed itself by now, but that's not the point. The initial separation was done rushed and forced, and there's no quick way to fix it. Now *go*, dear."

"But—"

"You don't have a choice." A female voice, haughty and hard, came from behind me. A cold hand was placed on my shoulder. Grandma's eyes widened with recognition, then nodded grimly at the unseen newcomer.

"Get her out of here," Grandma commanded whomever it was behind my back. She might've been surprised by the new arrival, but there was no mistaking the authority in her voice. Lost in the Internet or not, she was someone used to being obeyed.

Before I could spin around and see whom the newcomer was and beg Gran for more clues to help her, I was yanked from the pit and woke up in Gregory's arms. Ginny's website had darkened to the level of an opera house right before the show started, with Vera and Madeleine peeking at me over Gregory's shoulder.

"I was afraid you'd never wake up." Gregory blew out a breath of relief.

I didn't reply to him, and instead stared at the person standing behind everybody else, the one who took me out of the pit.

Cynthia.

21

ENEMY OF MY ENEMY

WITH GREGORY'S HELP, I got up. I had a lot to tell him, but here was not the time or place. Upon standing, I could see that there was someone else standing next to Cynthia—Esme. Save for the age difference, they looked like carbon copies of each other, all pale skin, green eyes, wine-red hair, and black pantsuit.

"Megan!" Esme ran to me. "I got your message as soon as we got back to the physical world. Then Mel told us where to find you and we're here. Are you alright?"

"I'm okay." Then I turned and glared at Cynthia. "Couldn't you have waited a few more moments? I needed a bit more time with her."

Logically, I knew I shouldn't be mad at Cynthia. Hack, Grandma basically ordered her to get me out of there. But a part of me simply rebelled at the idea that there was not much I could do to rescue Gran. Feeling angry beat feeling helpless.

Cynthia seemed unmoved. "The outcome would've been the same. You still have to leave her. And then you and your friends would have died because of the delay."

Trust Cynthia to be super blunt even during the worst situations. That was where Esme got her inborn abrasiveness from. Thank Hades a lot of it had rubbed off by having me in her life.

But regardless of her attitude, Cynthia had a point. I had my friends to think about. And Grandma seemed to be safe for now.

I took a deep breath, checked my arm, and found the arrow gone. I didn't feel any pain where the arrow had penetrated. Maybe that wasn't how it worked.

"It went limp and fell out around when you woke up." Madeleine showed me a thread caught between her fingers. "We should be able to get out of here now."

"Gladly," Vera said, taking her keyboard out again and began typing on it. Cynthia let out an exasperated sigh.

"Too slow," she said, lifting her hand.

Our surrounding dissolved and we were back in Mel's office again, the set of *Castle* felt like something I'd seen from a previous lifetime.

Wow, Cynthia managed to maneuver out of the Internet even better than a shade. That was truly impressive.

And yet, if someone like that had a hard time getting Grandma out, what chance did Grandma really have of ever escaping?

"You're back!" Candy cried, rushing to hug Gregory around the middle. "We weren't sure if you were going to make it."

"Of course we did, kiddo." Gregory ruffled the little girl's hair.

"Thank you," I said to Cynthia, my tone formal.

"You're welcome," she replied just as formally, even more so than her usual robotic voice.

To be frank, I had no idea what else to say to my father's ex-wife. Well, I was never anyone's favorite vengeance demon, especially these days, but Cynthia had more reasons than most to dislike me, even when she was helping me out upon her daughter's request. I was something that never should've happened if Dad and Cynthia were truly soul mates.

I'd had no time to dwell on that, though, because at that moment, Cindy shot from Gregory's side and came straight at me like a high-speed cannon ball. "Gregory told me you got hurt!" she said after giving me a fierce hug. "Are you okay?"

I hugged Candy back. "I'm alright. What's a little fainting between friends, right?"

"You should've waited until Mother and I could join you," Esme reproached me.

"I'm sorry." I turned to her. "I figured you were busy."

"I was. But you should've waited." Esme's voice was tight.

"I'm sorry," I repeated. Not sure what else to say.

"So, you broke the distortion spell," Candy stated, clearly excited by the feat.

I snorted. "For like, a few seconds. Did that give you time to download anything at all?"

Candy smiled smugly and showed me a stack of computer printouts in her hands. "I got about a thousand names before the blanket distortion was back up."

I took the stack of paper, staring at the names. What do I do with it, now that I knew what I knew?

"With that, I should be able to establish some patterns, figuring out what the conspiracy is," Mel said with satisfaction.

"Don't bother." Still staring at the names, I heard myself say. "I already know what's going on."

I proceeded to tell everyone what I saw in that pit with Grandma. Every detail of the vision, down to the description of each soldier in training. I saw the dawning horror on their faces, reflecting how I was feeling inside. Given what Boyce and the other innocents had been forced to endure, everyone knew what a Lucifer regime would look like. Gregory's face grew taut, and despair filled Vera's eyes. Even Cynthia seemed shaken.

"What are we going to do?" Madeleine whispered.

"As if one enemy isn't enough." Esme sighed. "Now we have a second one."

Yes, the Council wanting to take over was bad enough, now Lucifer wanted to, as well. And they were both dangerous. Well, the Council seemed more dangerous to me, just because I had personal experience with it, but there was no doubt they were both major players in the Cosmic Balance in their own right.

A light blub went on in my head.

"That's it!" I screamed, waving the name list around. "I'm going to see Lucifer."

"What?" Everyone else in the room yelled simultaneously. It took a while for them to calm down.

"I'm going to see Lucifer," I repeated. "You know that saying 'the enemy of my enemy is my friend'?"

"What about it?" Madeleine snapped.

"Well, the enemy of my enemy is *still* my enemy, but what's not to say these two equal powers could balance each other out and leave us alone?"

"What are you proposing?" Esme asked.

"I'll go to Lucifer with the name list." It was a reckless plan, and I wanted to get it out there before I lost my nerve. "Tell him I know all about his little army—maybe suggest I got the full list rather than the partial—and ask that he let the innocents go. He could grow his army organically, but not with participants others would have to be forced to replace in Hell. That ought to keep his army smaller but still a good balancing force against the Council."

Vera seemed cheered by the idea of her man being freed, but only cautiously. I didn't blame her.

"And what's not to say he'll just imprison you there to keep you quiet?" Gregory asked quietly.

"That's where everyone else here comes in," I replied, gesturing the entire room. "You all take a copy of the list and go into hiding. If I don't come back after a certain time, you make the list public so the Council will be on Lucifer's ass. That'll be my leverage."

"It's too risky," Esme protested.

"It beats going to the Council directly. That'll only tip the balance in the wrong way. And we still won't get Boyce and the rest of them back."

The day that working with the king of Hell became a more viable option was a sad one indeed, but here we were.

"I'm coming with you," Esme announced, ignoring the frown from her mother.

"So am I," Vera added. "I want to be there."

"No," I said firmly, "I need as many of you scattered out as possible to make my leverage work."

"Well, *I'm* coming with you," Gregory said. "Lucifer was our client. Still is."

Looking into his eyes, I knew there was no stopping him. So I nodded.

"You do realize there's always a price to pay dealing with Lucifer." Cynthia thinned her lips. "He is the Lord of Lies."

I sighed. "Don't I know it."

❦ 2 2 ❦

THE TOUCH

AFTER COORDINATING with everyone to make sure they were as widespread as possible across different planes and societal levels, Gregory and I said good-bye to them, with the promise to get in touch as soon as it was safe.

Then we teleported to the front of my duplex, checking in on Sophia and Rosemary before we headed to Hell. Neither of us would admit it, but we were wondering if this was the last time we would see our loved ones in a long time. We'd left instructions with our friends about caring for Sophia, Rosemary, and Sassy if something were to happen to us, but hopefully it wouldn't come to that.

Talking about Sassy, she greeted us at the front door with loud meows that sounded suspiciously like *where have you been* and *have you brought me any bad guys to munch on?* I laughed, leaned down, and rubbed my cheeks against her fur. "Oh, there were bad guys alright. But none I could bring home. Believe me, I would've loved that, too."

Sassy gave me a reproachful look and stalked off.

"Thank you," I told Gregory. "For everything."

"Not a problem." He let out a breath. "I guess I should go find myself a tux."

I frowned. "What are you talking about?"

"The easiest way to see Lucifer is to play along with his invitation and go through Hell's front entrance," Gregory explained. "It beats trying to surprise him in his own territory by using the service entrance. We never met him before so I'm not even sure where to go."

Right, the invitation. I'd almost forgotten about that, as busy as I was to argue for visiting the Lord of Hell, I'd forgotten the logistic of *how*. Using his invite would make the most sense. Unconsciously, I fingered my necklace, where the VIP pass was miniaturized and attached to its clasp.

"Let's go see Sophia and Rosemary first," I said.

The two ladies were both just as we'd left them. Gregory leaned over Sophia with an expression so tender that it strengthened my resolve to do what I had to do next.

I lightly touched one of his shoulder blades where his vengeance wings would come out of, and applied just a small amount of energy tailored to cancel out the frequency of his power signature.

Gregory slumped over his mother's bed, and I gently eased him into a chair nearby. He would be out for hours. Hopefully I would return by then. If not, there would've been nothing he could do about it, which was exactly what I wanted.

Generally, it would've taken some powerful magic to knock out a full-blooded vengeance demon, but I was using the knowledge of Gregory's own power signature against him —something I acquired being his business partner all this time, not to mention the fact that we had dated and kissed.

What I just did was considered so despicable and unsportsmanship-like, that only the lowest of the low would do it. I felt like a slimeball for tricking him like that.

But I did it because I had no intention of dragging Gregory along into my confrontation with Lucifer. As Esme said, it was too risky. In addition, there was a chance the VIP pass was only good for one person. I mean, Lucifer didn't send Gregory the flowers and card, now did he?

My eyes were moist as I stared at Gregory's still figure. Then I took a deep breath and started making the preparation to go to Hell.

I wished Rosemary was conscious, because I could sure use her advice in getting dolled up. To go through Hell's casino meant I had to dress up for it. Heck, Lucifer had asked me to do so outright in his own invitation.

Wear something nice. I shivered as I wondered what his true intention was. The idea of a professional interest was just as gross as a romantic one.

I started hunting down suitable formalwear for the occasion. I had a closet full of dresses from my mom, stuff spun with trickster magic that was designed to enhance one's sensuality. But considering that I would be trying to threaten my host, something a little more dignified would be preferred.

I turned on my heels and walked toward Rosemary's wardrobe. She always said I was free to borrow anything from there. As a chef, she was always more interested in her white aprons than the edgier stuff her fashion-designer mom tried to get her to wear. So in a way, I used the clothes given by my mom just as little as Rosemary did with hers.

From my roommate's closet, I picked out a cocktail dress of wine red and a flattering sweetheart neckline. I also borrowed a faux diamond tennis bracelet and necklace set. I was tempted by a pair of silver strapped sandals, but decided that a little polishing spell on my old black pumps would do just fine. New footwear always made me feel unbalanced, and tonight I needed to be on an even heel like no other time.

I washed up, changed, and left the house.

Let's pray I won't become a permanent guest in Hell, for Lucifer's amorous attention or otherwise.

❧ 23 ❧

HOT DATE

I STOPPED short on the front lawn, right when I was about to start the teleportation. While I might've had a VIP pass to be presented at the front gate of Hell, I still had to get there first. All I had ever done was travel with Gregory through the back door, and that was where the teleportation would've taken me.

I took out my cell phone, ignoring the passerby's stares as they took in my formalwear, and dialed a number.

"This is the main switchboard of Hell. Your call is very important to us, please wait for the next available person. Your estimated wait time is—" There was a pause. "Five minutes."

Five full minutes, plenty of time for me to wait around and feel absolutely miserable about how I'd just betrayed Gregory's trust. Not to mention the sheer helplessness regarding Grandma's situation.

Then the girl at the switchboard said "hello." I told her the extension number I wanted to reach and got connected with my guy in Hell.

"Hey, Megan," Tatus, the assistant of Leonard, bookkeeper of the Book of Life and Death, answered the phone, his tenor cackled over the cross-dimensional line.

Yep, that was my guy in Hell. Well, technically he was Gregory's guy, but that was just semantics.

"Are there any big sinners biting the dust tonight?" I asked.

He didn't ask me why I needed to know. That wasn't the reason why Gregory put him on a magical credit allowance. Tatus just said, "I'll be back."

I was on hold for only a few minutes, but in Hell it could've been hours or even weeks. I knew where Tatus was off to. He was taking a sneak peek at the Book behind his boss's back.

"A heart attack," Tatus said after he came back, and went on to give me the information of a medical emergency that was about to happen in an upscale restaurant in downtown Calgary, on the human plane in a little under two hours. The person involved definitely deserved a grand entrance into Hell. That meant through the soon-to-be departed I could hitch a ride all the way to the front gate of the Underworld.

Well, luckily I was all dressed up and would fit right in at a fancy restaurant.

I hung up on Tatus and teleported using the coordinates he gave me. Outside the restaurant, the sky was lit with a spectacular summer sunset, all clear-blue sky and hues of orange clouds. With Calgary being two hours behind Toronto, it was only about nine o'clock here, and night hadn't fallen at this time of year. On the sidewalk, patios were in full swing, with people mingling, chatting, drinking beers, and catching sport games on large TV monitors.

Inside the restaurant, I told the front desk I had a reservation. I didn't, but I laced my words with compulsion and was soon shown in. I made sure to take the table right in front of the heart attack waiting to happen. Literally.

Dark wood panels covered the walls of the restaurant, and each table had a single rose and candle in the center. Soft violin music played in the background. Couples were sitting together, bending their heads together in intimate conversation or holding each other's hands. I was the only single person in the room.

A glance at the logo on the front page of the menu revealed that the place served French cuisine. The cruel irony of it all, for me to be surrounded by frog legs and escargots, when that was how I envisioned my second date with Gregory to be.

That date was impossible now, after how I'd betrayed him. Even if it was for his own good.

My stomach rumbled. It apparently didn't care if my heart was breaking. It didn't matter that I'd spent a lot of time since my last meal not even being inside my physical body—it smelled food, it wanted some, and that was the end of it.

My stomach rumbled again.

"I see you've worked up quite an appetite." A mirthless chuckle sounded behind me, making me jump to my feet.

I turned around and my mouth fell open.

There was Gregory, standing behind my chair. How was he awake? How did he sneak up on me like that?

With a tailored suit, broad shoulders, and untamed brown hair, he looked as handsome as the...well, I guess I shouldn't say as handsome as a devil, given where I was heading this evening. It didn't matter that he'd only dressed up to blend in when he tracked me here, he was still looking the sexiest that I'd ever seen him, and I couldn't deny the effect.

"Well, aren't you going to invite me to sit?" he asked.

My jaw was still on the floor. All I could manage was, "H-how?"

Gregory sat down smoothly and gave me a cold smile. "You can't imagine this is the first time I'd ever been surprised by someone I trusted, right? Would you not think, that I might've developed some sort of defense against that?"

I narrowed my eyes. "You only *pretended* to pass out?"

"Of course."

I sat back down. "Listen, I—"

Gregory gestured to the server for a place setting for himself. He, too, had used compulsion, and the server did his bidding, never mind that my non-existence reservation was for one person only.

I opened my mouth again, but he held up a hand.

"We're a team, Megan." Gregory's eyes glinted with smoldering heat. "What you did wasn't only underhanded, but insulting."

His shoulders twitched jerkily as if his wings, in his agitated state, were begging to come out. His face was stormy. But under all that rage, his power signature hid a deep sense of confused hurt. And that was what made me feel like the slimiest grub ever.

I swallowed. "I was trying to keep you safe. I don't even know if my VIP pass would let both of us in."

"We won't know until we get there, now will we?" Gregory said, his voice determined.

"What about your adopted family?" I demanded. "I thought you don't want Lucifer paying any attention to Candy. There's also your mom to consider."

"I am doing this for them." Gregory ran his fingers through his hair. He closed his eyes, then opened them and looked at me directly. "Listen, if Lucifer is taking over, they aren't safe anyway."

"Alright." It was hard to turn him down when he put it that way. "And, er, sorry about the whole knocking you out business."

The corner of his mouth lifted. "*Trying* to knock me out."

"Yeah, that." My shoulders, which I never realized I was

tensing, relaxed. I'd really come to rely not only on Gregory's support, but his companionship. Having him by my side while I faced Lucifer would be a great asset. To be frank, I expected Gregory to be so furious with me for what I'd done that he would throw roadblocks to prevent me from going to Hell, or not speak to me for another three months. Perhaps having a foundation of a professional relationship before we'd ever contemplated dating was a good thing, as we could talk like grown-ups without a lot of hurt feeling got in the way.

"We have a bit of time before we hitch a ride," I informed him, checking my cell.

"I know." His eyes sparkled. His mood seemed to have picked up now that we'd settled the matter between us. "My guy in Hell told me."

"Hey, I thought he was *my* guy." I smiled.

"Nope. He's mine way before he's yours."

"Jerk," I muttered.

"Let's order." Gregory picked up the menu, effectively blocking the napkin I threw his way. "This is our second date, after all."

"Our second date?" I echoed.

Gregory's face turned serious. "Look. I have no idea what we're going to face in Hell. Let's treat this meal as a date, so that come hell or high water, we have this. Would you like that?"

Would I like that? Almost two hours together with him, where we keep the burdens of recent events at bay and simply enjoy ourselves? It sounded precious beyond compare.

But all I could do was choke out, "Come hell or high water? Is that supposed to be a pun?"

Gregory laughed, and I flipped open the menu with a grin.

Alright, there might be a little problem here.

The menu was in French, or they were describing items

that were in French. Other than frog legs and escargots, I knew basically nothing about French food. Would that be just as offensive as thinking Chinese food was all about spring rolls and sweet and sour chicken?

Our server approached, and I got busy listening to him talking about the various menu items. His voice was accented as expected, fake or otherwise, but I had no idea what the sauces were that he was talking about. Actually, I wasn't even sure if he was describing sauces, meats, or veggies. It all sounded French to me.

When I told Gregory that I wanted to go to a French restaurant, it was because it sounded so posh and romantic. But the truth was, other than the aforementioned frog legs and escargots, I really knew nothing about the cuisine. Sure, Rosemary cooked French dishes at home before—what self-respecting chef wouldn't?—but I'd never bother remembering their names because it wasn't like I had to order them at a restaurant.

Until now.

Gregory seemed perfectly content to let me order, either out of chivalry, or assuming that I must knew more about the cuisine than him since I was the one who suggested it. I was too embarrassed to admit to him how little I knew, and I couldn't exactly Google the dishes right in front of him.

See, no matter how they sliced it, there was a difference between sharing a meal and going on a date. Megan-the-mercenary- business-partner would never have a problem telling Gregory the truth. Hack, once we had to do a stakeout at a zombie nightclub, and I told him straight up I knew nothing about any of the uniquely flavored brain appetizers on the menu.

But the Megan who was on an unexpected date with a guy who just minutes ago was mad at her, found herself unable to admit to him her lack of knowledge.

I ended up nodding to whatever the server said was the specials of the day, and Gregory said he'd have the same. I gave a mental push, making sure the kitchen would know to make it a priority order.

After the waiter left, Gregory turned to me. "So, do you know much about the heart attack victim?"

I shrugged. "I was in a hurry. Just the name, physical description, and cause of death."

Our victim was a beautiful, if slightly artificially enhanced young woman by the name of Yelena King. She was seated behind us, in a booth with an elderly man old enough to be her grandfather, and they were flirting outrageously with each other. When I tilted my head toward the lower section of the booth, I could see Yelena's hand exploring the inside of the old man's thigh. Urgh. From the flushed look on his face, I wondered if Tatus got it wrong and it was the old man who was about to die of excitement.

Assuming Tatus was right, though, Yelena's cause of death was undiagnosed hereditary heart condition, to be triggered by the severe allergy attack she was about to receive from the aged rum in her dessert cocktail. Apparently, she'd forgotten to ask them to make it a virgin.

"So what's her crime?" I asked Gregory.

His eyes danced with amusement. "Why don't you take a guess?"

"Black widow." It was the most obvious choice. "Maybe like that McCain case we did with the woman who'd poisoned five husbands and took their life savings."

Gregory shook his head.

Damn. Usually the most obvious thing was the most likely. Not in this case. "Er, art theft. She's distracting the old man so her partner could clean out his safe."

"No." He was grinning smugly. Bastard.

"Corporate espionage. She's trying to get him to say things she could take back to his business rival."

"No."

"Oh, come on. Skipping out on the bill for her boob job? Crime of fashion?" I asked, eyeing the front slit of Yelena's dress, which revealed half her private parts.

"No."

I was stumped. "Tell me."

Gregory leaned closer. "Remember Rabbit Hill?"

My mouth fell open. "The man who was having unprotected sex with women knowing he was HIV-positive and didn't tell them? The one whose face we put a hundred warts on to make sure he's too gross to ever get laid again?"

"That's the one." Gregory chuckled. "Yelena is the female version of that guy. Except the list of her victims is so long that an early admission to Hell was scheduled."

"I *knew* it has something to do with what's she's doing with the old man!" I pumped my fist.

"But you didn't guess what she's after, now didn't you?" Gregory laughed.

I should've been peeved about guessing wrong, but truth be told, I was just enjoying the heck out of talking shop with Gregory. It might seem weird to some to talk about genital warts at the dinner table, but we were vengeance demons *and* mercenaries, and this line of conversation was just fine with me.

And a part of me wondered if after tonight we would have the chance to do so again.

I entertained him with tales of some of my childhood trickery adventures. I told him about that time when I enchanted the bingo marker belonging to Miss Neringa, the nosy giantess next door. During Friday night bingo, she gossiped as usual and found the circles she made with her marker disappear with each groundless, harmful speculation.

"I have to say, I'm impressed," Gregory said. "That was a perfect blending of vengeance and trickery."

I blushed. Hearing such a direct compliment from him was nice. Very nice. "I did it unconsciously. It took another decade before I realized I have to embrace those two sides of me."

A look of uncertainty passed over Gregory's face. "Megan, there's a question I've meant to ask you for a long time. But I wasn't sure if you'd be offended."

"What is it?" Oh no, he wasn't about to ask if I'd colored my hair, was he? And no, I wasn't on a diet, either. I was suddenly self-conscious that I was more full-figured than the average, stick-thin female vengeance demons. But then, he knew I was a hybrid—

"How did you ever survive four trickster brothers?"

I laughed. That was an easier question than I thought. "With a lot of intel gathering and sneakiness."

"How so?" Gregory's tone was full of curiosity.

"When I was very little, I was just surviving from one prank to another, you know? Then I realized that while tricksters love to trick, they also like to keep things fresh. Like, if I sat on a whoopee cushion this week, I most likely won't see it for another month. And my brothers don't like to do the same prank in the same week as others, unless it's a group project. So I started keeping careful track of who did what trick, and when. After that, it was just a matter of keeping an eye out for stuff that hadn't happen for a while, and save my energy on stuff that was just hot last week. And then Twitter came along, and it helped tons."

"Twitter?" He snickered.

"I follow all the major trickster groups. Tricksters love to brag about their Trick of the Week, and will sometimes even challenge each other to do quests and stuff. If it's Switcheroo Week, then you betcha I'm going to double check my homework before handing it in. Then I do some pre-emptive strikes, too, like hiding all the laxatives during the Week of Diarrhea."

"A lot of intel gathering indeed." Gregory sipped at the sparkling water we'd both ordered, his eyes glinting with admiration. It seemed a shame to be eating French food without some nice wine, but we would be going back to working mode soon enough.

Talking about being on limited time, I had something I'd been meaning to ask Gregory as well. I was feeling brave and closer to him than ever, so I might as well do it. "Mind if I ask you a question?"

"Sure."

"How did you meet Mel?"

Gregory gaze became faraway. He remained silent for so long I began regretting the question. Then his face softened. "Do you remember how in my mother's memory, she mentioned that I had been hanging out at the Field?"

I nodded. That was the spot where low-income vengeance kids went to practice their magic.

"As a rather angry young man, I'd gotten into my fair share of fights in school. Most of the time it's from people laughing about my heritage. I could take them calling me a bastard, but not when they called my mother a whore. So when that happened I invited them to the Field to settle our differences. In the beginning, I lost a lot. I soon learned to use my allowance to buy magical balm to hide my bruises from my mother. Sometimes it meant skipping a few lunches. But I never let an insult of my mother go unchallenged."

I winced. I remembered the memory showing Gregory as a four- or five-year-old who still loved his daddy, and the other one with him as a hardened young teen who had already started frequenting the Field. But what was not shown was that somewhere in between those two life stages was a young kid who got teased at school without the skills to fight back. My heart ached for that child.

But that child didn't stay that way.

"After a long while, I started winning," Gregory continued. "And I attracted the attention of a group of older kids. Some of them had parents who were mercenaries, some of them had started in the trade themselves. They were nice to me, and gave me tips on how to be a better and dirtier fighter. It was the first time in my life I was treated like a person, not defined by what my biological father did or didn't do."

I swallowed. No matter how bad I'd had it in school, my childhood world was anchored by having a set of loving parents and half-siblings that, no matter how much more spirited or straight-laced than I was, still treated me well in their own ways. Gregory never had that. He had his mother, but that was it.

"Then one day," Gregory said with wonder, "my new friends were talking about a job that needed doing. A job that paid well."

"What was the job?" I asked.

"They suspected one of the teachers in my school of touching female students in an inappropriate manner, and they needed to plant a magical recording device in his office. The device was similar to a human one, except that upon the collection of supportive evidence, it automatically triggered a glaring beacon in the Cosmic Balance."

"What's the beacon for?" I asked.

"It blares out a signal that's too annoying to ignore, forcing the licensed vengeance demons to make addressing the injustice a priority," Gregory said with grim satisfaction. "Without the mercenaries forcing their hands, it often takes the bureaucrats years before doing the right thing, and in the meanwhile more and more victims suffered. That's why there are so many unresolved cases of sexual abuse involving adults in positions of power. The job in question was contracted by the parents of a victim who committed suicide after the system failed her."

One would think that the safety of minors should've been a priority, but sadly, I wasn't surprised about the inefficiency of the process. It was, after all, being ran by the likes of the Council and the Greys.

"My friends would've gladly taken the job themselves, but there was a problem," Gregory explained. "All of them had dropped out of school by that time. And they had all left in such a manner that it would be impossible for them to return. They'd be barred from entry no matter what magical disguise they donned. The safeguards around the school were strong enough to do that, though it did nothing to protect those who were *inside* the school."

"But you could get in because you were still a student there," I guessed.

Gregory grinned, his pride for his first job shone in his eyes, making him look years younger. "And I did. Earned myself enough money to buy my mom a new design table. After I planted the recording device in the pervert's office, my friends took me to see Mel, who was the one who sent out the call, and he gave me my pay. He told me outright that mercenary wasn't some gang culture to aspire to, but a way of life that had a place in the Cosmic Balance, even though many believe otherwise. His words, and the realization that I'd helped not just myself, but the world that day, changed my life."

"How did you explain where you got the money when you gave your mom the new design table?" I asked.

Gregory shrugged. "I told her I worked part time at a magical supplies shop and she bought it. It also explained the many nights I was late getting home because of the fighting. People saw what they needed to see."

It was then that the server approached our table with the appetizers. I licked my lips in anticipation. This was going to be good.

There were the escargots. Then the frog legs, in what appeared to be a butter and garlic sauce.

But the server didn't stop there. He also put down shredded pork and apricots on slices of baguettes, salmon tartares, mushroom tartlets, and herb-and-lemon baby artichokes.

How could there be so many appetizers? And why was there double of everything?

Oh no. I must've said yes to all the appetizer specials of the day thinking they were main dishes, and Gregory had followed suit.

He didn't say anything as we dug in. I was too embarrassed to even look at him. The food, though, was delicious, especially the frog legs. And no, they didn't taste like chicken.

"Think about it," Gregory said after he polished off his salmon tartare, his tone casual. "We can pretend we're having Spanish cuisine. Then these would be tapas."

"I think the French chef would be horrified to have his food mistaken for Spanish." I giggled, my embarrassment forgotten.

Come what may, it was a fun date.

"So will you keep going out with me if I take you to eat frog legs every day?" Gregory teased as he pushed his own dish of frog legs toward me, watching me polish them off in quick succession.

"I don't know." I tapped my chin, pretending to really have to think about it.

"Oh." His face fell.

"Not the part about going out with you, silly," I hastily assured him. "But the part about eating frog legs every day."

"Because it's more of an occasional treat?" he suggested.

"No, I like it enough to have it often. But the growing worldwide demand for them is killing the frog population."

Gregory chuckled. "Oh, Megan. You're one in a million."

"You better remember it." I used the dessert menu to hide my own smile. With us saving some unexpected time due to skipping the main course, did I have time for a quick dessert? Maybe not a chocolate molten lava cake or anything time-consuming to make, but ice cream over warmed apple pie would be wonderful.

After the unfortunate appetizer-turned-tapas incident, sticking with classic dessert I could pronounce sounded like a great idea.

There was the sound of glasses breaking. We turned and found Yelena King breathing heavily like a fish out of water, her face turning blue. A broken cocktail glass lay on the floor, spilling its champagne-colored liquid onto the thick carpet. Her date frantically gestured the waiter to come over.

"That's the beginning of the end. I'm afraid our date's over," Gregory said regretfully.

"What? But how?" I checked the time on my cell phone. "She's, like fifteen minutes away from her time of death."

"Maybe she struggles for a while before dying," Gregory suggested.

"Oh." That was something I hadn't considered because I was in the business of punish and release, not eternal torment in the down under. Damn, no dessert for me then.

Gregory quickly paid the bill. It had taken a bit of magical persuasion to keep the ball rolling with the process, as the entire panicked staff was focused on caring for the dying woman or calling for help.

After the bill was settled, Gregory and I got up and made ourselves invisible with a spell that let us phase out of the surrounding mortals' minds in a gradual manner that wouldn't alarm them. Though if we were to be invisible to the ever-seeing reapers, we would need a lot more than that.

I took out a tube of gooey black paste from my purse and after taking a slab with my index finger, handed it over to Gregory. Holding my breath, I slathered it all over my forehead and cheeks. The tube was a just-in-case gift from Bonaventure the Third, and even with my breath held, a whiff of wet paint and rotten bananas got through.

Yes, the burning sensation on my face was the feeling of ground maggots from the Grimmian Forest seeping into my pores. It was poisonous and prolonged exposure would send us to the Underworld on a permanent basis. The slow heat soon blossomed into a sharp pain, as if my face was being sliced open with a letter opener.

I know. I know. It was absolutely disgusting to be touched by maggot paste, of all things, right after a romantic dinner. But we were, after all, professionals. It was the only way we could fool the reaper who would be coming for the soon-to-be departed into not sensing us.

"I guess we won't be doing the customary post-date kiss, huh?" I joked.

But soon I was in no mood for humor.

The longer I had the paste on, the heavier my heart grew. Physically I felt like a fifty-ton gorilla was sitting on my chest; emotionally, despair was settling into my very bone, whispering to me that all was lost and nothing in the world was worth fighting for anymore.

By now Yelena was clutching the left side of her chest with a pained expression on her face. Here came the heart attack.

A team of paramedics rushed into the restaurant just when she lost consciousness. As they started performing CPR on her, a quick glance at my cell showed that her time was near.

Yet there was still no sign of the reaper.

Gregory and I, unseen by the paramedics, each placed a finger on Yelena's shoulders.

"Come on, come on!" I muttered, willing the reaper to show up to end her misery and allow us to hitch a ride to Hell. Every second the maggot paste stayed on my body was excruciating.

"You know how they are," Gregory said. His tone was calm, but I saw his knitted brows. He must be in as much pain as I was.

"Yeah, I know." I rolled my eyes. Reapers 'R' Us, the organization that handled the dispatching of all angels of deaths, operated on a just-in-time business model like a Japanese car manufacturing plant, and preferred to have their reapers not show up until right before the big finale. "But would it kill them to leave a little margin for errors?"

"I'm going to call it," one of the paramedics yelled, causing her date to cry out in dismay.

Fifteen seconds to the true time of death. Often, there was a lag between the last sign of life was detected by humans and the soul actually leaving the body.

In the last five seconds, the reaper finally showed up. He wore a suit that was no less formal than those in the French restaurant, and his face had the gauntness that was the signature of his kind. He didn't seem to notice us.

Gregory and I exchanged a look of relief.

The reaper took out a notepad, confirming his target's descriptions, and began chanting the words "Go to Hell" repeatedly. It might sound like a curse to humans, but to the reapers it was just a mundane travel instruction for the spirits.

Yelena's soul separated itself from her body. Gregory and I made sure we kept our fingers on the real her, not her discarded corporal body. I clasped Gregory's arm with my free hand and he did the same with mine, and I repeated the reaper's words in my mind three times. Then the reaper gave Yelena a light touch on her cheek, and off her soul went, flying through the many layers of the Cosmic Balance, heading straight for the front gate of Hell, taking us with her.

❦ 24 ❦

VIP

WHILE IT WAS true that Hell was whatever you made of it, the grand entrance of the Underworld was the same for everyone— long, steep red-carpeted stairs leading up to an ultra-posh casino, with overhead lights from hundreds of bulbs bathing the steps in eternal brightness.

The now-dead Yelena, still clutching the left side of her chest, looked around her in confusion.

"How did I get here? Where am I?" she asked. Then she stared up at the lights above her and stopped talking, an expression of awe on her face. She dropped her hand to her side.

Every wrongdoer knew, deep down, that they were headed to Hell all their lives. They were simply too arrogant to admit there would be consequences to their actions, but they always knew.

In what could be a few seconds or an eternity—time moved differently here not just in relation to the other planes, but also for each individual—Yelena's expression went from shock, anger, fear, then finally resignation. Maybe those bright bulbs served as some sort of mental adjustment or something.

Then she tore her gaze from the lights and stumbled toward her new home. A bellboy opened the door for her politely. It was all very civilized up until the torture. He already had her luggage in a nearby cart, waiting—one piece of luggage for every major sin she committed. She would not be free of her baggage, literally, until she was properly punished. She walked into the casino and the bellboy followed suit.

The reaper assigned to her case was nowhere to be seen. That was expected. He'd already called in the delivery to the bellboy and needn't make a personal appearance during the package's arrival. What would be the point? No one escaped once they arrived in Hell.

Well, at least not in theory, anyway.

The first thing Gregory and I did upon our arrival was to take out specially formulated handkerchiefs and wipe the maggot paste off our faces. The tightness on my chest eased. With the scent of aloe vera filling my nose, I could feel cheerful again. In Hell, no less. A quick glance at Gregory showed that he, too, was doing better.

There were two security guards at the entrance. They noticed us and started making their way over. I should be keeping my eyes on them, but something on the left side of the stairs caught my attention, and I nudged Gregory and tilted my head toward that direction.

Each side of the stairs was lined with various golden statues, cast in the images of men and beasts. Standing out from amongst the expected deal-making demons, hellhounds, reapers, and vengeance demons, was a man with the face of Santa Claus.

Gregory's confused expression matched exactly with how I felt.

Yep, the statue got the face of Santa Claus right, but nothing else.

Gone was the jolly red snowsuit and the ridiculous curly white full beard. His body, looking more muscular then flabby, was covered in a dark, monk-like robe, and there was keen intelligence and seriousness in his eyes. He didn't look like he would clutch his belly and bellow "ho, ho, ho" any time soon.

Why the heck was Santa immortalized here, and in such a manner? Santa was all about handing out rewards, while Hell was all about dishing out punishments.

We had no time to dwell on that as the guards had now stopped in front of us.

"Can I help you?" one of them asked.

Unlike their nearly naked, stripper-like counterparts that served Leonard on the lower levels of Hell, these boys were the very cliché of the secret service guys in human movies—the black suit, the sunglasses, the headpiece, etc. But what the human CIA agents didn't have, but the guards of Hell did, was a hellhound on a leash. The hellhound was the picture of intimidation, all fangs and salivating, and it was the size of a small bear.

Each guard had a silk armband. One was emerald, the other one, holding onto the leash of the hellhound, red. I suddenly remembered what Lucifer said on his note:

...please come to the front of the casino and present the guards with the red armband with the enclosed VIP pass...

Well, what was I supposed to do when the two of them approached us together? Pull one aside? I lifted my hands, and the guards immediately went into fighting stance, making Gregory extend his vengeance wings in response.

"Chill, guys," I said, hastily spreading out my fingers to show that I wasn't up to any trickery, "I'm just taking out the proof that I have reasons to be here, okay?"

The guards looked at each other, and Gregory folded his wings as a gesture of goodwill. Looking a little more relaxed, the guards signaled me to proceed. I reached back slowly—no sudden, jerky movement there—and detached a small piece of paper the size of a microchip from the clasp of my necklace. I expanded the paper until it resembled a movie ticket on the palm of my hand.

My VIP pass into the casino of Hell.

I hadn't shown Gregory the pass before, in fear of having it drive home to him how Lucifer really did reach out to me behind his back. Knowing was one thing, seeing was another, and one tends to be a little territorial regarding one's *solus iungere*. I was right in my assumption, because Gregory's eyes narrowed at the sight of the VIP pass, and his fingers flexed as if longing to rip it apart.

The guard with the emerald armband stared at the pass and frowned. "I don't know what you're playing at, but I've never seen such a pass bef—"

He slumped forward and was caught by his colleague in the red armband. Initially I thought the latter was trying to help, until he let his buddy's body slide onto the floor. Minus the unconscious guard, there were now only the three of us on the front steps of Hell's entrance. I took an involuntary step toward Gregory.

Mr. Red Armband gestured for us to follow him. "Hurry, before they find us."

He turned and broke off into a run toward a non-descriptive side door off the entrance, taking the hellhound with him. Gregory and I looked at each other, at a loss of what to do. Inside the casino, there would be more of Lucifer's servants. Would we be safer in there, or go with just one guard to who-knew-where, when he already proved that he had zero hesitation in hurting one of his own?

And why the heck was I contemplating the issue of safety in Hell, of all places?

"Come on!" Mr. Red Armband yelled.

In the end, it was the color of the guard's armband that got me to make up my mind. Lucifer's note had made mention of it, and we were here, after all, to see Lucifer.

"I think we should go after him," I said.

"Agreed," Gregory replied.

We went after Mr. Red Armband, who was already at the side door. With one hand on the doorknob and the other tapping his headpiece, he spoke into it. "Code Cobra. I'm bringing them in."

❧ 2 5 ❧

THE CHOCOLATE FACTORY

ONCE THE GUARD opened the side door, a wave of heat hit us and I nearly staggered into Gregory. Never in all my time in Hell had I ever experienced such scorching temperatures before. The heat was almost a physical barrier, and moving an inch forward was like trying to swim across a pool of boiling spring water.

Mr. Red Armband stepped through the threshold with his hellhound, both of which didn't seem to have a problem with the heat. The guard looked back at us, saw our hesitation, and gave an exasperated sigh. "Move along. We don't have time for this."

I wetted my dry lips and tried to retort with a biting remark, but couldn't. I was close to passing out. From Gregory's labored breathing behind me, I doubt he was doing much better.

But we had to keep going. Too much was at stake. If this was Lucifer's way to test us, then that was more the reason we had to bring our A game.

Gregory took my sweaty hand in his and squeezed it before letting go, signaling his determination. Gritting my teeth, I forced myself to cross the threshold, knowing he would be right behind me.

What awaited us was a dark passageway that instantly made the bright and flashy front entrance all but a distant dream. Then a burst of eerily orange glow lighted up the space in front of us, followed by the distant sound of gurgling and a wave of scorching heat. The glow lit up our surroundings, showing stone steps winding a path downward. The same burst of light repeated every few seconds, suggesting that there must've been some sort of lava pool bubbling ahead.

My hand accidently brushed against the brick wall and came away covered in green gooey slime. Repressing a shudder, I pulled out the handkerchiefs I used for the maggot paste and wiped my hand on it.

The air was stifling, a mix of underground muskiness and pungent sulfur. The sulfuric smell was so pronounced, in fact, I could taste it on the tip of my tongue.

It was an inferno worthy of every human nightmare. I would say it was cliché if it wasn't what the supernaturals had come to expect of Hell, as well.

Must...go...forward...

One moment I was treading along, the next I was slumping backward onto the steps, overcome by yet another blast of heat. I got the vague impression of Gregory, who was behind me, trying to catch me, but I knocked him down with me as well.

At least I fell backward, and didn't pitch forward down the steps, bowling into the guard and hound who were ahead of me.

That was my last thought before passing out.

The next thing I felt was the sensation of a large tongue licking my cheek, and the smell of dog breath. *Ugh.*

Strange enough, as the licking continued, the temperature

in my surroundings became more bearable, as if someone had turned the air-conditioning on. I opened my eyes and stared into the face of the hellhound. His eyes shone with keen intelligence, and with his bark-like panting, and his tongue rolling out to the side of his large mouth, I swear that he was laughing at me.

Then the massive beast leaned past me, his fur tickling my neck, as he proceeded to lick something—or someone —underneath me.

"Alright, that's enough," Mr. Red Armband said, pulling the hellhound off me.

Wait, someone underneath me?

As quickly as I could manage, I turned over and got off Gregory. Poor guy, I practically squished him against the hard stone steps when I went down. He broke my fall when he could've gotten out of the way, and he was as heat exhausted as I was.

He was so getting a third date if we got out of this.

Gregory's eyes were closed, and his forehead was beaded with large drops of sweat. I gently pushed a stray piece of wet hair away from his face.

As I watched, his sweat disappeared. He blinked up at me.

"Let's go," Mr. Red Armband urged impatiently. "The hellhound's saliva should give you immunity against the heat. We have to hurry."

"What's the emergency?" I gave voice to the questions I'd had since he spirited us away. "Why aren't we going through the front entrance? Who are we hiding from? Why did you just attack one of your own? What the hell is 'Code Cobra'? Why was the invite addressed to me, but you're perfectly okay with Gregory here as well, as if you're expecting us?"

The only thing I could think of was that there had been some kind of mutiny within Lucifer's own camp, or another mass breakout. Either way, it didn't make very good timing for visiting Hell. But then again, had there ever been a good time?

Despite getting the immunity from the heat, which was a nice gesture despite the ick factor, it was about time we got some answers.

Mr. Red Armband buttoned his lips mulishly. "You're going to have to talk to the boss about it."

"Not. Good. Enough. Of. An. Answer," I bit out. "Oh, come on, you have to give me something."

"Fine." Mr. Red Armband sighed. "There has been a little, er, social unrest that the boss is handling."

Oh crap, I *was* right, and there was a rebellion of sort. *Maybe we'll come back another time* was at the tip of my tongue. But really, as I said there was really no good time to do this.

"There are those who, er, might take issue to your presence here," the guard added.

"But I've been here before," I protested.

"Not as a VIP," Mr. Red Armband said pointedly. "The boss would still very much like to see you, so I'm getting you in as discreetly as possible. We're taking a longer route, but we'll get there safely. That's as much as I'm going to say for now."

"Would you at least tell me your name?" I asked. There was always some measure of power in a name, if nothing else.

"No. You saw my red armband, and that's all you need to know."

I opened my mouth but Gregory gave me a *leave it for now* look. With a sigh, I helped him up, and along with the guard and beast, we continued our descent into the belly of Hell. After about a thousand steps, there was a small landing before the stairs continued down.

Mr. Red Armband stopped on the landing, and Gregory and I did the same. The guard gestured a small door by the landing and said, "This is Torture Chamber Section 2C567."

I paled. Just how many torture chambers were there in Hell? It wasn't like they actually teach us these things in the vengeance education system. Was Lucifer's idea of *talking* to us over some medieval torture devise and a glass of blood?

Seeing my expression, Mr. Red Armband snapped, "You want to meet the boss or not?"

Fine. I took a deep breath and squared my shoulder. Gregory gave me a nod, and when the guard opened the door, we followed him in.

Torture Chamber Section 2C567 was set up like a midway at a state fair. There was Ferris wheel, Gravitron, Haunted House, and many other carnival games, and together they lit up the dark backdrop with thousands of multi-colored neon blubs, twirling and flashing in a dazzling display. Plenty of people milled around, or lined up for rides. A pair of large stereo speakers was stationed at every ride, blasting cheerful carnival tunes of their respective adventure. The smell of funnel cakes, hot dogs, and cotton candies drifted to my nose, and despite having had dinner not so long ago, my mouth watered in response.

The giant Ferris wheel at the entrance was at least six hundred feet tall. Its speakers crackled as it played "My Favorite Things" from *The Sound of Music*. The wheel lumbered on, having just finished loading up a fresh batch of riders. The ride was quite popular, with the long lineup stretching all the way to the neighboring food stands.

My first clue that something was off was the realization that though this was an amusement park setting, nobody was entirely amused. There was no shared laughter, no chatting, none of the stuff that people usually did when they lined up for a fun time.

My second clue was the look of sheer terror on the riders' faces as the Ferris wheel suddenly jumped in speed. Then it went into turbo mode, and the song sped up so fast that Julie

Andrews was listing out all of her favorite things in under ten seconds. The riders hung onto their seats for dear life-well, maybe not life in their case—but it was futile. The momentum sent them flying into the air one by one, and soon the ground was littered by their broken bodies.

Gregory grabbed me, and together we dove under an unmanned, umbrella-covered hot dog stand. We reinforced the large umbrella, so that as the bodies rained down on it, they slide off with loud squishing sounds, but didn't puncture our barrier. I scraped my palm on the dirt floor in our hasty retreat, and it stung like crazy.

Mr. Red Armband walked over with his canine friend and said, "Take down the barrier. It isn't necessary. Those licks from the hellhound are already protecting you from the flying bodies, like it does for me."

A look at the guard indicated that he was indeed unharmed, and he'd been in the open the entire time. Maybe Hellhound slobber acted as some kind of condemned soul repellant? Gregory and I came out from our shields reluctantly. I would prefer to have some barrier, already being protected or not. It would make me feel better.

"We're supposed to wait in this area for further instructions, don't go too far," Mr. Red Armband said, tapping on his headpiece. "And when I say run, do that right away, okay?"

"Why are we waiting here?" I asked.

"For the right time, so we can get through this area while ensuring that we're not followed," he replied. "Every safeguard in Hell covers different geographical areas, and they shift over time, complementing and neutralizing each other in a complicated rhythm, creating pockets of safe zones that take particular traveling patterns to enter. The boundaries are not visible even to me, so I'm relying on instructions from my superior before we proceed."

"So is this about securing our safety, or your boss's privacy?" Gregory asked.

Mr. Red Armband shrugged. "Does it matter?"

I looked at my surroundings. Maybe while I was waiting I could learn something about the Lord of Hell from the way he ran things here. I could certainly use every bit of information I could get my hands on. From the way Gregory looked around him, he must be thinking along the same line.

The Ferris wheel, now empty, was slowly coming to a full stop. Though their bodies were broken, the riders on the ground didn't lose consciousness. They simply lay in their own pools of blood, crying out in pain. Then, incredibly, the pool of blood receded before my very eyes, and what was once broken—jaws, legs, arms, hips—seemed to get knitted back together. Yes, the broken bones were resetting themselves. Without the use of anesthesia. If the increased volume of cries were anything to go by, this process appeared to be even more excruciating than the business of sustaining the original injuries.

"Batch four of the Wheel of Broken Fraudsters, please report back to the line for further punishment. Batch five, please get ready to take your seats." A neutral voice announced over the PA system as the Ferris wheel started moving to load up a new round of passengers.

I wondered what had made them so agreeable to the arrangement, as most of them had a resigned look on their faces, whether they were lying on the ground or waiting their turn to end up in a similar fashion.

The freshly-injured-and-healed bunch stretched out their bodies gingerly, got up, and headed back to the line. People who did scummy things in life had a general disregard for the law, and it wasn't like there was a single underground law enforcement officer in sight, our own tour guide excluded. So why were the prisoners so accepting of their punishment?

No sooner did I ponder about that did a few of the recently punished made a run for it. Looked like there was some fight left in them, after all. They darted around the French fry stand, bulldozed over the beaver tail pavilion, and one enterprising fellow even rolled under the base of a Gravitron, hiding his entire body under there.

Mr. Red Armband's hellhound pulled at his own leash. The guard waved his hand, and the leash simply melted away. The hellhound doubled in size and bound after the escapees.

And he wasn't alone. At least half a dozen hellhounds came out of nowhere, racing to catch up with the prisoners. Once they did, they barked, bit, and pushed the escapees, including the one under the Gravitron, back in line like a herd of ill-tempered German Shepherds.

I guess if the hellhounds could drag people to Hell, then they were more than capable of keeping them there.

Gregory and I strode to the hot dog stand nearby, attracted by its heavenly smell. There was just something about carnival food that was as wonderful as they were unhealthy.

Suddenly he stopped in his tracks and steered me away from it, his face tight. "Let's go check out the other side."

I dragged my feet. "What's going on—"

"Would the prisoners whose names begin with the letter E"—the same neutral voice spoke again over the PA system —"please come to Hot Dog Stand 12C and pick up your penises. You're free to reattach it back to your body for the rest of the day."

Oh, those hot dogs that were rotating and grilling in their own juices weren't hot dogs at all.

My food lust toward the carnival food evaporated, and bile threatened to rise up within me once more. The disgust worked on two levels. As a vengeance demon, I'd been exposed to my share of gross retribution. But knowing that someone I'd sent back to Hell might've had their penises grilled because of me just made it that much more real.

In a desperate attempt not to puke my guts out, I turned to Gregory and said pleadingly, "Talk to me. Distract me."

Gregory looked at me, understanding dawned in his eyes. "What have you learned about this section of Hell thus far?"

Good, logical analysis. That I could do.

I took a shaky breath, trying to ignore the screaming of the tormented souls, the gruesome images of broken bodies, and the smell of burnt flesh. "For one, there were people being tormented from all walks of life here. Across all races and genders, supernaturals or otherwise."

"What else?"

"This whole section is automated. Other than the hell-hounds, there isn't a live agent on site."

"Live being a relative word here," he said dryly.

"You know what I mean. The place is run completely by machines." It was working, my sense of nausea was receding. I didn't care if Mr. Red Armband overheard us. It wasn't exactly any unique insight.

"But notice how everything is running at full capacity?" he asked quietly.

Now that he mentioned it, he was right. At most of the games and rides, just like the Ferris wheel, people had to wait quite a long while before they were up again. It was like a typical midway or amusement park in that aspect, except nobody minded the wait at all.

I paced around. "But is this the way things are meant to be run? These machines are so overworked. Do you hear that sputtering sound in their engines? They sound like at any time now they could give up the ghost. I thought the whole idea of having Leonard overseeing the Book of Life and Death is to manage Hell's occupancy in an efficient manner."

"Okay, I just got word we're good to go." Mr. Red Armband ran to us. "Follow me. We don't have much time."

He ran toward the carnival games. We darted around in a haphazard pattern that didn't make any logical sense. First, we sprinted toward the stand with water guns that spewed acid onto the prisoners, then we turned direction and headed toward a whack-a-mole machine with people rather than moles in their holes. At the last minute we dashed into a giant teacup and rode along in a crimson pond of menstrual blood —yes, it was as gross as it sounded, and smelled worse.

Man, with all the running around, was I glad that I had opted for glamming up my sensible black pumps rather than stumbling around on the fancy silver strapped sandals. I just wished the stink of menstrual blood could be washed out of my borrowed clothes easily.

After three rounds around the pond, we got off and headed straight to the True House of Horrors, which was between the pavilion for a singing competition for people with their throats slit open, and a small stage for an hourly show of *Death by A Thousand Cuts*.

The entrance of the True House of Horrors was blocked by a chain with the sign *Closed for Repair*. Mr. Red Armband came to a stop by the chain, lifted it, and waved us in. "We made it. The boss is waiting in there for you."

Alright, let's see what fresh hell this was. Literally.

✿ 26 ✿

THE CARETAKER

INSIDE THE TRUE HOUSE of Horror, in front of a range of distortion mirrors, was a man I supposed must be Lucifer. He was different than what I thought he would look like. Between the Medieval depiction of him carrying pitchforks, and the modern human pop-culture representation of him being ultra-bad boy sexy, the range was pretty broad.

What I got instead was someone not in the extremes at all.

He wasn't very young or very old. He wasn't super skinny or overweight. He was no geek, but not a gym rat, either. He was not a bureaucrat, but to call him sexy would be an exaggeration.

Truth be told, he looked like an urban, well-adjusted, friendly-but-not-too-friendly barista, with the dark clothes to boot. Brown hair. Brown eyes. Medium height. Cute, in a boy-next-door kind of way. But not entirely memorable.

But maybe that was the point.

On the contrary, the distortion mirrors behind him were making him taller, shorter, fatter, and skinnier, demonstrating the various forms the devil could possibly take.

"Hello," he greeted us in a tone that could've been used to ask if I wanted an extra shot and cream for my decaf soy latte. "Welcome to Hell. As you might've guessed, I'm Lucifer."

I crossed my arms, then uncrossed them when I realized that I was facing the devil. *The* devil. It was best to play nice. So I said, "Er, thanks for the invite."

Not really, but what could I say?

"And thanks for letting me come along," Gregory said politely.

Lucifer waved his hand. "I expected Megan would want you to come along. Thank you, both of you, for answering my summons."

There was sincerity in his voice, which was just as confusing as his physical form.

"Summons? Yeah, about that." Might as well get on with why we were really here. "We know about the wrongfully accused."

Instead of being flustered, Lucifer smiled. "Wonderful. So what are you going to do about it?"

Taken aback, I blurted, "I'm going to get you to back off. I got a full list of the wrongfully accused and all."

"No, you don't. Only partial." Lucifer paused. "And it isn't my army."

Gregory and I looked at each other, our mouths gaped. What the hell did he mean, it wasn't his army?

Lucifer continued, "That's why I invited you here. As the Lord of Hell, I'm not allowed to come to you, creatures of the living. I could only ask you to come to me, with the hope that after you found out about the army, you'd *want* to."

"How did you know we'd find out about the army?" I asked.

"How do you think Vera found out which mercenaries captured her man?" Lucifer grinned.

Oh crap, just how much of our journey so far had been manipulated by Lucifer?

"If it's not your army, whose is it?" Gregory demanded.

Lucifer gave Gregory a look.

The Council. Of course. There was no other player big enough to pull everything off.

I resisted a mental palm slap. The jailbreak from Hell didn't start until I joined forces with Gregory. Could it be that after my refusal to release the Absolute Good for the second time, the army was the Council's way of upping the game?

It made an awful lot of sense.

If the Council had enough muscle, they wouldn't need to release an ancient entity to make a whole pile of trouble. What would this mean to my friends and loved ones, who were mostly from one fringe group or another? Would they be forced to go on the run, or end up in concentration camps somewhere?

"I also have to thank you," Lucifer said as he turned toward one of the distortion mirrors. "For bringing me this."

He touched the surface of the skinny mirror, and it rippled. A tall man fell out of it, bound in chains made of cotton candy that was unbreakable despite his struggling. He glared at all of us, but was otherwise silent.

It was Tatus, Leonard's assistant and our guy in Hell.

Or maybe not so our guy, after all.

"He's an agent of the Council." Lucifer's eyes chilled. "I've been playing dumb for months, quietly trying to figure out how the Book of Life and Death came to be tampered with. My safeguard against prison breaks doesn't work on the innocent, and they escape easily. I had suspected that the culprit was close to Leonard, and that's why I asked you to come to the front instead. I had no idea he was already your contact."

I remembered how at the entrance of Hell, Yelena King

stared at the dazzling light bulbs overhead, and her demeanor changed into that of resignation. That must've been part of the mechanism that kept people in Hell. But I guess it wouldn't work on innocents because they honestly didn't do the crimes. Without that there would be no resignation to their fate. Hence the breakout.

"You used us as bait to lure him out," Gregory accused Lucifer.

"I believe he got close to you to monitor you to begin with," Lucifer said. "Then when he knew you were coming to Hell to confront me, he thought he could use the opportunity to figure out how much I really suspected, and I played along. He's been following you since the entrance of the casino, remaining invisible."

"But now you managed to ferret him out," Gregory pointed out.

"My trusted guard took you through the carnival in a pattern that made the traitor easier to detect."

"Wait"—I put up a hand—"all that dashing around and riding in menstrual blood was meant to get Tatus to reveal himself? There was no social unrest, was there?"

"Of course not."

And I guess all that talk about asking me to wear something nice was just a ploy to get me to blend in while they whisked me away, in case I was ever spotted. Should a girl be offended about that?

"Tatus is a servant of Hell." Lucifer's face turned stone cold. His eyes became black and bottomless like a coal mine. I shuddered, reminded again that he was, after all, the devil. "Ironically, that makes his betrayal harder to sense. But being a living creature, your essence wreaked havoc to his perfectly balanced disguise."

"My true master will rise," Tatus finally spoke, still struggling against his bind. "You'll all be punished."

"The world needs balance," Lucifer stated. "The pursuit of Absolute Good will destroy that."

With another wave of his hand, Lucifer sent Tatus back into the mirror. "I shall interrogate him thoroughly soon, but Megan and Gregory, I asked you here because I need your help."

Lucifer, the Lord of the Underworld, wanted our help? Gregory and I exchanged an uneasy glance.

"I know what the Council really is," Lucifer said. "And what you have to understand is that this is about more than the vengeance governing body being corrupted by the Greys, on the off-chance that they'll be successful at their hare-brained attempt to call back an ancient entity, or their army. There's something that's equally at stake here."

"What do you mean?" I couldn't think of anything else just as high stake.

"This is about the health of the entire Cosmic Balance. Do you know what Hell should look like?"

I shook my head.

Lucifer waved his hand, and we were back at the carnival again, except it was almost empty. There were a few people scattered on the Ferris wheel, and a couple on the merry-go-round, but all the lines were gone. The machines, which spewed out hot steam due to overworking on my last visit, were mostly shut down, their engines quiet. Some of the rides and food stands even had tarps draping all over them. Though the whole place was pretty much abandoned, it had a strange sense of peace that its noisier self lacked, like this was the place where punishment, though being dished out less often, actually meant something.

"This is how Hell is supposed to look?" I asked incredulously.

Lucifer lifted his hands to encompass his surroundings. "Hell should never have been at even half-capacity, let alone over-capacity. This has been a chronic problem for a long time now. My workers are overworked, my machines are over-worked, and I have to grant early release to many prisoners due to overcrowding."

"What happened?" Gregory asked quietly.

"Long ago..." Lucifer walked to the hot dog stand and stroke the tarp covering it fondly. "Back when the Cosmic Balance was first created, three followers of Fleur the Trick-ster—the Father, the Warrior, and the Caretaker—made an arrangement about how to manage the irregularities in their newly created system. The Father would raise the alarm when a person started doing bad things, the Warrior would give that person fair warning, and if failed, punishment, and the Caretaker removes the unrepentant, repeat offenders from the system. The 'care' in Caretaker applies to both the protection of the innocents from the wrongdoers, and the personal growth of the wrongdoers before they moved on to the next life. I'm the Caretaker. The Warrior, after many rein-carnations, became the modern-day Council. And the Father is—"

"—Santa Claus," I guessed, remembering the group of golden statues lining the stairs leading up to the front entrance of Hell. Santa was there, and he had a very out-of-character serious demeanor about him.

"Please don't call him that. He hates that name." Lucifer winced. "In popular culture he's been reinvented to be a joke of a man, some jolly old fellow who exists only to hand out gifts. It's insulting to do such a character assassination to one of the early founders of the Cosmic Balance."

"Is that the Council's handiwork?" If the three followers of Fleur had worked together, my own vengeance education sure as hack never covered it. Well, they never really gave Fleur due credit, either. Having Santa portrayed as a one-dimensional gift giver sounded like a smear campaign aimed to get people to not take him seriously, and the Council wasn't above that.

"Of course," Lucifer confirmed. "Nowadays the Council still purchases the Father's Annual Wrongdoers' Development Report for appearance's sake, but to say that they squander many opportunities to nip wrongdoings in the bud would be an understatement. Mass murderers, weapon dealers, and serial rapists, etc. should have been scared straight at their very first crime, before they even attempt bigger ones, and my realm would be at the capacity it's supposed to be at. Just as vengeance demons gain their magical credit through the correction of injustice, I receive mine through the repenting of sinners and the protection of innocents. For centuries now I've been spending more magic than I've gained, with sinners having created too many victims and too set in their ways to change by the time they come to me. That's why I came to rely on machines for the punishments. This imbalance in the Cosmic Balance hurts everyone and cannot go on."

Wow, the furthest they'd ever told us in school about the relationship between vengeance demons and Hell was that we should aim to "soften up" the wrongdoers before they moved on to eternal damnation. Nobody told us our job was supposed to be far more in-depth than that.

"Okay, but I still don't see where Gregory and I fit in," I said.

"In a way, you're both children of both worlds, and your experience has given you unique foresight and compassion. The Council was inefficient long before the Greys got to it. I'm talking about the revamping of the entire system. That's what it really needs. We each have a role to play in the Cosmic Balance, and this current state of things is hurting us all."

I allowed my senses to take over and felt the truth of

Lucifer's words. Yes, the large-scale injustices he mentioned had the Ring of Vengeance to them.

I looked to Gregory to see his reaction. Time and time again I was asking more from him than I'd intended, and I feared I had finally crossed the line. For Hades's sake, we were literally talking about conspiring with the devil here.

But there was no mistaking the fierce determination in his eyes as he looked back at me. He shrugged with deliberate casualness. "Well, on the positive side, we already sealed our fate when we went against the Council."

I bit down the joy that threatened to mist my eyes, and resisted the urge to run into his arms.

Well, I did join the mercenary life with the explicit purpose of building up contacts in my fight against the Council. I wasn't planning on reinventing the wheel altogether, but this wasn't the first day I knew the current system was inefficient. I'd seen unaddressed injustices all my life—starting with my own childhood bullying.

"What is it exactly you want us to do?" I asked Lucifer.

"For now, quietly obtain the full list of all the wrongfully convicted and their counterparts in the Council's army."

That could be doable, especially if I was able to get further help from Gran. Hopefully we could figure out a way for her to send me messages that were clearer than that confusing *rain raw* one.

"I'll take the list you have so far," Lucifer continued. "And set the innocents aside in an area of Hell where they can stay in relative comfort. We can't afford to return them home right now lest we alert the Council."

"Wouldn't they already know, with you capturing Tatus?"

"He won't remember it after I'm done with him." Lucifer's eyes glinted. "And I'll make it look like I dismissed your claim entirely and sent you on your merry way. Nobody will know that we're working together except us and those close to you."

"And what's the long-term plan?" Gregory asked.

Lucifer said simply, "We bring down the Council, and rebuild it with people who genuinely care."

Yeah, simple as you please. Bring down the Council. Despite the risk, I found myself drawn to the idea.

"So what do you say?" Lucifer asked.

What could I say? The devil I knew was better than...we all know the rest.

❧ 27 ❧

PURGATORY

As a gesture of goodwill, Lucifer allowed Gregory and I to observe the transportation of the innocents to their new home. Converted from a garden formerly known as Torture Chamber Section 4A290, it had six interconnecting greenhouses with everything from orchids, cactus, hibiscus, palm trees to ornamental banana plants. Every greenhouse either had a waterfall, a small pond, or a waterwheel. The eternal sunshine, the fragrant of countless flowers and the sound of water made it a tranquil environment, but given what I'd seen at the amusement park, I suppose all those innocent-looking plants could do quite a lot of damage. The cactus went without saying, but also the many blossoms that could be as poisonous as they were vibrant in color.

The innocents settled into the various alcoves and sitting benches, their voices hushed as if afraid that their sudden respite from torment would not last.

We found Boyce Armstrong kneeling by a rose bush with a trowel and a bucket of plant food pellets, his tattooed arms flexing as he worked at loosening the soil around the roots. Looked like he wasn't content to sit idle like the rest of them.

He looked rather out of place with his studded leatherwear, the same clothes he wore when we took him back to Hell. Since I'd gotten to know him through Vera's memory, he no longer seem as mean-ass as I initially thought.

I coughed. "Hey."

Boyce stopped the trowel and turned to us, but didn't get up. "Is it true my girl helped get me here?"

"News travel fast," Gregory commented.

"No, they didn't tell us anything"—Boyce shook his head —"but I figured it out. Vera never gives up."

"That's true," I agreed.

"But she had help, didn't she?" Boyce speculated.

"Yeah." I thought about what Lucifer said about pretty much siccing Vera on us. Every subsequent action took us that much closer to seeing Lucifer. Geeze, that guy sure had a plan. "You can't leave here, though. Not for a while."

Maybe a long while.

"I know." Boyce looked around him. "Tell my girl I love her. It's peaceful here. I always wanted to learn gardening. Maybe when I leave here I'll know enough about it to turn it into a career. Be truly legitimate."

"Good luck," I said with heartfelt sincerity. Boyce and Vera seemed like such an odd couple. But they seemed to genuinely care about each other, and I hope one day they could be together again.

Gregory looked deep in thought as we walked toward the exit of the former-torture-chamber-turned-paradise where Lucifer was waiting.

"How much of this have you manipulated?" Gregory asked once he reached Lucifer. His voice was controlled. Too control. I looked at him, but he only had eyes for the Lord of Hell. Just what the hack was Gregory talking about?

Lucifer blinked once. Slowly. "Do you really want to know?"

"I need to. It wasn't that I was *allowed* to come along with Megan using her VIP pass. You summoned us both. You've been keeping track of us every step of the way."

"I had to." Lucifer spread his hands. "I couldn't leave here. I could only observe and set the chess pieces from afar."

"How far did you go to make sure Megan and I would come here? That I'd be at her side?"

"All your feelings for Miss Aequitas are genuine. I simply... lowered your barrier so you would overlook a few silly doubts, that's all."

"What the hell did you do?" I snapped. Lucifer's words were freaking me out. So far I had, like, one and a half dates with Gregory. Not a lot by any measure. Even making it that far was somehow influenced by Lucifer? What did that say about how strong we were on our own?

"Very well, if you must know." Lucifer sighed and turned to me. "The issue of protecting Candy should've created more friction between you two. When you rendered him unconscious and he caught up with you after, he should've made you work harder to earn his forgiveness. Overall, given how his own father walked away, he should've been a lot more wary in the relationship. I put a mild filter on all that doubt and anxiety."

Oh crap, that was why Gregory never said out loud he thought we were indeed soul mates even as he was all for more dates to happen—he was charmed into not voicing his true opinion on that matter, and every other related matter.

What we felt on our dates—just how authentic was it anyway? How much of Gregory's sacrifices were truly voluntary?

"Make no mistake," Lucifer declared. "In time, you would've found your way through all that I'd filtered out, and the path you took would've been the same. Unfortunately, time is something I couldn't afford. Not with the army growing in strength every day. So I sped things up."

"Some things aren't meant to be sped up." Gregory bared his teeth. "We're supposed to have roadblocks and doubts in a relationship. We're supposed to fight and work through it. What you did robbed us of the opportunities to grow and to find our way back to each other. It's not right."

"War is not about being right or fair," Lucifer said simply. "You should know that."

———

Mr. Red Armband was charged with taking us back to the lobby of Hell. Rather than walking, we were going to teleport there. I was glad of the shorter trek, given how awkward it was between Gregory and I after what we were just told. He'd been silent ever since then, seemingly lost in his own thoughts. I had no idea how to get him to open up because I, too, was in shock. We needed our own space. Time to think and process it all. The sooner we got out of here the sooner we could do that.

How silly was I, thinking all along I was oh-so-lucky that Gregory was the reasonable sort of guy. I even convinced myself that the bond we formed from months of professional interaction must've somehow helped us skip some of the nastier fights we could have had. What a joke. Lucifer had been pulling our strings all along.

The question was, was what the puppet master did horrible enough to make us not want to join his cause?

No, Lucifer's intention was sincere, even if his method was underhanded. So there was only one course forward for the sake of Grandma and the rest of the Cosmic Balance.

Dammit.

"I'm sorry," Mr. Red Armband apologized right before we teleported directly to the lobby.

"Don't worry about it," I muttered. We already discussed the parts we would be playing for our exit from Hell. The little piece of upcoming drama was meant to be public, to convey Lucifer's displeasure of us after our supposedly disastrous confrontation.

We landed right in the middle of the lobby, which, unlike the entrance leading up to there, was jam packed with guards, sinners, and the bellboys that trailed after them with luggage.

Once we arrived, Mr. Red Armband pushed Gregory and I onto the ground, our bodies rolling on the soft red carpet. The guard yelled for all to hear, "The boss said you're not welcome here anymore. And all your freelance contracts with us are now cancelled. Now get outta here!"

With that, he lifted us up by our arms, dragged us to the threshold, and gave us a heavy shove from the back. I had a brief second of flying down the stairs, with a quick glance at the statue of Santa, before we got transported back to the French restaurant where we came from.

I sprawled onto the floor. Ouch, the hard tile of the restaurant wasn't as nice a landing pad as the lobby's carpet. I turned to check that Gregory got back alright.

Except he wasn't there.

A hellhound with a full coat of black, shiny fur stared at me. My first reaction was to scramble back. Somehow, Mr. Red Armband's hellhound must've traveled back with me instead of Gregory. But why?

Then I recognized the creature's brown eyes. Intelligent eyes. Gregory's.

This beast *was* him. His energy signature, though turned more animalistic, still had that sophistication and elegance that I'd come to recognize.

Damn, damn, damn! What the hell did Lucifer do this time? Was this really necessary? Hadn't he done enough?

Gregory twisted his neck left and right, staring at the fur on his shoulders in dismay and rubbing against it as if he couldn't believe what had just happened. Well, that made two of us.

I quickly glanced around us. Looked like we were still invisible to the humans around us, hence no one was screaming their heads off about our teleportation, or the big-ass hellhound in their midst.

Looked like not much time had passed on the human plane since we left for Hell. The body of Yelena King was still lying on the restaurant floor, with the EMS guy asking her distressed date some standard questions, the latter having no idea that he'd just dodged a bullet.

Lucifer's words came back to me.

...I'll make it look like I dismiss your claim entirely and send you on your merry way. Nobody will know that we're working together...

But did that also mean punishing one of us in a visible way for all to see? Was this Lucifer's way of making sure that the whole charade was believable? So Gregory would be a vengeance demon without his body, and a hellhound without being able to go back to hell?

Creature of both worlds, indeed.

I reached out to Gregory and placed my hand at the back of his head—since he was as big as a small bear, I wasn't even leaning down—and stroked behind his ear, taking comfort in his coarse but warm fur. We had so much to talk about, so much trust to rebuild—or whatever you called strengthening something that was initially inflated—and now he got turned into a dog.

He tilted his head to one side and gave me a look that said, "Really? You're going to scratch behind my ear like I'm a puppy now?"

I grimaced and withdrew my hand quickly. "Sorry."

Awkward. Again.

But wait, maybe for now being a hellhound wasn't such a bad thing for him. The Council might not dare to touch me because of what I could do for their master, but not when it came to Gregory. He could use the extra protection in the coming days, and hellhounds had their special blend of magic and were practically un-killable.

Was that why Lucifer did it, or was it only part of the reason?

Gregory put his paw in my palm, and gave me a short and decisive bark. I didn't have to know dog-speak to know what he was trying to communicate. Hound or vengeance demon, issues to resolve or not, came hell or high water he still had my back.

And we still had lots to do.

I folded my fingers over his paw. "Let's get out of here."

The wrongfully accused were no longer suffering, but not exactly free, either; Grandma was found and then lost again; Gregory was right by my side, yet not in his true form.

Everything was in purgatory. But I knew that it wouldn't stay that way. I would face the Council and bring it crashing down if it was the last thing I did.

Because Hell hath no vengeance like a demon on a quest.

THIS IS WHERE THE AUTHOR SHAMELESSLY BEGS YOU TO LEAVE A REVIEW...

Did you enjoy HELL HATH NO VENGEANCE? If so, I would really appreciate it if you could write a review on Goodreads and/or your online retailer!

ABOUT THE AUTHOR

Louisa Lo lives in Toronto, Canada with her husband, an aristocratic cat, and more cardboard boxes than she cares to unpack. She decided to write about vigilantes, because it seems like a better life choice than trying to become one and landing herself in jail. She just has that kind of luck.

Visit Louisa's website at **www.LouisaLo.com** where you'll find her social media links.

RECOMMENDED READING
SEQUENCE

Vengeance Be Mine (Vengeance Demons #1)
Before Vengeance (Vengeance Demons #0)
Vengeance Unclaimed (Vengeance Demons #2)
A Good Vengeance (Vengeance Demons #3)
Vengeance For Hire (Vengeance Demons #4)
Hell Hath No Vengeance (Vengeance Demons #5)

COMING SOON...

VENGEANCE DELAYED
Justice comes slowly, but surely...

BE A VENGEFUL VIXEN!

I'd love to have you join my Facebook reader group! Search "Vengeful Vixens Louisa Lo" on Facebook.

Sign up for my mailing list on my website for the latest news and offers!